VAMPIRES, WEREWOLVES, ROBOTS & PRINCESSES

Harry Challenge,

Victorian Supernatural Sleuth

! with Special Guest Appearances by !

The GREAT LORENZO

VAMPIRES, WEREWOLVES, ROBOTS & PRINCESSES

Harry Challenge,

Victorian Supernatural Sleuth

! with Special Guest Appearances by !

The GREAT LORENZO

BY

RON GOULART

WILDSIDE PRESS

Published by Wildside Press, LLC
www.wildsidebooks.com

CONTENTS

FOREWORD
Welcome Back, Harry!

Ron Goulart is one of the most prolific genre authors in America, with more than 180 published works. Twice nominated for the Mystery Writers of America's Edgar award, Ron is an acknowledged expert on comic books and "pulp," having written Cheap Thrills, an Informal History of the Pulp Magazine, and is also the author of approximately fifty science fiction books and twenty mystery novels, including a delightful series starring Groucho Marx as detective—which is a perfect example of Ron's ready wit and chutzpah: I mean, just think about the challenge of penning a huge supply of new "Grouchoisms!"

It is this risible ability that, wedded to the grand traditions of espionage, private investigation and the supernatural, that distinguishes my personal favorites of his work—the Harry Challenge adventures. Having come upon them many years ago, I craved more of the same, and when I was editor of H. P. Lovecraft's Magazine of Horror, I encouraged Ron to write new exploits of Harry and his flamboyant sidekick, the Great Lorenzo, and in the fourth issue of that now-defunct publication, I was pleased to offer just such a story; later, I was able to run two more of them in Sherlock Holmes Mystery Magazine.

At the time, I was under the impression that these were the first new Harry Challenge adventures since his first exploits, but I was wrong—Ron has written quite a few of them over the years (for details, see the Afterword.) Harry, the Great Lorenzo, and the intrepid reporter Jennie Barr have only appeared, however, in the two paperback novels which kicked off the series, The Prisoner of Blackwood Castle (1984) and The Curse of the Obelisk (1987).

I am grateful to Ron for writing these wonderful stories. They provided great pleasure to my late wife Saralee; they were among the last books that she read in the final months of her life. It therefore is a privilege and gives me much joy to present these splendidly tongue-in-cheek adventures in a single volume for your reading pleasure.

—Marvin Kaye
Manhattan, April 2011

AUTHOR'S INTRODUCTION

Born and raised on the West Coast of America in the 19th Century, Harry Challenge is an Operative with the Challenge International Detective Agency. He practices his trade chiefly in England and on the Continent, including small Middle European nations that have some similarities with Ruritania and Graustark. Unlike many of his contemporary Victorian rivals, he goes in for fisticuffs and gunplay, and he's far from celibate. Harry doesn't rely entirely on ratiocination. Also playing hunches, nosing around and using, when necessary, tipsters and informants.

Harry Challenge made his debut in 1984 in *The Prisoner of Blackwood Castle*. He returned in 1987 in *The Curse of the Obelisk*. Since then he's also shown up in about a dozen novelets and short stories in an assortment of magazines and anthologies.

The character grew out of my wanting to write some Victorian adventure tales but using a contemporary style. In my formative years I was a follower of the work of Anthony Hope (as the title of the first novel in this compilation indicates), H. Rider Haggard and, especially, Sax Rohmer. In fact, in my early teen years I wrote Rohmer a fan letter, which he answered.

I thought it would be fun, and something of a vacation, to write about a focal character who worked on detective cases involving some of the props and paraphernalia of the above-mentioned writers—sorcery, swordplay, castles, Satanists, criminal masterminds, secret societies, Egyptian curses, beautiful princesses, reanimated mummies, damsels in distress, etc. And I wanted a hero who had some of the qualities of a hardboiled private eye combined with those of a smart cowboy. I still enjoy writing about Harry and I sold a new novelet about him just a few weeks ago.

In casting the series, I wanted to come up with a recurrent cast of characters. Essential is a confidant/adviser. That function falls to the professional magician The Great Lorenzo. Quite possibly, as he often maintains, Lorenzo—Oops, you always have to refer to him as the Great Lorenzo—is the World's Greatest Illusionist. In addition to inventing awesome stage tricks, he devotes part of his time to wooing countesses, duchesses, actresses and other women of means. He's a plump gentleman in his fifties with ample sideburns, a bit of a dandy. He insists that he has no magical powers, but The Great Lorenzo seems to have a knack for foreseeing, albeit in sometimes fuzzy fashion, future events. Since he is frequently touring Europe, he bumps into Harry quite often. They are close friends and he serves as a sort of Jiminy Cricket conscience to Harry. He's a fair investigator on his own.

Despite his now and then involvement with princesses, lady spies and lovely blonde clients, the woman in Harry Challenge's life is a cute, slim auburn-haired young international journalist named Jennie Barr, whom he frequently crosses paths with all over Europe. Jennie works for the New York Inquirer and specializes in covering supernatural events. She's based in part on the real life 19th Century daredevil reporter who called herself Nellie Bly, partly on a character from Robert Barr's 1899 novel Jennie Baxter, Journalist, partly on my cute, feisty, auburn-haired writer wife.

Lily Hope, second rate soprano and first rate international spy, and Dr.

Grimshaw, the World's 2nd Best Criminal Mastermind (Moriarty keeps beating him on the charts) both came later in the series. Possibly you'll encounter them if the stories are eventually collected.

I'm pleased to see *The Prisoner of Blackwood Castle* and *The Curse of the Obelisk* returning to print and I want to thank Marvin Kaye and John Betancourt for engineering this.

—Ron Goulart
April, 2011

THE PRISONER OF BLACKWOOD CASTLE

Chapter 1

Zevenburg in the spring of 1897 was a magnificent and glittering city. Capital of Orlandia, that small sovereign nation on the eastern fringes of the vast Habsburg Empire, Zevenburg was known worldwide as a metropolis where existence is more beautiful, joy more easily obtained and trouble more quickly thrown away than anywhere else. Its overall mood was especially festive that spring, because its splendid Quadricentennial Exposition had opened only three weeks earlier, and eager visitors were flocking to this gleaming city on the River Fluss from all over Europe and beyond. True, benevolent old King Ulrich was rumored to be slowly dying in his shadowy chambers in the ornate palace on Mariahilferstrasse. But he had had a long happy reign and would be succeeded by the popular and beautiful Princess Alicia. Business, in everywhere from the great hotels to the tiny shops, had never been better, and the weather had held pleasant and serene for nearly a full week.

And so nearly everyone in Zevenburg on the tranquil spring evening on which our story commences was content and happy, with the exception of old King Ulrich, who was justifiably downcast about his imminent death, and Harry Challenge.

Harry had just been thrown out of the palace, thrown out by two gilded and overdressed footmen on the explicit orders, so they claimed as they tossed Harry onto the hard cobblestones of the twilit Maria-hilferstrasse, of Princess Alicia herself.

"Well, damn," remarked Harry, rising up from beside a curb-side border of freshly bloomed flowers and glancing around for his bowler hat.

"Your hat, swine!" called one of the burly brass-buttoned footmen as he pegged the dented headgear out through the high wrought-iron gateway of the palace grounds.

"Much obliged." Harry caught the sailing hat out of the air, poked out the most conspicuous dents and tapped it onto his head.

A closed carriage went clopping by, heading for the Ulrichplatz and trailing light feminine laughter.

Harry was a man of middle height, lean, clean-shaven and a shade weather-beaten. He was not quite a year beyond thirty, and in the course of pursuing his profession he had killed several men. In fact, beneath the coat of his dark suit he wore a Colt .38 revolver in a snug shoulder holster. It was one of his rules, however, never to shoot anyone in anger.

Besides which, the two louts who'd heaved him out into the growing dusk had apparently been acting on orders from the fair Alicia.

"Women are changeable," Harry reminded himself as he brushed the dust of Mariahilferstrasse from his clothes and started walking away from the high-walled palace grounds. "No reason for the princess to be any—"

Slowing, he glanced back over his shoulder. The new electric lamps were lath in coming on tonight, and the darkness that stretched out behind him was thick. Harry narrowed his eyes, scrutinizing one particular linden tree some hundred yards behind him.

After a few seconds, he decided there wasn't anyone watching from behind that tree after all. He lit one of the thin black cigars he favored and resumed walking.

"Things sure can change one hell of a lot in just over a year," he said to himself as he thought of the lovely golden-haired princess.

* * * *

Zevenburg was noted for its profusion of sidewalk cafes, and one of the most popular, as many know, was Penzler's. Located in a twisting lane off Prinz Rollo Strasse and bordered by a row of lilac trees, it was always crowded with a mixture of discriminating local denizens and well-to-do tourists.

At a few minutes past the hour of seven on the evening in question, a portly man in a gray suit, flamboyant double-breasted waistcoat and astonishing green silk cravat was pointing impatiently at three overturned demitasse cups that rested on his small table next to one of the lilac trees. "Come, Rudi, my boy, it's painfully simple. Don't dawdle so."

The small frail waiter hunched, shifted his feet, tugged at his black bow tie, rubbed his perspiring palms once again on his long white apron. "Well, Herr Lorenzo, I think maybe perhaps—"

"My boy, what did I tell you my name was?"

Rudi smacked himself on the temple with the heel of his hand. "Forgive me, my mind was wandering," he apologized. "Well, Herr Great Lorenzo, I think maybe the cube of sugar must be under..." His hand, trembling slightly, hovered over the center cup in the row of three and then darted to the one on the left. "...yes, under this cup."

"Ah, what a pity," sighed the Great Lorenzo. "You're wrong once again, Rudi, and that makes six more free brandies you owe me. Plus the five éclairs from our earlier round of fun."

At a nearby table a handsome red-haired woman in a satin dress began giggling over something her thickset gentleman companion had said. Her fluffy feather boa nearly slipped from her shoulders as she swayed in her chair.

"Might I," inquired the waiter tentatively, "see for myself it isn't under there, Herr Loren—Herr Great Lorenzo?"

"Eh? You doubt my—Ah, but of course. I am a stranger in your land." The Great Lorenzo fluffed his graying muttonchop whiskers. "To you I am merely a wandering minstrel who happens to be starring, twice nightly, in a magical extravaganza at the nearby Rupert Theatre. Were this America, my boy, were this my own, my native land, you'd be fully aware that the Great Lorenzo is a man of unimpeachable honesty and unassailable integrity. Two years ago in Chicago, in fact, I was prevented from running for a prestigious public office on the grounds that I was simply too honest." Giving a shrug, he lifted the cup the waiter had tapped.

There was nothing beneath it but crisp white tablecloth.

"Forgive me, Herr Great Lorenzo, for ever doubting—"

"Think nothing of it, my lad." The Great Lorenzo made a dismissing gesture with his plump beringed right hand. "Now, rather than cringing here and delivering any further tearful apologies, why don't youinstead trot into that inspired kitchen of yours and fetch me the first of my hard-won éclairs, eh?"

"At once, at once, Herr Great Lorenzo."

"Good thing this isn't New York." Harry Challenge sat down opposite the magician. "They'd have given you the heave-ho long ago for trying such an obvious flimflam on—"

"One of the chief advantages of an outdoor bistro, Harry, is that there are no swinging doors to be flung through," observed the Great Lorenzo. "Speaking of which, you look as though you've had the proverbial bum's rush applied to your person not long since."

"I got tossed out of the palace."

"Serves you right for trying to mingle with your betters." The portly magician uprighted the trio of cups he'd been using in his shell game. The sugar cube wasn't beneath any of them. "Since you won't be spending the evening in amorous pursuits, why not, as I earlier suggested, join me for dinner at some—"

"Nope. Believe I'll just head back for the hotel."

"To sulk?"

"I might do a little of that," admitted Harry.

The Great Lorenzo waved his right hand through the air and a bright yellow theater ticket appeared between his fingertips. "Take in my second show at the Rupert, my boy. I'm planning a new variation of sawing a lady in half, and dear Sara may—"

"I've told you a little about the princess, haven't I?"

"A little? When I encountered you last year in Manhattan, you poured gallons of syrupy reminiscenses into my sympathetic ear," replied the magician. "Of course, you'd just returned from last year's visit to this jeweled city in the crown of European visit to this jeweled city in the crown of European real estate and were bubbling over with—"

"I was last over here late in the winter of ninety-five said Harry, puffing absently on his cigar. "A government minister wanted the Challenge Interattional Detective Agency to handle a case for him and my father sent me—"

"How is your dear papa these days?"

Harry frowned. "Ogres usually don't change much," he answered. "At any rate, I met Alicia, shewas just twenty-one then and—"

"I know, I know. A great and wondrous romance blossomed, but in the end, alas, duty forced you to return to American shores, and the fair princess, with heavy heart, turned her attentions once again to the demands of her kingdom."

"You make it sound like a dime novel, Lorenzo."

"Everyone's life is a dime novel, my boy," the ma gician said with a wistful sigh. "It's when one gets to thinking his life is a Shakespearean tragedy that the trouble commences."

A gaggle of some half dozen street musicians, decked out in crimson and gold, went marching lazily down the middle of the narrow street, filling the gaslit air with brassy militant music.

Eventually Harry said, "Maybe I am making too much of all this."

"Would you care to join me in a brandy? Or an éclair?"

"The thing is," continued Harry, "when our agency was hired to escort Mr. Katjang Otak and his crown jewels from New York City to the Burmese Pavilion at the Exposition here, I let myself get the idea I could pick up where—"

"Zeverburg has many another pleasure to offer, ample, I am doing two magnificent shows nightly at the very threshold of the Exposition grounds.

"You're absolutely certain you don't want even one éclair?"

"When I sent in my card tonight," said Harry, "these two louts came out of the damn palace to throw me in the direction of the gutter."

"Are you and your dear old dad still using that business card with the staring eye and the catchy slogan, 'A Wide-Awake Detective Agency' emblazoned upon it? That's been known to annoy some otherwise placid individ—"

"Alicia's changed, I guess."

"Her father is said to be at death's door. Perhaps, Harry, that accounts for—"

"Okay, King Ulrich's dying. She could still have sent a short note explaining—"

"Would you like me to introduce you to my assistant, Sara? A charming lass, titian-tressed and quite surprisingly well-read. She can actually recite interminable stretches of Browning," said the helpful magician. "That ability, coupled with her impressive bosom, might well distract you for a bit."

"I've been thinking, Lorenzo, that there's no real reason for my staying in Orlandia at all," Harry said. "The jewels are now safely on display inside the Exposition and—"

"Stay on," advised the Great Lorenzo. "You've hardly even taken in any of the sights and wonders of the Exposition itself."

"Excuse me, Herr Great Lorenzo." The frail waiter was again beside the table, a pale blue envelope held against his narrow chest. "The boy brought this for your friend."

"Which boy?" inquired the magician, glancing around.

"The lad over by the lady with all the feathers in her—Ah, but he seems to have vanished, sir."

With a shrug the Great Lorenzo took the envelope and passed it across the table. "Smells romantic, my boy."

Harry had recognized the handwriting on the envelope face before he even took hold of it. Opening the envelope, he extracted a folded sheet of blue notepaper.

Harry dearest:

    Please forgive what occurred when you attempted to call. I do want to see you again, but not here. Can you meet me tonight at eleven in the Pavilion of Automatons on the Exposition grounds? I have much to tell you.

    Love, Alicia.

The Great Lorenzo drummed his fingers on the table edge. "Ah, how well I remember the last time I received an amorous missive penned upon notepaper with a royal crest. 'Twas in Bosnia nearly a decade ago, shortly after I had introduced my sensational Floating Lady illusion and the whole of the nation was atwitter and agog over my—"

"She wants to see me after all." Harry folded the note, returned it to the envelope.

"At the palace?"

"At the Exposition."

Nodding, the magician said, "Good, the ground is much softer thereabouts. If you get heaved out again, aim for one of the flower beds or a patch of verdant sward. Although—" He ceased speaking, a look of pain suddenly spreading across his plump face.

His chair creaked as he sank back, bringing one hand up to press against his chest.

"What's wrong?" Harry was on his feet.

The magician waved him down. "Nothing, my boy, not a thing." His voice was a bit dim and throaty. He coughed into his hand before continuing. "I keep forgetting I am but a stage illusionist and not a true magician."

Settling back into his chair, Harry slipped the pale blue envelope into the breast pocket of his coat. "You saw something?"

"Nothing at all, no," said the Great Lorenzo. "I have to keep reminding myself I can't really see the future and that these occasional flashes, these unbidden peeks ahead, mean absolutely nothing. Merely, no doubt, the result of mixing éclairs stuffed with clotted cream and rather inferior brandy."

"Your latest vision had something to do with me?"

With a slow sigh his portly friend answered, "If you must know, my boy, I saw you stretched out upon a floor of black and white mosaic tiles. That assignation invitation was clutched in your hand, and there was a handsome sword of some sort thrust into you in the vicinity of your heart."

"Vivid," said Harry, exhaling smoke.

"As I say, not at all a dependable glimpse ahead," the magician assured him. "Don't let me spoil your evening, my boy."

Harry grinned. "Why would your predicting my death spoil my fun?"

"Even so," the Great Lorenzo said, "it wouldn't hurt to be as careful as you can this evening."

Chapter 2

The weather changed a few minutes shy of eleven that evening. A fine, misty rain began to fall, and the thousands of lights of the Exposition grounds became faintly blurred. The music and laughter and the babble of hundreds of excited conversations seemed suddenly muffled, too.

Harry was making his way through the crowd circling the main fountain when the rain started. The two arched dolphins were spouting streamers of purple water, the single naked water nymph was spilling a cascade of gold from her tilted horn of plenty. Cutting through a flower garden and then double-timing along a path of slick white gravel, Harry reached the Streets of Cairo Exhibit just in time almost to collide with a plump matron riding one of the fair's hundred and some white burros.

"Please, whatever you do, don't annoy the brute," the gray-haired Englishwoman pleaded. "Whenever he becomes annoyed, I tumble off."

Grinning and tipping his hat, Harry eased around the woman and her mount. He'd been to Cairo once on a case for the Challenge International Detective Agency and this crooked block-long alley, with its low white houses and mosques, over-hanging upper stories and multicolored awnings, looked fairly authentic. But it smelled much better than the real Cairo ever had.

A small ragged Egyptian boy of ten or so thrust a wooden bowl into Harry's midsection as he passed the alcove the boy was huddled in. "Baksheesh," the boy requested.

Harry fished out an Orlandian coin of modest denomination and flipped it into the bowl.

"My mother tell your fortune for—" The boy had stopped talking and was staring up into Harry's face, mouth slightly ajar.

"Aren't you going to finish your sales pitch?"

"It is of no matter." The boy dodged around him. "Don't waste your money, for you have no future." He went scurrying away among the legs of the tourists.

"Damn," reflected Harry as he continued on his way, "people are sure going out of their way to predict dire things for me."

Well, maybe it wasn't all that damn bright to be pursuing Alicia again anyway. She was Princess Alicia, after all, and fairly soon she'd be Queen Alicia. Best thing to do would be to forget what had happened between them over a year ago.

That wasn't altogether an easy chore, though. Alicia had been unlike any other woman Harry had ever met. She was beautiful and—

"Dime novel stuff again," he warned himself.

At the end of the Egyptian lane there was a stretch of park-like land, dotted with trees and wrought-iron benches. On the far side of this small park loomed the Pavilion of Automatons, a large building with a domed roof. Its walls were of pale imita-tion marble, its curving roof was made up of bluish glass panels set in a fretwork of white metal.

The rain fell heavier now. Harry ran when he reached the grassy area.

At the doorway of the pavilion two British seamen were just turning away.

"No use, guv," one of them informed him. "She's closed up

for the evenin'."

"'Ad me 'eart set on seein' that clockwork dancin' girl," muttered his mate.

Turning up the collars of their peacoats, they hurried away.

Harry, frowning, approached the closed metal and stained-glass doors of the darkened pavilion. Affixed to one of the glass panels was a hastily written note.

Temporarily Closed.

Hands in pockets, Harry stood with his back to the door. The rain hit down on the metal awning that sheltered the doorway. There was no sign of the princess anywhere.

Behind him a door creaked and a thin piping voice called out, "We are not closed to you, Herr Challenge."

It took Harry a bit more than ten minutes to determine he was the only living person inside the dimly lit Pavilion of Automatons. He was certain he was sharing the place with just the two dozen clockwork figures arranged in alcoves and upon low pedestals. He'd long since noticed that the floor was made up of black and white mosaic tiles that formed giant serpentine patterns. He reminded himself that Lorenzo's predictions quite often didn't come true.

Nearest the doorway stood the dancing girl the sailors had been anxious to see. She was a little over five feet high, dressed in a spangled Gypsy costume. She was poised on one foot with a tambourine raised high above her kerchiefed head. In the flickering light provided by the two gas lamps that had been left on she looked almost real.

"Almost," said Harry as he began another slow circuit of the long room.

Next to the immobile dancer sat a tiny golden-haired boy clad in a red velvet lace-trimmed suit. On his tiny lap rested a tablet, and he held a quill pen in his pink, pudgy right hand.

There was a clockwork flutist and a fortune-telling old witch, a caged mechanical canary and a juggler. At the far end of the room two life-size young men in fencing costumes faced each other holding sabers.

While Harry was studying the two realistic figures, the dancing girl's tambourine rattled. He spun.

She didn't appear to have moved.

The only sound he heard was the night rain hitting on the dozens of glass panels high above.

Then he noticed that the feather pen in the little boy's hand was flickering.

Harry went sprinting over there.

The mechanical boy had stopped writing by the time Harry reached him.

Scrawled across the white sheet of paper was a message for him.

Leave Zevenburg. It is not safe for you.

Harry took a step back from the little automaton. Lifting off his hat, he scratched at his dark, curly hair. "Well now, I'll tell you," he said aloud, his voice echoing. "I was aiming on leaving the whole damn country bright and early tomorrow. Now, though, I'm not so sure."

"Too bad, too bad." The old fortune-teller had spoken in a dry, rattling voice. "Now you'll die, now you'll die."

Above the drumming of the rain Harry heard heavy footfalls. He turned to see one of the fencers walking, quite gracefully, toward him. The blade of his saber caught the light of one of the bracket gas lamps and sparkled once.

"Clockwork or flesh and blood," Harry warned the approaching figure, "you're not going to take a slice out of me." He reached inside his coat for his revolver.

The gun was no longer there.

Somebody out in that crowd, the Egyptian beggar kid most likely, was a damn good pickpocket.

Keeping his hand inside his coat, Harry started backing for the doorway. "I'd sure hate to shoot up a valuable piece of machinery like you," he told the swordsman, who was now less than twenty feet from him.

All at once Harry tripped.

He fell over backward, arms flying wide.

The little velvet-suited boy had gotten behind him somehow, unseen and unheard. Making a chittering, giggling noise over what he'd done, the small cherubic automaton went scurrying away into the darkness at the edge of the room.

Before Harry could scramble to his feet, the swordsman's blade, sharp edge outermost, came swishing down toward his head.

Harry rolled.

Rolled right into the mechanical man, toppling him over.

The figure landed hard and made a rattling clang.

Harry dived to his left, got to his feet and ran for the end of the room. The other fencer was still unmoving on the pedestal. Harry shouldered the figure off his perch, at the same time grabbing the saber free from his waxen hand.

It was a British-style saber, its blade of finely tempered steel and about an inch shy of being three feet long. Harry'd been taught to use a saber by his father, starting back in his fifteenth year. Quite probably even a murderous automaton wouldn't be as nasty an opponent as his father had been.

The mechanical man who was trying to kill him was upright again, coming slowly his way.

"Might as well make this sporting." Harry saluted his opponent with his borrowed weapon.

Stopping a few feet short of Harry, the fencing automaton returned the salute. He immediately thereafter launched a running attack.

That was an approach Harry's impetuous father had frequently favored. He parried the mechanical man's thrust, retreated and then lunged.

The automaton met the blade of Harry's saber with a blocking parry and their blades clanked.

Harry prevented his opponent's riposte with an unorthodox wrist flick. Grinning bleakly, he tried a running attack of his own. Lunging, he passed his blade over the point of his adversary's, raised the other saber and then achieved a touch.

When the point of his saber hit the chest of the automaton, there was a small rattling metallic sound. His clockwork opponent closed with him suddenly and neither of them could use his blade.

This close Harry could see a faint reddish glow behind the glassy eyes, and he was aware of a faint scent of machine oil.

They moved free of each other and the bout continued. Their blades clicked against each other in the silent shadowy pavilion. The rain was falling hard now, pounding on the blue glass dome overhead.

As he fought the automaton Harry realized something. Although the mechanical man had been built to do a bit of assassination now and then, he was basically only an expert fencer. Expert, but quite traditional and conservative. His parries and ripostes were all by the book.

"No reason for me to get skewered by this gadget," Harry decided. "So let's quit fighting fair."

Grinning more broadly into the waxen face, Harry lunged again and then, unexpectedly, kicked the mechanical swordsman in the crotch.

"Yow!" exclaimed Harry, finding the groin area of the automaton untraditionally hard and unyielding.

Nevertheless, his kick succeeded in knocking the machine man off balance.

Hopping on his pained foot, Harry swung his saber in chopping fashion at the off-balance automaton.

The cutting edge of his saber bit into the face, sending chunks of pink-tinted wax flying. The skull beneath was of polished metal.

Pivoting as the mechanical man attempted to strike him with his blade, Harry executed another kick.

This one caught his opponent in the backside.

The automaton stretched out in the air like an enormous jumping jack. Then he fell over onto the black and white floor.

Harry followed him down, crouching over him and hacking at the wax and metal head with his saber.

The fallen machine man made tinny choking noises, arms and legs starting to jerk convulsively. Then his scalp, dark imitation hair and all, popped clear off his head. The silvery metal top of his skull quivered, swung open and vomited out gears, wires and intricate twists of metal. A small rainbow-tinted pool of oil was spreading swiftly across the mosaic tiles.

Sucking in air, Harry stood back and away from the dead machine.

Glancing around carefully, he made his way to the doorway of the Pavilion of Automatons.

Crouched in the shadows near the doors was the writing boy in the little velvet suit. "We won't forget," he chirped in his small voice. "We won't forget."

"Neither will I," promised Harry.

He was outside in the heavy rain, walking through the Chinese Street, when the stares and murmurs of the damp tourists caused him to realize he was still carrying the borrowed saber.

Harry threw it away in the first flower bed he came to.

Chapter 3

Harry was attempting to concentrate on the front page of the morning paper. There was political unrest in Ruritania, a severe earthquake had struck the farmlands of Graustark, there'd been an assassination attempt in Valeria. He set the newspaper aside and picked up his coffee cup.

Two tables over, a wealthy middle-aged American tourist couple were discussing their itinerary for the day. The woman, plump and muffled in fur and feathers, held a red-covered

Baedeker as though it were a hymnbook. There were few other patrons as yet, since the hour was early. The six bright yellow canaries, each in its own gilded cage dangling from one of the gold hooks around the dark-paneled restaurant walls, were singing happily. They were apparently not bothered by the fact that little of the morning sunshine penetrated the heavy shutters of the leaded windows. Illumination in the Hotel RitzZauber's restaurant was provided by a huge crystal chandelier and crystal wall lamps recently converted from gas to electricity. The maroon carpeting was so thick it killed all sound of movement.

The Ritz-Zauber—even Baedeker agreed on this—was one of the best hotels in Zevenburg. Harry didn't much like the place and found it too frilly and fancy, yet he always stayed here. His father felt that any partner in the Challenge International Detective Agency must always reside in a top hotel. As the only partner besides his formidable father, Harry didn't exactly agree, but he didn't argue.

He glanced at the front page once again, then sipped at his coffee.

"...wet umbrellas and parcels must be left in the cloakroom," "the plump American tourist was reading to her husband." "Then one is ready to stroll along the echoing corridors of the renowned Kunsthistorisches Museum to view the many—"

"It isn't raining," interjected her small gray husband.

"Well, of course, it isn't, Silas."

"Then why bother to tell me what to do with my wet umbrella? Seems to me, Fanny..."

Harry slid the blue envelope out of his breast pocket, removed the note he'd received last night. After unfolding it and spreading it out on the crisp white tablecloth, he ran his fingertips over the royal crest at the top of the page. He was damn sure this was a real sheet of Princess Alicia's notepaper, and equally certain the handwriting was hers.

She'd written him fifteen letters during his last visit. And Harry had saved them.

"Schoolboy stuff," he murmured. "A wonder I didn't tie them

up with a pink ribbon."

"I didn't realize I had a hangover until I heard those nitwit birds," announced the Great Lorenzo as he settled in opposite Harry. "My own fault, drinking champagne out of the duchess's slipper after our intimate midnight supper."

Harry slipped the letter away. "Which duchess is this?"

"Duchess Hofnung," replied the portly magician, who was decked out in a bottle-green frock coat and fawn trousers this morning. "A petite, though aging, beauty who is possessed of uncommonly large feet. Her slippers, as a result, held—Cease that vile chirping!" Twisting in his chair, he gestured at the nearest birdcage.

All six canaries fell suddenly mute.

"Nice trick," observed Harry.

"Not a trick, my boy, simply an exhibition of mental telepathy," explained the Great Lorenzo. "Since my brain—my critics and detractors to the contrary—is superior to that of a canary bird, there's no real—Whatever is that plutocrat babbling about?"

The tourist was poking at his plump wife. "Fanny, what's wrong? Why can't you speak? I didn't mean to be snide about the Spaniscue Hofreitschule."

"Ah, a little spillover," realized the magician. "I didn't mean to include you, madam." He snapped his pudgy fingers.

"'... no one should miss the lyric singing of the famed Sevenburg Boys' Choir,'" resumed the befurred matron.

The magician said, "One must be most careful not to abuse power. Now, before I regale you with a fiery account of what befell me last evening by simply complying with the hitherto unknown duchess's written request to teach her a few simple card tricks, fill me in, my lad, on your own amorous adventures. What did that mysterious billet-doux lead to?"

Harry drank some of his coffee. "Alicia wasn't there."

The magician blinked. "Not a very auspicious beginning for a tempestuous romance."

"However," said Harry, grinning, "one of the automatons did

make a try at killing me. That was right after I was warned to get out of town."

The Great Lorenzo pressed his hand to his waistcoat. "Then my vision was at least partially accurate," he said thoughtfully. "There was death awaiting you at the pavilion last night."

"Yep, and from a sword, too." Harry gave his illusionist friend an account of what had happened to him the previous evening.

When he finished, the magician plucked a Turkish cigarette out of the air and lit it with his fingertip. Exhaling smoke, he said, "Perhaps, my boy, those clockwork gadgets gave you sound advice. As you yourself pointed out last evening, your work in Oriandia is done. Why not journey over to Ruritania or—"

"Nope, not yet."

Clearing his throat, the magician leaned closer to Harry. "Do you have any notion how expensive one of those mechanical men is, my boy? Anyone who would construct one for the sole purpose of doing you in is a blackguard with an impressive budget. He may be willing to spend even more to speed you to your grave, Harry."

"Even so," he said, "I think I'll look into the situation."

"But why? Whether or not the princess sent you the note, there looks to be little chance of rekindling your former romance," his friend pointed out. "I hear, by the way, that Princess Dehra of Valeria is quite a looker and very personable. Why not run over there to—"

"Somebody wants me dead," cut in Harry. "I'd like to know who and why."

"Forgive me, gentlemen, for not hastening to your table sooner," apologized the tall, gaunt waiter who materialized beside their table. "The maitre d' had me trying to coax our birds to sing again and thus, sir, I failed to note your arrival until now." He bowed to the Great Lorenzo. "Might I take your breakfast order?"

"I happen to be," the magician told him, "a leading ornithologist. I'm confident I can cure these poor feathered creatures and have them harmonizing in no time."

"You could? How wonderful. What, sir, would be your fee?"

The magician dismissed the notion of money with a lazy wave of his hand. "I would do it simply out of my love for canaries," he explained. "If, however, the management could see its way clear to provide me with a plate of bratwurst and sautéed potatoes, with three fried eggs on the side and a large pot of tea, my good man, I would greatly appreciate it."

The waiter bowed once more. "I am certain that can be arranged, Herr Doctor," he said. "And will you cure them immediately or—"

"Right after my breakfast," promised the Great Lorenzo.

Bowing even more deeply, the gaunt waiter withdrew.

"I probably could've gotten them to toss in a bottle of wine as well," the magician reflected. "Ah, well, a bit early in the day for that." He fluffed his side-whiskers. "Where was I? Yes… Harry, my lad, your wisest course is to leave Zevenburg."

Harry nodded. "Yep, that probably is the smart course, Lorenzo," he agreed. "However, what I'm actually going to do is dig into this for a couple of days."

"How?"

"Well, first off I'm heading back to that Pavilion of Automatons this morning," he replied. "Take a look at the place in the daylight. Also want to see if I can find that Egyptian beggar boy who more than likely filched my gun."

"Since you no longer have a weapon, Harry, why not—"

"Always carry a spare in my valise." Grinning, Harry patted his shoulder holster.

"I still maintain—But what's this?"

Their waiter was hurrying silently back toward their table across the thick carpeting. He held a yellow envelope. "Herr Challenge, is it?"

"I'm Harry Challenge, yes."

He thrust out the envelope. "A cablegram just arrived for you."

"Thanks." Harry took the envelope and the waiter eased

away.

"I hope," remarked the Great Lorenzo while he was opening it, "you're being summoned to come at once to Guatemala or some other lush—"

"From my father." Harry read the message, passed the cablegram to the magician.

Dear son. Get your miserable lazy carcass over to the Grand Imperial Hotel there in Zevenburg. See Jack Mariott and sister. He's hired us. Rich as sin. Don't dawdle. Your devoted father, the Challenge International Detective Agency.

When he finished reading, the magician leaned back in his chair. "Although this doesn't get you out of town, my lad, it at least will keep you from poking your nose any further into the Princess Alicia matter."

"It would," said Harry," if I was going to pay any attention to it."

Chapter 4

The morning was bright and clear, and a very gentle breeze drifted across the vivid green meadows and woodland glades of the Volksgarten Park. On the other side of the tree-lined lane a white-suited vendor was selling multicolored ices from an umbrella-shaded cart. When three uniformed college students came speeding by on their bicycles, the tiny brass bell on the cart gave a sympathetic jingle.

Harry, after taking his leave of the Great Lorenzo on the marble steps of the Ritz-Zauber, had cut across the sun-bright park toward the Exposition grounds.

He slowed now and stopped, pretending to be debating whether or not to cross over and buy an ice. Actually he wanted to take a careful look behind him. For the past several minutes he'd again had the feeling he was being tailed.

Two French sailors were sharing a stroll with a giggling blond local girl. A bewhiskered gent was feeding strudel crumbs to some blasé park squirrels. A small, pouting little boy in a velvet suit was being taken for a reluctant walk on a leash by his hefty nanny.

No one else was to be seen behind him at all.

While Harry was standing there an old woman who sold flowers started to cross the road from his side.

"Look out!" cried the vendor.

From around a bend in the road a black stallion came galloping. The man in the saddle was dressed all in black. His face was lean, his dark hair was close-cropped and a puckered white scar snaked across his left cheekbone.

Although the horse was heading right for the flower seller, the dark rider made no effort to rein up or swerve.

Harry had started running while taking all this in.

He reached the old woman, grabbed her by the arm and yanked her back clear out of the charging animal's path.

The rider said, "Swine!" at Harry and kept on his course.

"Hey, you damn fool!" called Harry at the retreating horseman. "You came—"

"No, no, sir. It is nothing, please," whispered the old woman, clutching her basket of flowers closer to her.

"Nothing? That idiot almost—"

"You want no trouble with him." She crossed herself awkwardly, watching the horse and rider gallop out of sight. "That was Dark Otto."

"Was it now?" Letting gc of the woman, Harry lifted off his bowler. He dusted it, popped it back atop his head. "Baron Otto Van Horn, huh? Didn't recognize him right off. He's even uglier than he was last time I—"

"You mustn't say that, sir," the flower vendor warned as he guided her across the roadway. "For even though Dark Otto is not in favor with his fam ily, he is a powerful and vindictive man."

"I thought the royal family had an agreement with their black sheep," said Harry. "Otto was supposed to stay at his chateau in the Blackwood Forest and never visit Zevenburg except on rare formal occasions."

"Because our poor monarch is so ill…" She made another sign of the cross. "Dark Otto is allowed to breach the rules."

"That's not smart."

"It isn't, no. Yet you ought not to say so." She selected a white carnation out of her wicker basket, handed it to him. "Thank you for helping me, sir."

Grinning, Harry adjusted the flower in his buttonhole. "Thank you for filling me in on the political situation." From his pocket he took a silver coin and dropped it in her basket.

He resumed walking.

Harry had covered another half mile when a closed carriage caught up with him. It was drawn by two handsome gray geldings.

He casually reached inside his coat toward his Colt .38.

"By George, that was quite splendid," called a youthful voice from within the carriage. "The way you snatched that poor creature from the very jaws of death. Smashing."

Harry nodded, saying nothing.

The door of the carriage swung open, allowing him to see a blond young man of about twenty-five, clad in a tweedy Norfolk suit and matching cap. The youth smiled approvingly out at him.

"I'm very impressed," said the blond young man, "and more than ever convinced we've picked the right man."

"You've picked me for something?"

The young man hit his forehead with the heel of his hand. "I'm going about this backward I fear, forgive me," he said. "Amy's forever pointing that out to me. Should've brought her along, except she's on a shopping tour with a delightful English girl we met on the boat. Stop the carriage, won't you?"

The driver obliged.

The young man hopped lithely free into the morning sunlight. "I'm Jack Mariott," he explained, holding out his hand.

After making certain no one else was going to come popping out of the dark carriage, Harry extended his hand. "Harry Challenge."

"Yes, I know. That's why I've been pursuing you, you see." He shook Harry's hand with vigor before letting go. "Tried to catch you at your hotel, but apparently just missed you. A helpful old gentleman, who seems to have the knack of plucking cigars out of the thin air, suggested I'd find you taking your morning constitutional in the park here. I'm quite fond of exercise myself."

"Actually I'm on my way to a business meeting and—"

"We're most anxious, Amy and that you begin working for us at once," said Mariott. "Would a bonus, perhaps, persuade you to drop everything else?"

"I can get over to your hotel first thing tomorrow. The Grand Imperial, isn't it? That way—"

"I am prepared to offer you an additional ten thousand dollars." He reached inside his Norfolk jacket.

Harry took a step back, sizing up his new client. "What fee did you and my father agree on?""Twenty thousand dollars," answered Mariott as he took out his wallet. "Reasonable enough, considering the nature of the case and the excellent reputation of your detective agency."

Harry glanced up at a pair of doves on a tree branch overhead. He and his father split everything fifty-fifty. Meaning he'd make fifteen thousand dollars for handling this fellow's case. And if he agreed to drop everything, he'd have ten thousand dollars right now.

Mariott was counting out new hundred-dollar bills. "I only have about two thousand on my person. At the hotel, though, we—"

"Why the rush, Mariott? Couldn't your case wait a day or so until—"

"It is, Mr. Challenge, a matter of life and death."

Harry tapped the pocket that held his father's cablegram. He looked from the hundred-dollar bills to the doves and back again. "Okay," he said, taking charge of the cash. "I'll come along with you now to your hotel."

"Splendid!"

* * * *

The sommelier had a cold. Every time he sneezed, the gold keys on the gold chain around his neck rattled and clanged faintly. That barely detracted from the overall splendor of the world-renowned Garden Court Restaurant of the Grand Imperial Hotel. The place was immense, accommodating well over one hundred tables. At this hour, a few minutes past noon, every table was filled, and more anxious patrons could be seen crowded behind the plush crimson rope that guarded the main entry. The restaurant interior was two full stories high, covered over with a domed ceiling of white-painted metal and faintly rose-tinted panels of glass. Midday sun was streaming down, filling the interior with light and illuminating the profusion of potted plants and trees that gave the famed dining place its name.

Harry had the feeling he was lunching in a vast greenhouse. "Go on," he urged Amy Mariott.

She was a blond young woman of no more than twenty, pretty, though a shade too plump for Harry's taste. She wore a simple satin frock with a high collar. One of her plump hands rested on the copy of the second volume of the Tauchnitz edition of Anthony Trollope's Can You Forgive Her? that she'd been reading when Harry and her brother had joined her.

Amy had paused to glance over at the sneezing wine steward. "Poor man, a dose of sulphur and molasses would fix him up fine," she said. "But I don't suppose they have any in this entire country. You can't help wondering—"

"Amy, you're being discursive," her brother pointed out. "You always accuse me of—"

"Oh, tush," said Amy, feigning a pout. "I can come to the point faster than you any old day, Jack, and not go around Robin Hood's barn doing it."

Four musicians, clad in tailcoats, were mounting the elevated dais in the center of the room. As soon as they were seated, the cellist was hidden from view by a luxuriant banana palm.

"Perhaps I better go ahead and explain to Mr. Challenge why we hired him. Amy, since you—"

"I can do it much better than you, Jack." She gave Harry a brief dimpled smile. "You've no doubt heard, Mr. Challenge, of the Great Boston Tea Company?"

"Most everybody has," he answered. "Fact, I read an interesting article in McClure's a few months—"

"That was mostly a lot of radical nonsense," said Mariott firmly.

Harry snapped his fingers. "You're that Mariott family."

"Our uncle, Jonah Mariott," confirmed the girl, "is president and chairman of the board of the Great Boston Tea Company. It's no secret he's a millionaire many times over. Although that wicked magazine story exaggerated the extent of his wealth and influence considerably."

"The point is," added her brother, "after our parents were taken from us in a railroad accident five years ago, we became Uncle Jonah's sole heirs."

"I see," said Harry. "And now somebody's trying to come between you and your uncle's money."

"Marvelous!" Amy clapped her hands. "A very perceptive deduction."

Resting his elbow on a patch of sunlit table, he told her, "You'd be surprised, Miss Mariott, how many similar cases we've handled."

She smiled at him again, a bit longer this time. "It isn't just the money," she said. "Jack and I have a very comfortable trust fund that was thoughtfully set up for us by our dear departed parents. I shan't, though, play the hypocrite and pretend we'd rather Uncle Jonah's money went to that quack doctor than to us."

Harry inquired, "He's involved with someone you believe is a charlatan?"

Amy nodded. "We've met the man, had a very unsatisfactory interview with him at his sanitarium, and there is no doubt in my mind he's a complete and utter fraud."

Harry nodded toward her brother. "Who is the man?"

"He calls himself Dr. Mayerling."

Amy shuddered. "He's residing in a dreadfully bleak castle in the Blackwood Forest."

"That where your uncle is?"

Jack said, "He's been an alleged patient there for the past five months."

Reaching out, Amy took hold of Harry's hand. "We are convinced, Mr. Challenge, that Uncle Jonah is a virtual prisoner in Blackwood Castle."

"How does your uncle view the situation?"

"We haven't been able to see him or communicate with him." Amy increased the pressure on his hand. "The castle lies a day's rail journey from here, near the town of Dunkelstein. Jack and I traveled there last week, shortly after our arrival in Orlandia."

"I must admit," said her brother, "that Dr. Mayerling was very cordial to us. But he insisted our uncle was not yet ready to receive visitors of any kind."

"Imagine that, after we'd traveled all the way from America and I was so dreadfully seasick for days on end."

Harry retrieved his hand from her grasp, used it to scratch at his chin. "I've heard a little something about this Mayerling," he said. "He's gained a reputation among the older and wealthier as being able to make them young again. Is that the pitch he gave your uncle?"

"Dr. Mayerling is subtler than that," said Mariott. "He isn't one of those patent-medicine quacks one finds advertising in the back pages of our popular magazines, promising cures for the most deadly diseases. Oh, no, the doctor merely implies that his rejuvenation process has been known to make certain of his patients feel younger."

Harry glanced from Mariott to his sister. "Why'd you two decide to come over here?"

Mariott answered, "Originally Uncle Jonah was to have stayed at the sanitarium for just four weeks. After nearly two months had elapsed, however, he had yet to return."

"Then we received the most strange and unsettling letter from our uncle," picked up Amy. "He claimed that Dr. Mayerling had changed his life, endowed him with an entirely new point of view. He intended to stay on at that dreadful pile for an indefinite period."

"The letter was authentic?"

"Yes, unfortunately," answered Mariott. "We immediately considered the possibility of forgery, even though the handwriting did appear to be that of our uncle. We consulted our attorneys, and they put us in touch with a well-thought-of professor at Harvard who specializes in such things. He assures us the writing in the letter matches that of the samples we provided."

"You have that letter with you?"

Amy shook her head. "I told Jack we should have brought it, but he—"

"Since it was authentic, I saw no need."

Turning, Harry watched the string quartet play for a half minute or so. "Why'd your uncle decide to come over here in the first place? How'd he hear about Dr. Mayerling and his sanitarium?"

Amy blushed. "We haven't, I fear, been completely candid with you," she admitted. "There was—Well, Uncle Jonah had met a woman, a handsome widow many years his junior, and he started contemplating marriage. Then, when one of his cronies at the Union Club mentioned the supposedly marvelous results Dr. Mayerling was getting, Uncle made a direct inquiry to the doctor here in Orlandia."

"This widow didn't tout him on to the place?"

Jack smiled. "She wasn't, I don't believe, all that interested in a serious relationship with our uncle," he said. "Uncle Jonah, nevertheless, convinced himself that were he to appear a few years younger, he'd have a much better chance of winning her."

"I hesitated to mention the lady," said Amy. "Since I didn't wish you to think we two objected to his marrying again. We'd love to see him happy, even if it meant losing our rightful inheritance."

Harry asked, "Your uncle's been paying Dr. Mayerling's fees himself?"

Amy replied, "Exactly. Not only that, though the fees are outrageously high. No, in the past three months Uncle has also apparently donated an additional two hundred thousand dollars to the sanitarium."

"When we learned this," said Mariott, "we decided to come to Orlandia immediately."

"Our attempt to see Uncle Jonah failed miserably," said his sister forlornly. "We'd returned to Zevenburg from the Blackwood Forest to arrange for passage home, when Jack said, 'By George, what say we hire a crackerjack detective?'" She spread her hands wide, smiling at Ham'. The sunlight made her blond hair sparkle. "I do believe, after this delightful interview with you. Mr. Challenge, that we have surely hired the right man for the job."

Harry asked, "How old's your uncle?"

"Oh, we ought to have mentioned that sooner," said Mariott. "He's sixty-six."

"Sixty-eight," corrected Amy. "Uncle likes to shave a few years off his true age. He's sixty-eight."

"You saw him before he left for here?"

"At the dock in Boston," replied Mariott. "We made every effort to dissuade him from making the trip, but to no avail, obviously."

"He was in possession of his faculties?"

"He's not senile, if that's what you mean," said Amy. "At least he wasn't then."

"What exactly do you want me to do?"

Amy straightened in her chair. "Why, we want you to rescue him, of course."

"He may not want to be rescued."

"But he's a prisoner," she insisted. "We know that."

"I can go to Dunkelstein, nose around some," said Harry. "I can try to see your uncle. But you have to understand that I can't take him out of there against his will. The government of Orlandia, along with those of several other countries over here, allows us to operate in a limited way within its borders. Kidnapping isn't one of the things they let us do."

Mariott said, "You'll do what you think best, Mr. Challenge."

"We're absolutely certain," said Amy, "that Uncle Jonah would leave that castle if he could."

"Okay, I'll see what I can find out," promised Harry.

"Smashing," said Mariott with a pleased smile. "There's a crack train leaving this evening at seven. I've taken the liberty of arranging a first-class compartment for you."

Harry frowned. "I was figuring on departing tomorrow or—"

"That extra ten thousand dollars," reminded the blond young man, "was to guarantee your giving our case your immediate attention."

After contemplating that for a bit, and listening to the string quartet play Mozart, Harry said, "Give me the train ticket."

Chapter 5

The twilight brought rain, a fine misty rain that drifted down gradually through the darkening sky. The echoing platforms of the Zevenburg railroad depot were roofed over with massive canopies of iron and stained glass. Rain drifted down through the spaces between the roofs, the drops glistening as they were caught in the glow of the gaslights and the beam of a hulking train engine.

The Great Lorenzo was bundled in an Inverness cape and, his abundant side-whiskers were pearled with rain. "It will be a long, dreary odyssey, my boy," he was saying to Harry. From out of the dusky air he plucked the latest issue of The Strand magazine. "You'd best add this to your—"

"Lorenzo, Lorenzo, my adorable spaetzle," chided the petite Duchess Hofnung from amid her furs, "don't overload your handsome young detective friend with going-away gifts. He merely travels to Dunkelstein, not the ends of the earth."

Harry, wearing a gray travel suit, was clutching a large wicker basket bursting with fresh fruit, a wreath of yellow roses, a tinned ham, a picnic hamper, an assortment of English language magazines and several newspapers.

"I'm especially curious about these flowers you materialized, Lorenzo," he mentioned, jiggling the floral piece. "Why does the ribbon say 'Farewell to Our Loyal Member'?"

"People oft say farewell when one of their bosom chums departs," replied the Great Lorenzo.

"Your carriage passed the Zevenburg Municipal Cemetery on the way to the station, didn't it?"

Narrowing one eye, the portly magician picked a green and crimson Easter egg out of the air. "Hard-boiled egg?"

"Lorenzo," cautioned the smiling little duchess, "your strapping young comrade has already enough to feed a regiment."

"You never know when you'll want an egg." He deposited it in Harry's fruit basket.

"I appreciate your coming to see me off," Harry told him. "Now I'd better find my damn compartment so I can dump all this—"

"Fritzi, you wait in the carriage for me now," suggested the Great Lorenzo. "I have a few things I wish to discuss with Harry in private, eh?"

"You men. Always secrets, secrets. Worse than chambermaids." Her small blond head emerged from among the furs and she gave Harry a warm, moist, scented kiss on the cheek. "So very pleasant to have met you, Herr Challenge."

"Same here."

"Twenty-two A," said the magician, catching hold of Harry's arm and guiding him along the platform, "is right down here someplace, my boy."

Unlike American trains, those on the Orlandia rail lines had cars with doors on both sides.

Harry's compartment proved to be only a hundred yards from where they'd been standing. "Could you maybe make some of this accumulation disappear again?"

"Nonsense, you'll make use of it all before you arrive at your destination." He opened the door. "I understand, too, that the food on this train is not a gourmet's delight. You'll more than likely have to subsist on fruit and eggs."

Harry unloaded all his bon voyage presents on one of the leather-covered seats. "I appreciate your—What's wrong?"

The Great Lorenzo, pale, was pressing his hand to his chest and grimacing. "That chap in the tweed suit," he whispered.

Harry thrust his head out of the open doorway to look down the platform. A small dark man of about forty was walking briskly away from them. He halted now, opened a first-class compartment door and stepped in. "I see him. Don't know him."

The magician was almost breathing normally again. "Nor I," he said in a voice easing back toward normal. "Yet I had a most uneasy feeling when he passed us by."

"Another premonition?"

Shrugging, the Great Lorenzo readjusted his cape. "Be watchful of him. There's something…dangerous about him."

"You don't have to stay until the train pulls out." Harry climbed back into his brown-hued compartment. "The duchess is waiting and—"

"Handsome woman, isn't she? For her age."

"She can't be much more than forty, Lorenzo. That's not ancient, especially since you yourself are pushing—"

"I'll slip in and talk with you for a few moments." Nudging the gifts aside, he sat facing Harry.

Harry pulled the door shut. "One thing," he said. "I don't want you to go poking into what happened to me at the pavilion last night while I'm away. If, when I get back from Dunkelstein, I'm still curious, then I'll investigate the setup. Understood?"

"Perfectly, my boy. You, after all, are the detective, and I merely a humble entertainer." He dug into the fruit basket, selected a golden apple and took a hearty bite out of it. "You put even less faith in my premonitions than I do. Still, I do feel I ought to mention that I've…seen a few things since last we met."

"Having to do with what, the Princess Alicia business or my work for the Mariotts?"

Shaking his head, the Great Lorenzo answered, "I'm not certain, Harry. All I know is, I had a very sharp and upsetting flash of you being hunted by a pack of wild dogs. Later I saw you in a coffin. Very ornate one it was, made of bronze and filigreed all around. You weren't dead, though, merely stretched out in the thing."

"That's comforting at least."

"Perhaps yes. Perhaps no. I am not clear as to what these two visions might mean." He noticed the copy of The Strand." Ah, a new Rider Haggard yarn. Might I borrow this, my lad?"

"You can take along the hard-boiled egg, too."

The magician tucked the magazine under his arm. "I wish you well. Contact me as soon as you return." He opened the door and stepped out onto the platform. "And should you need any—

"Stay right there, don't move for a minute," cautioned Harry all at once.

He ducked, grabbed up one of the newspapers. Hastily unfurling it, he brought it up in front of his face.

"Creditor?" The magician looked around casually, saw only a slim young woman with freckles and auburn hair striding by. She wore a checkered travel suit and was carrying her own heavy suitcase. "Say, isn't that Jennie—"

"Hush," suggested Harry from behind the shield of his news-paper. "I'd just as well she didn't know I was aboard this partic-ular train."

"Why? Publicity never hurt anyone."

"Is she out of range yet?"

"Climbed into a compartment two coaches ahead of yours. Very trim ankle the lass possesses, by the way," said his friend. "That was Jennie Barr, the daredevil girl reporter of the New York Daily Inquirer, was it not?"

"Yep, that's her." Slowly he lowered the paper, but kept it ready in his lap.

"She wrote a rather perceptive article about my last show in New York. Taken from the unusual angle of—"

"She's continually trying to poke her damn nose into the agency's business."

"A pretty nose it is."

"Maybe so, but a detective agency wants privacy, not notoriety."

"Come, my boy, neither Pinkerton nor Burns shares your view."

"Well, neither of those gents happens to be my father," Harry pointed out. "He hates publicity, and I'm not all that fond of it myself. So I prefer to avoid Jennie Barr."

"Pity, since she's a bright and comely lass."

"Train'll be pulling out any minute now, Lorenzo."

"I doubt that, since an Orlandian train hasn't left or arrived on time since right after the thaw of ninety-four.

"Even so."

"The hint is perceived and acted upon." He rotated his palm once and another hard-boiled egg, purple and silver this time, appeared. He dropped it into the fruit basket. "Want some salt?"

"No, don't conjure up any. Just close the door and let me lie low until the train's out of the station."

"I seriously doubt you can avoid the young lady from here to Dunkelstein."

"I'm sure going to try."

"I'll wager you won't succeed." He chuckled, tipped his slouch hat and went strolling away down the platform.

Harry pulled down the shades on all the windows of his compartment. "Wonder what the hell Jennie's doing on this train."

Chapter 6

An hour out of Zevenburg, rolling swiftly across flat farm country, Harry's train ran into a storm. The fun moon suddenly vanished from the night sky, massive black clouds closed in and hard rain began to pelt the train.

Outside his compartment window, Harry saw an image of himself floating. The rain sliced at it, and when lightning sizzled across the fields of grain, the reflection thinned and was gone. Lights of farmhouses flickered far off in the wet darkness. Another flash of lightning showed him a bareheaded boy riding a white mare hell-for-leather for a great yawning barn.

There were several deep rumbles of thunder, drowning the clacking of the train wheels.

Then Harry saw a second figure floating out there in the rain-swept night.

He spun to face the corridor door, hand diving beneath his coat for his gun.

"I knocked," said Jennie Barr on the threshold.

Bringing out his hand empty, Harry told the reporter, "I have nothing to say to the press."

"Malarkey." She came on in, shutting the door behind her, and settled on the other seat amid his scattered gifts. She tucked her legs under her, grinned at him.

She really was a very attractive young woman, twenty-six years old, slender, with pale reddish hair and a light dusting of freckles. She wore the checkered skirt of her traveling suit and a puff-sleeved white blouse, and she was carrying a shoulder bag.

Harry said, "I was hoping you wouldn't find me on board."

Jennie laughed. She had her auburn hair pulled back and held with a tortoise-shell comb. "You get yourself seen off by a half-baked magician who's all but pulling rabbits and pigeons out of his sleeves and you expect to be inconspicuous?"

"Lorenzo's a friend of mine, old friend. Naturally he—"

"I wouldn't mind being your friend, Harry, except—" Her pretty nose wrinkled. "You must have noticed, being a fairly astute detective, that many kids grow up to resemble their parents."

"I have, yes."

"Settling down with you might be fun for a while," she told

him as the lightning crackled outside. "The hitch is, see, you'll probably end up being a dead ringer for that crusty old father of yours. Who'd want that?"

"Never having met your folks, I can't—"

"I never did either. I'm an orphan."

Harry watched her for a moment. "Left on a doorstep in a basket pretty much like that one there?"

When Jennie shook her head, a strand of hair fell free. "My parents, whoever they were, apparently couldn't even afford a basket. They delivered me to the steps of a Detroit orphanage in ad old faded floursack. Even so, I managed to look quite sweet, so the sisters later informed me."

"This is bringing tears to my eyes."

"Hard-as-nails Harry Challenge." From her shoulder bag she extracted a stenographer's notebook and a stub of pencil. "Well, enough smart chatter, Harry old pal. I'm after—"

"No interviews."

"Malarkey. You might as well talk to me, since I already know you're going to Dunkelstein. It figures that—"

"How'd you find out where I was heading?"

"By batting my eyes at the conductor. You ought to try it, simpler than using brass knuckles to get information out of people."

"Jennie, a detective is sort of like a priest or a doctor. He takes a vow of—"

"Mother O'Malley!" She laughed aloud, shaking her head. "A little more of that, Harry dear, and I'll expect to see a halo sprout right over your head."

"C'mon. We've run into each other enough in New York for you to know I don't believe in—"

"I know your grouch of a father doesn't like the press, but then he doesn't like kittens and puppy dogs either."

Out in the corridor chimes sounded. "Last call for dinner."

Harry stood up. "I haven't eaten yet."

Jennie stood up. "Thank you, Harry. I'd be delighted to dine with you."

* * * *

As they moved along the swaying corridor to the dining car, the small dark man in the tweed suit came toward them.

He didn't seem especially dangerous or formindable, although Harry noted a nasty look to his small gray eyes.

The man smiled at Jennie in a nervous, quick way. "Good evening, Fräulein Barr."

"Evening, Mr. Gruber." She pressed back against a carriage wall to let him go shuffling by.

"Know him?" inquired Harry, opening the dining car door for her.

"Name is Gruber. He's a traveling salesman in cutlery. He introduced himself to me this evening earlier when, so he claimed, he entered my compartment by mistake."

"Lorenzo didn't take a fancy to him either."

A plump waiter with a handsome yellow moustache escorted them to a table beside a dark, rain-washed window.

"Oh, does your magic friend know Gruber?"

Harry said, "Noticed him on the platform and…" He paused, grinned. "Lorenzo has premonitions sometimes."

"Second sight. Sister Patricia had that, at the orphanage." She picked up the small menu. "Although you don't have to be a mind reader to tell that Herr Gruber's an unsavory character. The sauerbraten sounds good."

Harry had his menu in his hand, but he was looking out the window. Great forks of blue lightning were dancing across the immense darkness of the sky. "I should have Lorenzo along. He's very good at conning people out of free meals.

"Sports editor friend of mine does admirably with a trained cockroach." She dropped her bag on the empty chair next to her. "Now shall we talk about Dr. Mayerling?"

Harry opened his menu. "Might as well," he said finally.

"I won't, since I'm your dinner guest, take notes."

"You're going to Dunkelstein on account of the good doctor?"

Jennie replied, "I suspect he's a confidence man and nothing more. There's no evidence he attended any legitimate medical school in Europe, England or America within the past thirty years."

"And he's been fleecing a number of wealthy Americans."

"Right, exactly. That's the angle that appealed to my editor. Is Dr. Mayerling taking advantage of our gullible native aristocrats? Who is this mystery man who does business out of a haunted castle? Since I was coming over to Orlandia to cover the Exposition anyway, we decided—"

"Is Blackwood Castle supposed to be haunted?"

Jennie shrugged one shoulder. "To Daily Inquirer readers all European castles are haunted," she answered. "Besides, with a name like that, it's bound to be cluttered with spooks."

Harry said, "What do you know about Mayerling's persuading his patients to donate substantial sums, above and beyond their treatment fees, to him and his sanitarium?"

"That's one of the items I'm going to be looking into. Now suppose you tell me something."

"Can't give you the name of my client," he said. "So let's just say I'm working for someone who's concerned about one of Mayerling's patients. And with whether or not this patient is staying at the castle voluntarily."

Nodding, Jennie reached into her bag. "That's another of the rumors about Dr. Mayerling I intend to investigate." She produced her notebook, flipped it open to a middle page. "Let's see now. I have the names of the following rich Americans who are presently residing within the castle. Mrs. Esme Watt-Evans, Colonel Evan Marshall, Mr. and Mrs. Melvin Shestack, Ogden Whitney III, Jonah Mariott, Daphne St. Claire and Hugh S. Scott." She shut the book. "Your eyes flickered only on Mariott's name. Is he the one you've been hired to extricate from Dr. Mayerling's clutches?"

"Jennie, it's one of those on your little list. That's all I can tell you right now."

The freckled reporter smiled. "I have contacts in Dunkelstein," she told him. "I'm darn good at finding out things, as you already know, Harry. Be much more sensible for us to team up and—"

"Nope, I've heard about your idea of teamwork. Gent on the Chicago Tribune mentioned the time on a steamboat on the Hudson when you were supposed—"

"Heck, that was with another reporter," she said defensively. "Nobody expects you to play fair with your own colleagues, not in the newspaper game. You're different, though. You're a detective and not a journalist, so I'd play fair with you. On top of which, Harry dear, we're friends."

"Be that as it may, I am going to work alone. Solo. Without you."

Her smile returned, broader. "Okay, pretend to yourself that's the way things are going to be," she said. "I intend to win you over before we even reach—"

"Excuse me for intruding," said the yellow-moustached waiter. "I don't like to interrupt a young couple so obviously enamored with each other, yet I must inform you the kitchen will close very soon now."

Jennie said, "I'll have the sauerbraten."

"The same," said Harry.

"Alas, my heart grows heavy," sighed the waiter."We're all out of sauerbraten."

Chapter 7

By midnight the train was chuffing its way through the Schweigen Mountains. Thunder rumbled, echoing across the dark chasms, and rain lashed at the windows of Harry's compartment.

Absently he peeled the colorful shell from one of the hard-boiled eggs. "Wish Jennie was off chasing a story in another part of the world altogether," he said to himself.

But did he?

He returned the egg to the basket. Restless, he stood up, shrugged back into his jacket and left the compartment.

The corridor was empty, dimly lit. The sound of snoring came from several of the rooms he passed. Harry moved quietly through the rattling train, heading for the smoking car at the tail end.

The smoking car was empty, thick with stale grayish air. Only one wall lamp was lit, making a cone of light in the middle of the car.

Harry sat down in a tufted armchair beneath the lamp and took a cigar from his breast pocket. He held it in his hand unlit.

You could really hear the rain back here, drumming on the roof and slamming at the windows.

Harry slouched in the chair.

"Let's consider Jennie first," he said inside his head. "Was she really sent out here to do some newspaper articles on Dr. Mayerling?"

Or had the reporter somehow gotten wind of the fact that the Mariotts had hired him? Was she just tagging along to see what he came up with?

"And what about those blond Mariotts?"

Could any two people, especially now in the waning years of the nineteenth century, really be so clean-cut and innocent? They could very well be fakes, ringers, sent by somebody who wanted to get him out of Zevenburg.

"But Jack Mariott's paid me ten thousand dollars in cash," Harry reminded himself. "Be a lot cheaper just to kill me."

That had been tried already, though, at the Pavilion of Automatons last night. They'd failed and maybe decided to just buy him off the scene.

Lord knows, enough people were aware that he, like his father, was mercenary as hell. Money could sure be used to lure him.

"That would mean, then, that this all has to do with my trying to call on Alicia.'

Why would that be so damn important? Worth maybe ten thousand dollars, worth killing him for.

Their romance was over. Alicia would soon be the ruler of

the country. That would put more than enough barriers between them.

"And what exactly do I really feel about her? A year ago I was sure—"

Someone else had entered the shadowy smoking car. A figure was standing just beyond the circle of light cast by the oil lamp.

"Evening," said Harry, eyes narrowing. "Mr. Gruber, isn't it?"

Gruber edged nearer, smiling ruefully. He had bad teeth. "You'll forgive me, Herr Challenge," he said in his thin nasal voice.

"This car's open to anyone."

Gruber rubbed his hands together. "I meant about what I have to do." He shuffled closer to Harry. "Selling knives and forks isn't all that bad." Gruber's quick laugh was like a bark. "Oh, that was a lie. Told to a pretty fräulein."

"Trying to impress—" Harry noticed the man was bare-footed. "Sent your shoes out to be shined, did you?"

"I find it helps if I'm not wearing shoes when it happens," he explained, rubbing his hands more vigorously. "The first times, many years ago when I was young, I left them on and it was painful. So now I…" The sentence blurred and shifted into a snarl.

Gruber's shoulders were shrugging spasmodically, and he was crouching lower and lower. The lips were pulling back from over his jagged teeth, his nostrils were flaring.

Bristles of dark hair began to sprout on his face. Not just where a beard ought to be, but everywhere. His cheeks, his low forehead, his ears. His jaw seemed to be growing, and his nose and mouth were changing. When he brought his hand up to scratch at his face, it was more a paw than a hand now.

Harry had left the chair. He took three steps back and then reached for his shoulder holster. "Wouldn't advise you to try anything foolish, Gruber." He drew out the Colt .38.

Gruber's only answer was a snarling roar. Teeth bared, he leaped straight at Harry.

In Zevenburg the Great Lorenzo had concluded his second magic show of the event; a few minutes shy of midnight. Here in Orianda he liked to finish with his new and improved version of his famous Floating Lady illusion.

He caused his handsome assistant Sara, who was clad in a scant costume of white satin, to seemingly rise high above the dark stage in a rigid horizontal position.

Then the magician reached beneath his scarlet-lined black cape to produce a pistol with a long filigreed silver barrel. He paused for an instant to cast a fond glance up at Duchess Hofnung in her box.

"Dear ladies and gentlemen of the audience," he announced while taking aim at the floating lady, "let us see if we can bring this lovely creature down to earth again."

He fired two sudden shots at the figure of the young woman. The attentive audience gasped.

Sara vanished in a great cloud of purplish smoke, and a small shower of rose petals fell down, gently, to the stage.

As enthusiastic applause broke out the Great Lorenzo bowed across the footlights. Then the heavy velvet curtain fell and hid him from view.

Straightening up, the magician hurried backstage. He was anxious to change and then escort the duchess to a quiet supper.

The Great Lorenzo slackened his pace. He came to a stop beside a prop table. His left hand, over which he seemed to have lost control, grabbed up the magic slate he'd used earlier in his show.

His right hand picked up a stick of yellow chalk and scrawled a message across the slate.

Shaking his head, as though just awakening, the portly magician held the slate at arm's length to see what he had written.

As regards Harry. It all ties together.

"Not a very impressive handwriting," muttered the magician as he reread the message.

"What's wrong, Lorenzo?" Sara, wearing a Japanese dressing gown over her scant costume, had just come up from the below-stage area where the trapdoor had deposited her just before the dummy replica had gone rising upward.

"Eh?"

"You look somewhat pale and shaken. Are you mooning over that scrawny duchess?"

"Fritzi is petite, not scrawny," he corrected. After taking one last look at the message, he rubbed the slate clean with a red silk handkerchief.

"Your hand's shaking a bit," noticed his assistant. "Remember that time in Graustark when we were playing the Royal Theater and you came down with the grippe? It started exactly this—"

"Fear not, child." He patted her on the shoulder. "I'm not ailing. It does appear, however, that I'm going to have to break my vow to Harry and do a bit of investigating."

Chapter 8

The wolfman had foul breath, a mixture of stale wine and decay. His initial leap knocked Harry over.

Harry's head hit against the claw-footed leg of a chair as Gruber landed atop him.

He snarled and snapped, trying to get at Harry's throat with his teeth.

Straining, Harry brought up his knees and dealt the wolfman a heavy blow in the crotch.

Gruber howled in pain, momentarily preoccupied.

Harry rolled free of him, rose to his knees. He aimed his .38 revolver at the wolfman. "Back off or I'll use this."

Growling, Gruber lunged again. His paws raked at Harry.

Harry fired.

Again.

Twice more.

The bullets thudded into Gruber's shaggy carcass. But they

failed to stop him, or even slow him much.

He managed to get a grip on Harry's neck, struggled to sink his jagged teeth into Harry's flesh.

Blood was coming out of the bulletholes in Gruber's tweed coat and rumpled white shirt. The blood was reddish muddy stuff, and it was dripping onto Gruber's furry hands, matting the thick hair. Yet he didn't seem bothered by the wounds at all.

Harry broke the wolfman's grip on his neck, swung his pistol up. He shot Gruber smack between the eyes.

The bullet bored clean through Gruber's head. Tufts of fur, splotches of blood fragments of bone and brain went flying, splattering the rose-patterned wallpaper of the swaying smoking car.

The wolfman was unfazed. He was growling deep in his chest, still intent on tearing into Harry's throat.

Harry wasn't in favor of that. Gritting his teeth, he shoved hard at Gruber's chest with both hands.

He succeeded in getting him up and off.

While Gruber was tottering, Harry grabbed an unlit lamp off a table and swung it at the wolfman.

The lamp connected with his muzzle, hard enough to smash the glass and splash oil.

"Stay clear of him, Harry!"

Two pistol shots followed.

Gruber stretched up straight, as though he'd suddenly decided to try to leap up and see if he could touch the ceiling. "No, this isn't—" he said in a bloody, bubbling voice.

The life went sighing out of him. He dropped, knees first, to the floor. Then he pitched over onto the shattered lamp and was still.

"Much obliged," said Harry after taking a deep breath.

Jennie Barr dropped her .32 revolver back into her shoulder bag. "I thought you might need a little help."

"How come your gun brought him down and mine didn't?"

She smiled. "Don't you know, Harry dear, you need silver bullets to kill a werewolf?"

* * * *

Harry opened his smallest suitcase. From within it he took out a bottle of brandy and two small metal cups. "I told you you should've stayed inside."

Jennie was standing near the window of his compartment, examining the wet splotches on her ankle-length skirt. "I've never seen anyone toss a dead wolfman off the back of a moving train during a thunderstorm before," she said. "I didn't want to miss it."

After pouring brandy into both cups, he handed her one. "Thanks again for saving my life, Jennie."

"Cheers." She clicked her cup lightly against his. "I imagine you'd do the same for me. Wouldn't you?"

He narrowed his left eye. "Probably."

"I think we did the right thing, disposing of Gruber and cleaning up as much of the mess as we could." Sitting down, she took a sip of her brandy.

"Dead wolfmen are tough to explain to the authorities." He settled opposite her.

"Some people maintain a dead lycanthrope will revert to his human form a few hours after death," she said. "That, though, would be even tougher to explain."

"Jennie," he said, watching her freckled face, "how did you happen to have a gun loaded with silver bullets?"

She patted her bag. "Always prepared, that's my motto. I also carry a bottle opener, a skate key, a sewing kit, a compass and—"

"C'mon, don't treat me like one of your newspa per colleagues. Did you know Gruber was going to change?"

"Not him specifically, no," she replied. "See, Harry, I had a hunch Herr Gruber was up to no good. When I just happened to spot him go skulking out of his—"

"Just happened?"

"Well, I guess the fact I was sort of spying on him helped me some." She drank a bit more of the brandy. "I followed him, saw him transform himself to attack you and…came to the rescue."

"That still doesn't explain the silver bullets."

She glanced toward the window. "Storm's quieting down," she said. "Well, Harry, I didn't tell you absolutely everything at dinner exactly."

"For one thing, you know a lot more about Dr. Mayerling, don't you?"

"Some," she admitted. "I really do have informants in Dunkelstein. One in particular, a brilliant old gentleman who's an expert on things occult, has given me a lot of information. It's possible, Harry, that the doctor is a lot more than just a quack and a confidence man. He's probably a sorcerer or worse."

"That's impossible, Jennie."

She smiled at him. "How about werewolves, are they impossible, too?"

Harry answered, "Always thought so. Until tonight." He shook his head. "Okay. Was Gruber in cahoots with Mayerling?"

"Not certain, though it seems darn likely," Jennie said. "Dr. Mayerling surrounds himself with some very strange associates at that castle of his."

"But he is conning his patients out of money?"

"Yes, but I believe that's mostly to finance his work, his other work."

"Which is?"

She shrugged her left shoulder. "He's supposedly interested in immortality. In carrying on the work of gents such as St. Germain and Cagliostro."

Remembering his cup of brandy, Harry drank most of it down. "If Gruber was working for Mayerling, then it's the doctor who's been wanting me dead."

She eyed him. "Sounds like this wasn't the first attempt."

"Back in Zevenburg," he said. "There was—Hell, Jennie, all of this sounds incredible. At any rate, somebody rigged one of those fencing automatons at the Exposition to come at me. With a saber."

She blinked. "That's…bizarre, isn't it?"

"Yep," he agreed. "First a mechanical man, then a werewolf. Beats most anything I ever encountered in the States."

"Orlandia is a very old, and fairly mysterious country," Jennie said. "You've never met Dr. Mayerling?"

"Not under that name," he said. "Hell, I didn't even know myself I was going to be involved in investigating him when the first attempt was made."

"It might be all this has something to do with your celebrated romance." Standing, she handed him her cup.

"What celebrated romance?"

"The one with Princess Alicia last year. You must be aware it was gossiped about all over the place."

Harry said, "Hadn't occurred to me, no."

"I'm turning in." She eased to the door. "What about my suggestion we team up?"

"I'm considering it," he said. "Seriously."

"Good night, then." Raising up, she kissed him briefly on the lips. "Yell if you need any more help." Smiling, she let herself out of his compartment.

Chapter 9

On tiptoe the Great Lorenzo made his way across alternate stripes of sunlight and shadow toward the carved wood door of the duchess's vast bedchamber.

While he was still several yards from making his getaway, the small marble and gold clock on her dressing table began to chime the hour.

"Renzo, my darling Renzo, wherever are you sneaking off to, fully dressed and all?" called the Duchess Hofnung from the fourposter far across the room.

"Fritzi, m'love," he said, turning to face her, "I have some serious business to take care of."

She was sitting up in bed, arranging her lace negligee and pouting. "So serious you must sneak off before breakfast with me?"

"It has to do with my friend Harry Challenge."

"Ah, your handsome young detective friend? Is he in trouble?"

"He may be soon, my pet, unless I cease dawdling and find out who—"

"Very well, go then, dear Lorenzo." She made a dismissing gesture with her small right hand. "You may use Bruno and the carriage if you wish."

"This task calls for a certain amount of secrecy." He headed for the exit. "Racing around in a gilded carriage pulled by two white stallions with plumes is not the most subtle way to get about town. Thank you, my sweet, for the offer all the same." He plucked a dozen red roses out of the air, flung them in the general direction of the bed.

While she was still clapping her hands with delight, he made his escape.

The Great Lorenzo took an indirect route across the sprawling Exposition grounds toward the Pavilion of Automatons. He wanted to be absolutely certain not a soul was interested in his activities.

He strolled, swinging his gold-headed cane, along the American Street, and even paused at the simulated soda fountain to buy an ice cream cone. Then he toured the Lusitanian Pavilion and admired the jewels and relics therein.

Quite a few people in the midday crowds recognized him, since his show was a popular one, yet no one seemed to take an undue interest in him.

He wandered slowly along the Cairo Street but couldn't spot the beggar boy Harry had mentioned. A fresh-scrubbed goat nuzzled him when he paused to scan a pottery vendor's wares.

The sign pasted to the door of the Pavilion of Automatons read:

Closed Until Further Notice. Sorry.

After scratching at his two chins with the head of his cane, the Great Lorenzo unscrewed the head and glanced discreetly around.

No one in sight.

He plucked a lockpick out of the hollow head of the cane and used it deftly on the simple lock of the doors.

Inside, while reassembling his cane, he took a slow careful look around.

There was no evidence anything unusual had ever occurred here. Down at the other end there were once again two fencing automatons standing stiffly, facing each other.

Nodding to himself, the Great Lorenzo studied the floor at his feet. "Exactly the pattern I saw in my vision," he confirmed.

Swinging his cane, he started along one row of still, silent mechanical figures.

He halted in front of the cherubic boy with pen and tablet. The topmost sheet was blank. Squatting, puffing, the magician looked the little figure straight in his dead glass eyes. "Any messages, my little man, you'd like to pass on?"

The mechanical boy remained motionless.

"They are lifelike, aren't they? I don't blame you for talking to him."

Lorenzo straightened and slowly pivoted.

Standing in the doorway was a girl dressed in a simple skirt, white blouse and kerchief. Her hair was a pale blond, worn in two braids. She was twenty or twenty-one.

"Were you looking for something, my child?"

Timidly, she crossed the threshold. "I am looking for someone, yes," she answered. "When I saw you unlock the doors, I assumed you must be an official of some sort. Is that so, sir?"

After clearing his throat he said, "In a manner of speaking, yes."

She sighed, smiling. "Ever since I arrived last ight I have had a very difficult time, trying to find anyone who is directly connected with the Pavilion of Automatons." She walked slowly across the mosaic tile floor. "I am Helga Spangler, of Munich." She watched his plump face hopefully.

"Spangler..." He tugged at his side-whiskers. "Spangler... Ah, would you, dear child, be the daughter of Wolfgang Spangler?"

"I am, yes." She gave a relieved laugh. "Then you do know where he is."

"He's not in Munich?"

Helga's smile vanished. "When you said you knew him, I thought..." She began, quietly, to cry.

"I know of him, Helga," explained the Great Lorenzo. "Anyone in my line of work quite naturally has heard of your gifted father. Without doubt Wolfgang Spangler is the best builder of automatons and clockwork figures in all of Europe."

"In all of the world," she amended. "That's why he was sent for, brought here to Orlandia. Over five months ago, to work on these exhibits..." Sniffling, she began to walk by the row of figures. "Yes, most of these are his work and yet..." She shook her head, her braids flickering. "They're not exactly his work either."

"Am I correct in assuming your father is missing?"

"Yes," she answered. "At least, I believe so. We haven't heard from him in over four months. As soon as I was able, I came here to see what had happened to him."

"What have you found out so far?"

"Only negative things," said Helga. "I went first to the rooming house, which is located on the Nussdorferstrasse, where my father was supposed to have been staying. They maintain he never lived there, that they have no knowledge of him whatsoever."

"And the officials of this Exposition?"

Her shoulders hunched forlornly. "The few I've been able to talk to have offered little help," the girl replied. "One or two say they may have seen my father, months ago when the Exposition was being built, but they have not the slightest idea where he might be at present."

Scratching his chins with the head of his cane, the magician asked, "What of the gentlemen who are in charge of this particular pavilion?"

"I haven't been able to find any of them. This exhibit was suddenly closed down a few days ago and no one knows exactly why."

The Great Lorenzo said, "Do you know who hired your father in the first place?"

"Oh, yes," she said, nodding. "His name was Sir Andrew Mainwaring, a very wealthy Englishman. He offered my father such an impressive fee that he did not feel he could refuse."

"Did the money actually arrive?"

"Yes, half of the amount was paid in advance and most of that is safely in our bank in Munich."

The magician commenced pacing, down as far as the old crone fortune-teller and back. "This must tie in as well," he said, mostly to himself. "Yes, it has to. The missing Spangler, the automaton assassin, Harry's investigation of Dr. Mayerling—"

"Beg pardon, sir?"

He halted beside her. "Do you have a place to stay in Zevenburg, my child?"

"At an inexpensive hotel on the other side of—"

"No, won't do. I want you someplace safe where you can be looked after," he told her. "Yes, we'll have the dear duchess put you up in one of her guest rooms. She's got dozens of them, each more rococo than the next."

"A duchess? I don't under—"

"Allow me to introduce myself, Helga." He plucked a large business card out of the air and passed it to her. "I am none other than the Great Lorenzo."

Frowning slightly, the girl looked from the boldly engraved card to the magician. "I'm afraid I've never heard of—"

"Never heard of me? Incredible, since we played to sold-out houses for seven weeks in Munich as recently as eight years ago."

"Oh, you are that sort of magician then. A stage magician

and not a true one."

"That remains to be seen," he said, fluffing his whiskers. "Come along now, we'll get you installed in Fritzi's menage."

"You intend to help me find my father?"

"Yes, most certainly," he assured her. "I make it a practice to help young damsels in distress, especially when their problems are linked up with mysterious cases I am already investigating." Producing a dozen yellow roses and handing them to the girl, he guided her to the doorway.

Chapter 10

Harry stepped out of his compartment and nearly bumped into what appeared, at first glance, to be an ambulatory bouquet of white roses. "Oops," he said, halting in the brown-carpeted corridor.

"We've got something of a problem," said Jennie, who was carrying the enormous array of roses. "I brought this down to show you."

"Is Lorenzo around?"

"No, this is—Take a look at the card."

Locating the buff card attached to the green paper that shrouded the dozens of flowers, Harry read the inscription, which was written in a bold, clear hand, aloud. "'To a fine girl and a splendid fellow journalist! Ever, Peter.'"

"Did you happen," inquired the young woman, lowering the huge bouquet enough to look over its top at him, "to hear an enormous thud while we were halted at Froschstadt around dawn?"

"Nope, must've slept through it. Why?"

"That was Peter."

"Doing what?"

The car vibrated as the train went speeding around a woodland curve.

"They were hooking his private car on to the end of our

train." She decided to drop the flowers, propping them against the wall. "Peter Starr McMillion."

Putting his hands in his trouser pockets, Harry gazed up at the swaying ceiling for a few seconds. "The soldier of fortune of the newspaper world? England's answer to Richard Harding Davis?"

"That Peter Starr McMillion, yes. The man who disguised himself as a desert tribesman to interview Sheik Mirhad Waraq, *et cetera, et cetera.*"

"Is he pursuing you or a story?"

"Possibly both," she replied, kicking at the bouquet, tentatively, with her button-shoed foot. "With Peter, though, you can bet the story is at the top of his list."

"And that story must be the same one you and I are interested in?"

"Afraid so, Harry. He's bound for Dunkelstein. Odds are he's interested in Dr. Mayerling's doings."

Taking her arm, he escorted her into his compartment and shut the door. It was late afternoon, and the forest they were speeding through was filling with shadows.

Harry said, "From what I've heard of McMillion, he'll use both fair means and foul to make sure he gets to a story first."

"He will," she said, sitting. "But he really does seem to be fond of me. I mean to say, Harry, Peter's never tried to seduce me off a story."

"Far as you know," he grinned, "and he is a handsome devil."

"Malarkey," she responded, nose wrinkling. "He's Charles Dana Gibson's idea of a handsome fellow. Most women prefer more unconventional faces, such as yours."

"Who's McMillion working for?"

"Most likely the London Graphic, although he's also been doing exposés, very polite ones, for the Gentleman's Monthly."

"If it's the Graphic, he's got Sir Rollo Shestack's money behind him."

Jennie nodded. "Plus his own family money. I imagine Peter's paying for the private railroad car out of his own pocket," she said. "Did I ever tell you what sort of gift he sent me while he was trying to find the headwaters of the Orinoco River with the Sheepstone Expedition?"

"A shrunken head," answered Harry.

"I did tell you before?"

"Nope, I deduced."

Jennie folded her hands. "He knows I'm going to Dunkelstein; he's probably found out about you, too," she said. "Oh, and he's traveling with a loathsome man who's part valet and part thug. Name of Tubbs and quite handy with a blackjack."

"Amazing the variety of interesting people one meets traveling." Harry fished his watch out and consulted it. "We aren't due to arrive in Dunkelstein for another two hours yet. It's already growing admirably dark."

"What are you contemplating, Harry dear?"

"His car is hooked on to the rear of our train?"

"Just behind the smoking car where we had such fun with the late Herr Gruber, yes."

"Has McMillion invited you to join him in the dining car for tea?"

"Matter of fact, he has. By way of a note that came along with that ton of roses. He suggests we meet in a half hour."

"Accept," Harry told her. "Only tell him you can't make it for an hour. Send a note, don't go anywhere near his car yourself."

It was raining in Dunkelstein, a heavy, determined rain that slapped down hard on the roof of their horse-drawn carriage. The town was a quaint one, old-fashioned, its two- and three-story houses and shops leaning close together and possessed of slanting red tile roofs, ornately carved shutters and trimmings, colorful chimneys that tilted at odd angles. Rainwater coursed along tile drains, came splashing down on the winding cobblestone streets.

Jennie sat close to Harry, a plaid lap robe over her knees. "Wherever did you acquire a knack like that?" she was asking while plucking the petals from a single white rose.

"States, out West," he answered. "Back almost ten years ago, from my father. It isn't all that difficult."

"And Peter won't be hurt?"

Harry shrugged. "Seems unlikely."

Jennie laughed. "It seems somewhat cruel." She laughed again. "Uncoupling his private car, setting it adrift as it were, while poor Peter was no doubt freshening up for his anticipated rendezvous with me."

"We've only delayed him a few hours," he reminded. "So, soon as we get checked into the Zilver Inn, we better start working."

"Exactly," she said. "I'll start contacting my informants tonight. Do you want to come along or—"

"No, I'm going to try a direct approach on Dr. Mayerling."

"Tonight?"

"Yep, in the dark."

"This may sound superstitious, but Mayerling seems like the sort of fellow best approached by daylight, bright sunny daylight."

"By the time we get our next sunlight hereabouts, Jennie, Peter Starr McMillion will be in town."

The auburn-haired reporter nodded at the curtained window. "Dunkelstein doesn't have a single telephone yet, you know."

"I do, which is why I'll arrange for a carriage to take me out there. Blackwood Castle is only about fifteen miles out of town."

Finished with the rose, she slipped both hands under the robe. "I bet at night, traveling through the Blackwood Forest," she said, "it'll seem a heck of a lot longer."

* * * *

Harry, alone and whistling softly, took a walk through the lanes and byways of Dunkelstein. The rain had subsided into a gently falling mist.

A hired carriage would call for him at nine at the Zilver Inn. The innkeeper had arranged for the transportation, insisting that Harry must pay double the usual fee because the destination was Blackwood Castle and warning him the driver must leave the vicinity of the castle well before midnight struck.

Jennie had taken off from the inn a few minutes ahead of Harry, bound for a meeting with the occult expert who was one of her sources of information.

She'd looked very pretty in her rain cape.

"Not as pretty as Alicia, though," Harry felt obliged to remind himself.

He whistled a slower tune, pausing to look into a toymaker's dimly lit shop window. Rag dolls were sprawled in a heap, at least a dozen of them, floppy arms and legs tangled and twined. A long parade of soldiers stood frozen in front of the tumble of fat dolls. Dangling down from above was a blond ballerina puppet.

Harry moved on.

From a pastry shop cafe spilled yellow light, loud conversations and the strong scent of cinnamon.

"...no, no, that is not the way it goes, Max," someone was arguing inside.

"I am right, Moritz."

"No, no, Max. The man takes the sheepdog up to the front door and..."

Harry turned a corner to find himself walking down a steep incline. There had been a fire on this street recently; the black smell of it was still hanging in the damp air. The two shops on his right were gutted, a jumble of broken wine bottles could be seen in among the charred and fallen timbers of one. It was impossible to tell what sort of business had been carried on in the other shop.

Just beyond the ruined stores was a narrow twist of alley. Huddled in it, on her knees, was a dark-haired young woman in a dark cloak.

Standing over her was a wide-shouldered young man in a tattered peacoat. He had a butcher knife in his raised right hand.

"...please...don't," the fallen girl pleaded in a faint voice.

"I don't think you'd better touch her," said Harry. The youth spun, facing Harry. His face was soft and moonlight white, his eyes small and red-rimmed. "Mind your own damn business, outlander."

Saying nothing, Harry suddenly kicked the young man in the knee. "You ought," he suggested, kicking him in his other knee, "to be cordial to tourists, lad. They're good for the local economy."

The young man was howling in pain, doubled over, trying to rub at his knees.

Harry next dealt a paralyzing blow to the youth's knife arm, and the blade clattered to the slick cobblestones.

"Swine!" Turning, he went hobbling off, picking up speed the farther downhill he got.

"People keep calling me that," murmured Harry, watching the departure.

"Thank you," said the dark-haired young woman. She was standing now, cloak wrapped tight around her. She was tall, nearly as tall as Harry, and quite attractive. "I should be all right now."

"How far are you from home?"

"Only a mile or so," she answered. "I am certain I shan't have—"

"Still and all," he told her, "I'd better see you home."

"Very well," she said, smiling faintly. "That would be most kind of you."

She put her hand on his proffered arm. He could feel the coldness of her touch through his coat sleeve.

Chapter 11

Harry dropped more sticks into the small fireplace. The fire crackled and sputtered but still didn't seem to produce much heat.

"You've been most kind," said the dark-haired young woman, who'd introduced herself as Naida Strand. She sat, dark cloak still wrapped around her, in a carved wooden chair close to the heatless fireplace.

Carved serpents chased frightened hares up the thick legs of the chair.

"You're certain," inquired Harry, "you don't know the gent who attacked you?"

"I haven't any notion who the man was, no." She held both pale hands out to the thin fire.

They were in the parlor of her cottage, a stunted gray-stone and red-tile place on the edge of town. The walls were a dead white color, slanting oddly inward, as though the room had been designed by someone with a faulty sense of perspective. The only light, besides the feeble fire, came from a hurricane lamp on the small wooden table beside Naida.

"I wouldn't have figured Dunkelstein," said Harry, "for a town with many footpads and robbers roaming its streets of an evening."

My stay here has been peaceful and untroubled...until tonight." She stood up, slowly and gracefully. "Might I offer you a cup of tea before you take your leave?"

Harry tugged his watch from his watch pocket. "Sure, if you're up to fixing it."

"I am." She moved silently out of the chill room. Hands in trouser pockets, Harry took a slow stroll around the grim parlor.

There were only two small windows, both high up and made of jigsaw chunks of thick stained glass. Tree branches scratched at them. A lame claw-footed table stood beneath one window, its surface covered with a varied collection of objects—a dumpy pewter vase filled with dusty straw flowers, three small glass globes housing snow scenes within, a crystal egg. One of the globes, which Harry lifted and upended, had a ruined castle inside. The make-believe snow swirled around its broken battlements.

All along one shadowy wall ran a series of dark wood shelves. Fat old leather-bound books mingled with small stuffed birds, polished stone lizards and toads and tiny little people made of blown glass. The gilded titles of most of the books were blurred, not legible. Selecting a book at random, Harry opened it. The pages were musty and foxed. Once, long ago, someone had pressed a yellow rose between them. It was brittle and nearly black, with the stem twisted like the tail of a lizard. The text was in Latin.

"Do you read Latin?" asked Naida behind him.

"I was able to while I was in high school," he replied, closing the book and returning it to its place. "The knack's long since deserted me."

She was wearing a full-length gown of dark velvet, held in at the waist with a thin cord of gold. A ruby pendant hung around her neck on a golden chain. You're an American, I assume." She set the copper tray she was carrying on the table beside her chair and poured two cups of tea from the plump purple teapot.

"Yes, from New York." He accepted the cup of tea she handed him.

"An exciting city, I hear. Do you prefer it, say, to London or Paris?"

Harry sipped his tea, which was strong bitter stuff. "You didn't include Zevenburg on your list."

A very thin smile touched her face. "It is a charming city, yet I don't believe it compares with Paris or Vienna," she replied. "Although I did pick up this lovely brooch in Zevenburg." She lifted the chain and the lamplight flashed in the deep red stone. "It's quite fascinating, don't you think?"

Harry had to be interested in jewels professionally, but he wasn't much fascinated by them otherwise. "It's—" Yet this ruby, ticking slowly back and forth on the glittering chain, was fascinating.

It pulsed, like a small beating heart, and he couldn't keep from watching it.

Seeing, in fact, nothing else.

The walls and the floor were growing dim, dimmer, fading away, swallowed by deep shadows. The ruby was there.

And Naida's eyes.

Then there was nothing but shadows.

* * * *

Peter Starr McMillion said, "Look on the bright side, Tubbs."

His stocky valet was bent under the weight of the steamer trunk he was lugging across the misty courtyard of the Zilver Inn. "There hain't no bloody bright side to this 'ere fiasco, guv," he growled.

Swinging his small valise in his gloved hand, the tall handsome McMillion said, "We had a pleasant and invigorating climb up the mountainside once we made our way out of our derailed private rail car, Tubbs old man," he pointed out. "Then a brisk and healthful hike over the pastoral highways and byways of this delightful—"

"Muddy is what it were."

"One can never have enough exercise." The journalist pushed open the doors of the inn. "Don't forget, Tubbs, we rode the final fourteen miles."

"In a bloomin' wagon full of goats. Foul beggars, they was." Tubbs dumped the trunk down on a bright throw rug. "An' me carryin' this blinkin' wardrobe trunk on me poor frail back till me bean-tosser fair to fell off."

"I'm on a mission," McMillion said as he approached the deserted desk. "I need my disguises."

"'Ow the bloomin' 'ell are yer goin' ter hutilize a complete wog disguise in this 'ere benighted 'ole? These wooden 'eads don't know a burnoose from a bullock's tallywag." Tugging a polka-dot handkerchief out from a lumpy pocket of his mud-spattered greatcoat, he wiped at his forehead. "Or 'ow about your southern darky costume, guv? That'd merely scare these Krauts out of—"

"One never knows which disguise will be called for. Hence, Tubbs, we must bring them all." He rapped the hardwood desktop with his fist.

"The deep-sea diver outfit, that's another what weighs a bloody ton," grumbled Tubbs as he sat on the muddy trunk he'd been hefting. "Complete with 'elmet. You'd think we was halways on the bloomin' verge of hattendin' a blinkin' fancy dress ball. Hit's enough ter give a man a pain in 'is ruddy gravy-maker."

No one emerged from the tiny office behind the registration desk to attend to the new guests. "I say," McMillion called in a polite, but louder voice, "might one be shown to one's room?"

"Might one get a boil on one's fundament waitin'."

Tubbs dug a hand under his greatcoat to scratch at his armpit. "I'll tell yer once hagain to 'oom we owe this fine feathered predicament, guv. That skinny freckled grummett, is 'oo. Never did like 'er, special after that time in Valparaiso when—"

"I'll thank you, Tubbs, not to refer to Miss Barr as a grummett. Whatever that might be."

Tubbs spit into his fist. "Makes a bloomin ransom for merely scribblin' words on paper, yet don't know that a grummett is a bellydingle, a camnikin, a—"

"Yes, I suspected as much." Deftly, he reached behind the registration desk and brought up the register. Opening it to the page for that day, he scanned the names of the guests. "Ah, speak of the devil, as it were. Miss Barr is registered here at this selfsame inn."

"'Ooray fer that news. Might be you an' me can dress up like a wog an' a red Indian an' take 'er dancin' in the rain."

"Jove, Harry Challenge is here as well."

"Hin the same bloomin' room as the quiff, I'll wager."

"Now then, Tubbs, no more of that," warned the renowned journalist. "Miss Barr is certainly not that sort of young woman."

"Just 'cause you been unhable to get inter 'er knickers, guv, don't mean this 'Arry is so dumb," observed his valet. "Them Hamericans is quick as weasels. The ol' twanger can slip in afore—"

"Enough," cautioned McMillion again. "Ah, but here comes our boniface now."

The heavyset, white-haired innkeeper had come puffing out of the kitchen, face flushed, wearing a white apron over his dark suit. "Forgive me, sirs," he apologized as he ducked behind the desk. "I didn't realize you were waiting out here. You should've rung the little silver bell there."

"We didn't 'ave the strength, guv," said Tubbs, arising wearily from the trunk.

"Eh?"

"Merely a jest," explained McMillion. "I am Peter Starr McMillion. I have a reservation for myself and my man."

"Of course, of course." He turned the register toward him. "We are honored, sir."

Tubbs was scowling at the knickknack shelves on the wall. "I don't himagine they 'as one decent bordello in this 'ole bloomin' town," he observed.

Chapter 12

In the article she'd written about him for Scribner's magazine two years ago, Jennie had described Professor Wilhelm Staub, then the head of the history department at prestigious Zevenburg University, as being leonine in appearance. Here in his comfortable, tidy study, the word still struck her as apt.

Staub, retired now, was a large, broad-shouldered man with long straw-colored hair. Although he had given up tobacco, he still liked to chew on a disreputable pipe. He wore rimless spectacles low on his wide, flat nose and looked over them as often as through them.

The professor was seated behind his large wooden desk, open books and a sheaf of papers neatly in front of him. He had a half-full beer mug resting on a wooden coaster near his right elbow. "I've learned a good deal more since last I wrote to you."

Jennie, sitting in a large leather armchair near his desk, had been staring into the blazing fire in the deep stone fireplace. "Beg pardon?"

"Thinking of something else, little Jennie?"

"Someone else," she said.

"You did not come alone to Dunkelstein?"

"I intended to, but I ran into—well, a friend of mine on the train."

"A good friend, judging by the tone of your voice." He took a sip of his beer.

"I have mixed feelings about that," she said. "I'll tell you about him, and the unusual things that happened on our trip here, in a while. First tell me what you've learned, Willie."

Staub picked up the handwritten pages. "Three hundred years ago," he began, "in the wild mountain region of the country of Lusitania, there flourished a gentleman named Karl Mayerling. He was a scientist of sorts who—"

"Any relation to our Dr. Mayerling?"

"It is the same man."

Jennie suddenly sat up straight. "How the heck can he have stayed alive all these—"

"Mayerling engaged in very dangerous scientific and magical researches," the professor said, tapping the manuscript with the bowl of his pipe.

Jennie said, "You're trying to tell me, Willie, that he found the secret of immortality?"

"Not yet, no, but he continues to work on it. This rejuvenation sanitarium has been set up mainly to provide him with disciples who'll supply financing for his researches."

"Wait now," the reporter said."If Mayerling didn't find out how to become immortal through science and magic, how'd he manage to hang around so long beyond his alloted three score and ten?"

"By becoming a vampire," the professor answered.

The carriage creaked and groaned as it rolled along the forest road. The window on the righthand side was broken, and misty night air drifted in through the jagged opening. The tall dark trees were tangled in mist, too.

Harry sat gazing out the empty window, hands folded in his lap. Gradually, as the carriage rattled along, he commenced shivering some.

There was something he ought to be doing, but he couldn't quite remember what it was.

"Let's see now," he said to himself, "I'd better review the facts of the case."

What case?

That question presented a problem.

He was going somewhere, that much was obvious. "Blackwood Castle," he recalled.

He'd arranged to have a carriage call for him at the Zilver Inn at nine, to take him out to the castle in the Blackwood Forest.

"Simple enough."

Except he had absolutely no recollection of having stepped into his carriage.

He hadn't even, he was nearly sure, gone back to the inn after...

After what?

"I went for a walk."

Right, a walk. The toymaker's, the cafe, the burnt-out wine shop. But after that...

"There's a gap," he realized, taking out his gold watch.

The hour was ten-thirty.

"The last time I checked the time it was..." He couldn't remember that.

The carriage came to a dead stop.

Harry looked out.

There didn't seem to be anything about but trees.

This might be," it occurred to him, "a hell of an appropriate time to have a chat with my driver."

He located the door handle after a while. When he opened the door and looked down, he couldn't see the ground, only the thick gray mist.

After hesitating a moment, Harry stepped into the night.

The road wasn't exactly where he anticipated, and he stumbled, went down on one knee.

Something scurried away into the crosshatch of dark trees and branches.

He got to his feet and, by bracing one hand on the side of the chill, damp carriage, made his way around to the front.

There were two black horses in the traces, both standing silent and patient.

But there was no driver.

"Funny," remarked Harry as he glanced around. He noticed a faint glow a hundred yards or so up the misty night road.

"Must be the damn driver."

Harry started walking.

The light was a lantern.

A woman in a gray cloak was holding it. Not a young woman, someone in her late fifties.

He walked another dozen feet before he recognized her.

It was his mother.

Harry was very anxious to talk to her, because up to now he'd been under the impression she'd been dead for over six years.

Chapter 13

Twirling his gold-headed cane like a baton, the Great Lorenzo was walking briskly along the Nussdorferstrasse. He had roughly forty-five minutes, the time between his first and second shows, to accomplish what he had in mind.

This section of the city was modest yet well-kempt. The streetlamps were still of the gas variety and they glowed hazily in the night mist. Far up the block a delivery wagon was being pulled by a woebegone gray mare. Just around the corner, unseen, two stray cats were either courting or squabbling.

"Ah, my sought-after goal." The portly magician bounded up the steps of the narrow three-story boardinghouse.

Spying no bellpull, he rapped on the glass panel of the front door with his cane.

In the poorly lit corridor he saw a door A thin, tall man in a faded silk smoking jacket emerged and came hobbling to the door.

"We have no rooms," he called through the glass. "Good night, go away."

"I am not in need of lodging, my friend," boomed the magician. "I am Herr Doctor Korkzieher, the noted attorney, come to see you about your legacy."

"Eh?" The man's sharp nose pressed against the glass. "Is there money?"

"Immense quantities."

The door swung open. "From where?" inquired the landlord.

"You do, or rather did, have a great uncle named Gustav Dirks?"

"No, I never heard—Ah, but you must mean dear Uncle Gus? Is he the one who—"

"We have much to discuss, Herr Kummer." The Great Lorenzo took hold of his arm, urged him along the hallway to his open door. "We can talk in your suite. Are you alone this evening?"

"Yes, Herr Korkzieher. My wife is visiting with her—"

"Jolly. Then we needn't bother her with all the financial details, eh?"

"No, Elana has no head for figures. How much did my poor uncle leave me to—"

"They haven't finished counting the money yet," explained the magician as he shooed Kummer across his own threshold.

"So much then?"

"Your dear departed uncle was an eccentric man, as you well know."

"Oh…yes, yes. We often remarked of it in the family."

"Precisely. He had wads of money hidden here, bundles of bank notes stashed there. A real mare's nest and a great challenge to my clerks."

"I can well understand that."

The parlor was cluttered. Ponderous furniture, chairs, tables, sofas, stood everywhere. There were bell glasses covering plaster statues, vases of artificial flowers, books and bookends, all crowding on tabletops. Hassocks and stuffed pillows filled the floor space on the thick flowered carpet between the heavier pieces of furniture.

"Before we get down to business," said the Great Lorenzo, "I'd very much appreciate your looking at this gold medallion."

"My uncle left this to me as well?" Kummer squinted at the coin-size medallion that was rotating between the magician's forefinger and middle finger.

"We're not certain. What I'd like you to do, sir, is look at it. Carefully...that's right...look at it...look while I gently rotate it in my supple fingers...look at it...forget everything...think of sleep...sleep and rest...very good... Now sit yourself down on the godawful purple armchair... Fine..."

The hypnotized landlord sank into the fat chair.

Nudging over a tufted hassock with his knee, the magician sat facing him. "Some months ago you rented rooms here to one Wolfgang Spangler."

"I'm not supposed to talk about that."

"Ah, yet you will. That's the very reason I've bothered to put you in this classy trance, my boy," the Great Lorenzo explained. "Now then. Tell me all about Spangler."

"He only stayed a week."

"And then?"

"They took him away."

"Who performed that little service?"

"I was paid not to tell. To deny he was ever here."

"You'll tell me, though."

"They didn't think I knew who they were really working for," droned Kummer. "Think I'm a fool. But I recognized one of them. I'd seen him once when Mama and I were vacationing in the Blackwood Forest. He pretended to be the head man when they came here, but I knew he was the minion of..."

"Continue."

"I shouldn't give his name. He's a very powerful man. He could order harm done to me."

"You will tell me. That's the splendid thing about hypnosis. You'll give me the name of the man you suspect is behind all this."

"Dark Otto."

"Baron Otto Van Horn?"

"The same. He will kill me."

"Highly unlikely," the magician assured him. "Where did Dark Otto's men take Spangler?"

"That I don't know."

The Great Lorenzo drummed his fingers on his knee. "What were your instructions?"

"Should anyone come looking for Spangler, I was to say he'd never been here," answered the entranced landlord. "Whatever mail came for him I was to hand over to them."

"Where?"

"I took it and left it at the Pavilion of Automatons, at our Exposition."

"Dark Otto," muttered the Great Lorenzo, standing. "Most interesting. You've been a joy to converse with, Herr Kummer, even though you're not an especially admirable fellow." He made his way around the furniture to the door. "You'll fall completely asleep now, then awaken in one hour with no memory of my little visit at all. Oh, but you'll have a desire to buy the most expensive seat you can get for an early performance of the Great Lorenzo's magic show. You won't feel right until you've seen that spectacular entertainment at least twice. And you'll advise all your cronies to do likewise... He bowed. "Good evening, sir."

* * * *

Jennie had stood up. "I have to get back to the inn," she told Professor Staub, "right away."

"What's wrong?" He too rose.

"If what you say about Dr. Mayerling is true, then—"

"It's true, the fellow is a vampire." He thumped the papers upon his desk. "There can be no doubt. But why—"

"My friend, Harry Challenge—He's a private investigator from New York who—" She gave an impatient shake of her head. "Oh, there isn't time to go into the darn details. Harry's planning to drive out to Blackwood Castle tonight to confront the doctor. He doesn't know Mayerling's a vampire and—"

"Yes, you'd best warn him to stay clear -of that place by night," agreed the professor, anticipating what she was going to say.

The clock on the mantel chimed for the quarter hour.

"I've only got fifteen minutes to catch him." Jennie hurried to the door.

"Bring the young man back later, if you can." Staub opened the door for her. "We should talk, all of us."

Stepping out into the misty night, Jennie called back, "I will, yes. Goodbye for now, Willie."

She walked rapidly, in the long-striding tomboy way she used when she was anxious and in a hurry. The rain had a cold, gritty feel on her face.

Heading back for the Zilver Inn, she thought she was retracing the route she'd used going to the professor's house. Somewhere, though, she took a wrong turning.

Jennie found herself skirting a tiny park area. It had a rusted wrought-iron fence enclosing its weedy, overgrown half a square block of grounds. The nearest gate was sprung, hanging at an odd angle.

Stopping still, Jennie glanced around and sought to get her bearings. It was very difficult, with the mist closed in and the buildings blurred, to spot anything like a familiar landmark.

The high grass in the abandoned park was rustling, swaying as though something was moving through it close to the ground.

Jennie started walking back the way she'd come. The rustling kept up. Whatever it was in the grass was keeping pace with her.

She crossed the street.

All the houses and shops huddled along this unknown street seemed dead. There was no sound, no light.

Someone was waiting for her.

Up ahead, leaning against a lamppost. A small man in a gray suit, rubbing his hands nervously together.

She recognized him when she was fifty yards off. "But that can't be," she whispered to herself. It was the man she'd killed on the train. Gruber.

Chapter 14

She called to Harry across the foggy night and the voice was absolutely right. The woman standing there in the night woods, no doubt about it, was his mother.

"Come along now, son, there's a good deal we have to talk about." Lowering the lantern to her side, the gray-haired woman turned away and began walking deeper into the forest.

Harry was still a distance from her. "Wait, Mom," he said. "Give me a chance to catch up."

She moved swiftly, almost floating, away from him. The light bobbed and danced between the trees.

"I thought you were dead," Harry called as he followed her. "I'm glad to see you're not. This way...when you died I was out in Chicago on that swindling case. I...you know, by the time I got back home you were gone. There were things I'd intended to say..."

He couldn't get any nearer to her. She was up ahead, walking fast.

When he was a kid, that would happen. His mother'd be thinking of something, get to walking fast. Harry'd be looking into shop windows or watching the street life. All at once they'd both realize what had happened. She'd stand there and wait; he'd go running to catch up.

Yes, and she was doing that now. Up ahead. His mother had stopped, waiting, beckoning him to hurry to her.

"The thing is..." He slowed, struggling to catch an idea that was trying to form.

"Harry, please, come along," she urged.

"The thing is," he said aloud, "you're dead and gone."

Yes, he came home from Chicago in time for the funeral.

He'd seen her in her coffin.

Harry took a deep breath, shaking his head. His fists were clenching and he was shivering. He made himself stop walking.

They were only a few feet apart now, Harry and his mother.

"Come here, Harry darling." The lantern was resting on the mossy ground, her arms were open to him.

"You're dead," he told her. "This has to be…an illusion…a hallucination…"

"Harry, oh, don't say that. You'll spoil everything."

"Mayerling… This has to be Dr. Mayerling," he said. "He had that damn Strand woman…slip me something…do something." He was sweating, breathing hard. It was a fight not to go closer to his mother.

"Harry…"

She began to fade, slowly shimmering away to nothing. Even the lantern vanished, giving way to darkness.

The ground changed, too.

Harry looked down to find he was standing at the very edge of a pit. Hands shaking some, he lit a match.

The pit was some sort of animal trap. The bottom of it, six feet below, was lined with sharp-pointed sticks, all pointing up at Harry out of the grave-smelling earth.

Carefully, he took a step back and then another. He turned, began making his way to the road.

He thought he heard his mother call after him once, faint and far away.

He kept walking away from there.

* * * *

Gruber said, "Good evening, Fräulein Barr." His voice was dry, rasping.

Jennie thrust her hand into her shoulder bag. "I still have the same gun," she warned, tugging it out into the open. "I killed you once, I'll do it again."

His walk was a bit off. He lurched, swayed, as he came for her. "That won't, I fear, work this time," Gruber informed her.

"I would like you, please, to come along with—"

"Like heck!" She fired two silver bullets into his chest.

They made dull clanking sounds.

This wasn't Gruber at all. This was some kind of simulacrum, one of those clockwork figures Harry'd told her about.

Then the thing to do was disable it.

Aiming at the approaching automaton's head, she prepared to shoot again.

Something hit her in the legs, hard, from behind. Jennie stumbled, caught a glimpse of a large black dog. It must be the thing that was in the park.

She swung the gun up.

But Gruber was right there. He swung his heavy fist.

The blow hit her in the temple. Her teeth rattled. She let go, not meaning to, of her gun.

The next two blows were harder.

She fell, but never had the sensation of hitting the damp cobblestones. Instead, she was swallowed up by mist.

* * * *

"Hit makes yer ponder," observed Tubbs as he tested the mattress on Jennie's spoolbed with his backside. "With locks so easy ter pick hin this 'ere hinn, why, nobody's valuables is—"

"Do try to be less boisterous, old fellow," cautioned McMillion. He had the lady reporter's suitcase open on the floor and was kneeling beside it. "We don't want the innkeeper—"

"Gor, 'e's deaf as a post." He settled on the bed, short legs dangling, to watch his employer search through Jennie's belongings. "'Ow do yer feel 'andlin' 'er underwear? Pal o' mine in Lime'ouse, ever' time 'e so much as squinted hat a pair of knickers, why, 'is fiddlestick grew to a henormous—"

"Hush," advised the journalist. "We don't have that much time before Miss Barr may return from her visit to—"

"She's more 'n likely carousin' in some low dive, hif they 'as such a thing in this rinkydink town, with 'Andsome 'Arry the detective."

"No, Tubbs, the innkeeper assured me they'd gone off separately. Miss Barr, furthermore, had inquired as how best to reach Wissenschaftstrasse."

"The innkeeper hain't the smartest bloke on this green earth, guy. 'E wouldn't even know where 'is rumpsplitter were hif it weren't attached to—"

"Ah, this is quite interesting." He was holding an envelope in his gloved hand. "Written to Miss Barr from a Professor Staub of 72 Wissenschaftstrasse, this town." Nodding to himself, he extracted the letter from the envelope.

Tubbs left the bed to prowl the white-walled room. "'Ow about this now?" he said, picking up a small framed photograph from atop the heavy chest of drawers. "Didn't I tell yer 'Arry was dippin' the ol' plowshare inter—"

"Quiet." McMillion was reading through the professor's letter, frowning. "Things are much more serious than I was aware."

"Is the prof rollin' in the 'ay with Jennie as well?" McMillion's frown deepened. "This has to do with Dr. Mayerling."

"The very bloke you've come all this bloomin' way to get a yarn on?"

"The same, yes." He'd refolded the letter, was rubbing it across his handsome chin. "According to this Professor Staub, the doctor is involved in much more than fleecing foolish British millionaires. The original focus of my article must be severely modified, I'm afraid."

"What's the doc up ter?"

"Black magic and sorcery."

Tubbs chortled. "Ar, there hain't no such thing. You can't really, guv, believe—"

"Don't scoff, Tubbs," warned McMillion. "In my travels around this giddy globe, old man, I've encountered a good many strange things. No, I most certainly wouldn't rule out the possibility that Dr. Mayerling is indeed a sorcerer of sorts."

Shrugging, the valet held up the photo he'd discovered. "Suppose yer take a gander hat this," he suggested. "Hindicates the wench his far gone on friend 'Arry." It was a small studio portrait, sepia-toned, of a younger Harry Challenge. He was standing in front of a pastoral painted backdrop, his elbow resting on a marble pedestal.

"Not inscribed, I notice," said McMillion, returning his attention to the contents of the young woman's suitcase. "In fact, one imagines the Challenge International Detective Agency, being a vulgar and aggressive organization, hands such photographs out as advertisements."

"Be 'at as it may," said the smirking Tubbs, passing the framed photograph under his mangled nose, "this smells orful sweet, guv. I'd say she keeps it close to 'er much of the time. Therefore, yer chances of—"

"Allow me to conclude this search. Time is running out."

"What do we do arfter this bit of snoopin'?"

"Ah, here's a list of those in Dunkelstein Jennie intends to call upon. Jolly." He gazed at the newfound list for a few seconds. "There, got it memorized. What were you asking, old fellow?"

"I was curious, guy, has to what fun-filled hactivity we'd be engagin' in once we left this bloomin' 'ole. That is, when yer through diggin' inter m'lady's underwear."

"I have a hunch we'd be wise to follow in Miss Barr's footsteps this evening," replied McMillion. "Yes, one imagines that might well lead to something of interest."

Chapter 15

A rooster crowed as Harry came trudging toward the outskirts of Dunkelstein. Yawning, Harry brushed at the sawdust that was still clinging to his trousers.

He'd gotten a ride to within a mile of town in the back of a woodcutter's cart.

The day was about to commence; the last of the night was fading away. The grass along the side of the road was thick with dew. Birds were twittering.

And Harry, although he had recovered from whatever potion or spell Naida Strand had used on him, was a shade confused.

"They keep trying to kill me," he reflected, passing the first of the thatched cottages at the edge of town. "With a demented automaton, then with a wolfman." He spit at the road. "And, hell, I don't even completely believe in werewolves."

Then last night they'd set up that whole business with the dark-haired Naida. Turned him near stupefied, tried to lure him into toppling down into that damn pit full of sharp stakes.

"Would've looked like an accident. Tourist, not too bright to begin with, gets lost in woods and falls in animal trap."

Why, was Mayerling going to all this trouble? Just to keep him from talking to Jonah Mariott?

"They didn't even know I was on the case when they turned that mechanical man loose on me," he reminded himself again.

He was anxious to talk to Jennie, to find out what she'd learned from Professor Staub and her other contacts in town. Harry had decided he had to be better informed before he went up against Dr. Mayerling.

A bread wagon rolled by, trailing the pleasant scent of fresh-baked bread.

Harry knew there was no sense going back to Naida's cottage. He didn't figure she'd still be residing there.

"Damn, if that fake attack on her had been staged on Broadway, I never would've fallen for it."

Over here in the Old World, though, he'd let his guard down, acted as gullible as a hick tourist.

A plump little black pup came barking at Harry when he entered the early morning courtyard of the Zilver Inn.

"Hush, hush, Otto," ordered the stableboy in a loud whisper.

"Another Dark Otto, huh?" Harry said to the animal.

Tail wagging, the black pup circled Harry once before running into the stable to attack a pile of straw.

The desk area was deserted. A lazy horsefly was walking over the counter top.

Harry bounded up the stairs, hurried along the hall and

knocked lightly on the door of Jennie's room.

His knock caused the unlocked door slowly inward.

Harry was just taking in the fact that no one was in the room and that Jennie's bed hadn't been slept in when a pair of powerful arms grabbed him from behind.

"Bloody barbarian," grumbled Tubbs. He was sitting on a low stone wall, legs dangling, rubbing at the new welt on his forehead.

"That'll be quite enough, old fellow," instructed McMillion.

He and Harry were walking slowly around the little flagstone square near the inn. Early morning sunlight was starting to brighten the area, making the water in the circular fountain glitter.

"Toss a hinnocent workin' stiff inter a bloomin' wall," said the aggrieved valet, scowling at Harry. "When hall I was doin' were hinvitin' 'im to a little rendezvous with me—"

"Hush."

Harry, hands in his trouser pockets, said, "Where's Jennie?"

"That's just it, old man. I don't know, don't have the faintest idea."

"She didn't come back to the inn last night?"

McMillion shook his head. "One realizes the habits of American journalists are somewhat more relaxed than those of us in England who—"

"She didn't spend the night with anybody," Harry told him.

"Exactly the point I'm making, Challenge," said the handsome journalist. "You are rather keen on her, though, aren't you?"

"Look, I didn't agree to this meeting just to play advice-to-the-lovelorn with you, McMillion." Halting, he took hold of the man's arm. "I want to find Jennie. So you—"

"'Ere now! Don't go man'andlin' the guy," warned Tubbs from his perch, "else I'll climb down an'—"

"I don't," said Harry, turning briefly to stare at him, "want to hear one more single goddamn word from you."

"Gor." Tubbs closed his mouth tight.

"There's no need for any internecine fighting, old man. I'm very concerned over Jennie, too, Challenge. If you'll but hear me out—"

"Get on with it then."

"She left the Zilver Inn last evening shortly after eight," said McMillion, "to call on a Professor Staub."

"That I already know."

"To be sure, yet I wager you don't know that the professor was the only one she called on."

"How do you know that?"

"I happen, by the merest chance, to have had access to a list of her intended interviewees," he explained, watching the dolphin spray water into the pool of the fountain. "She left Staub's residence at approximately nine. Nothing is known of her activities thereafter, I'm afraid."

"You've talked to Staub?"

"I have," replied McMillion, coughing into his gloved fist. "He was, I must admit, deuced difficult. Gave me, don't you know, only the curtest of answers. He did imply, however, that he would be much more open with you, Challenge, which is one of the reasons I've sought you out."

"And what the hell do you get out of all this?"

"Jove, man, I'm concerned about Jennie." He drew himself up, throwing his broad shoulders back. "I also have a story to do, concerning the activities of this Dr. Mayerling chap."

Harry released his arm. "You talked to the others on the list."

"There were three. I sought out each and, although it involved rousing them out of slumber in two cases, questioned them thoroughly," said McMillion. "None saw Jennie Barr last evening."

"Unless one of them is lying."

"They wasn't," contributed Tubbs. "When I sits in on the hinterviews, you gets very little lyin'."

Harry said, "I'll go see Professor Staub right now, then see if I can pick up Jennie's trail."

"No doubt we'll find Dr. Mayerling's hand in this affair."

"Probably," said Harry. "But before I head out for Blackwood

Castle, I want to talk to Staub."

Smiling, McMillion said, "Splendid, Challenge. Together we ought to be able to—"

"I don't intend to work with you on this, McMillion."

"But, I say, that's damned unsporting. After one's confided one's innermost—"

"And if you send that lunkhead after me again—"

Harry jerked a thumb in Tubbs's direction. "I'll do more than just bounce him off the wall."

He went striding off across the flagstones of the square.

* * * *

"You believe all this?"

"Don't you?"

Harry drank some of the coffee in the mug the leonine Professor Staub had provided. "Guess I have to."

Staub was behind his massive desk, notes and manuscript pages spread out before him. "There can be little doubt that Dr. Mayerling is a vampire," he said.

"And you got Jennie interested in doing a story about him?"

"She is a very capable young woman, as you well know, Herr Challenge." He shook his head. "Many times before she has faced danger."

"Sure, but this is a mite different from tribal wars and tenement fires," Harry said from the leather armchair. "There's sorcery and—"

"Evil. You shy at the word."

"Evil then." Putting his cup on a marble-top table, Harry rose. "What do we do now?"

The professor steepled his fingers. "There are two possibilities we have to face, neither one pleasant."

"Yeah, either Jennie's dead or she's a prisoner of Mayerling." He went to the windows, stared unseeing at the morning street.

"I'm inclined to think the latter," Staub said. "Alive she has some value to him as a hostage, someone he can use to pressure you and his other enemies."

"I tried to get out there last night to see him, but—"

"Blackwood Castle is a dangerous place after sunset," said the professor. "Even in the brightest daylight it—"

"He's got Jennie and he'll want to bargain. I'm going to talk to him."

"It might be best to—"

"I'm way beyond doing the wisest thing," Harry told him. "I don't want to do some damn fool thing that'll jeopardize her, but I'm going to see Mayerling today."

From a desk drawer Professor Staub took a silver religious medal. Saying nothing, he handed it to Harry.

Chapter 16

The horse Harry rented from the livery stable at the edge of town was an amiable roan mare. She carried him that morning at a steady gallop through the Blackwood Forest.

By day the woodlands weren't particularly ominous. Sunlight came slanting down through the high branches, birds sang, squirrels scurried up and down the broad trunks.

Although he was on the lookout for the spot where his carriage had stopped last evening, he wasn't able to find it. It was the same road, yet not all of it was familiar. He had a momentary uneasiness, wondering if he'd see his mother again, the image of her beckoning him from beside the roadway. But that passed.

When Harry was roughly a mile from his destination, he began to notice the silence. No birds called, no animals moved in the brush. The sun didn't feel as warm as it had.

"Imagination," he told himself.

He rode his mount around a bend in the forest road, and there was the castle.

It rose up from a clearing a hundred yards ahead, an immense brooding structure of dark gray stone and dark tile. There were turrets, towers, battlements. A high stone wall surrounded the three acres covered by the castle and its grounds.

And riding out through the open oaken doors of the court-yard came a neatly dressed young man on a bicycle.

"Whoa," Harry suggested to his mare, reining up.

A trio of dark broad-winged birds took flight from the north tower, cawing loudly as they circled higher and higher into the thin blue of the morning.

"Would it be Mr. Challenge?" inquired the young man when his bicycle was opposite Harry. He was clad in a Norfolk suit of grayish prickly material, had a straw hat on his head, and wore gold-rimmed spectacles. He stopped his black bicycle, smiled up at Harry. "I am Dr. Mistley."

"Pleased to meet you." Harry swung down out of the saddle. "No need to give you my card, Doctor, since you already know who I am."

"I practiced medicine in Manhattan for nearly two years," said the smiling doctor. "I'm not as young as I look. At any rate, I heard a good deal about you in those days, and you were pointed out to me on more than one occasion."

Nodding toward the huge gray castle, Harry asked, "You work with Mayerling?"

Mistley removed his spectacles, polished the lenses carefully with his white pocket handkerchief. When he took off the glasses, his pale blue eyes began to water. "He's doing remarkable work here," he answered. "I'm quite proud to be associated with him."

"I've come to see him."

Replacing the spectacles and grinning, Dr. Mistley said, "You're much too early for that, I'm afraid. Dr. Mayerling is a late riser."

Harry was looking at the castle. "Indeed?"

Vampires were supposed to sleep by day. Maybe Professor Staub was absolutely right about Mayerling.

"I might be able to arrange an interview with Dr. Mayerling late this afternoon."

"Little after sundown maybe?"

"About then, yes," said Mistley. "However, I'm familiar with the entire functioning of our sanitarium and—"

"You have a patient named Jonah Mariott?"

"Of course. A fellow American and an amiable gentleman. He and I have had many an enjoyable evening of whist since his—"

"Could I talk with Mariott?"

"Now, do you mean? Today?"

"Soon as possible."

"You're not related," said the young doctor.

"I'm working for his niece and nephew, both of whom are very concerned about—"

"He's in excellent condition, both physically and mentally, Mr. Challenge. I can assure you that Dr. Mayerling's treatments have worked veritable mirac—"

"Not that I doubt your word, Doctor," cut in Harry. "Until I talk to him direct, though, I won't be satisfied."

"That's only natural, yes," admitted Dr. Mistley. "If you'd care to come into the castle now, I'll arrange an interview for you with Mr. Mariott." He climbed off his bicycle, started walking it back toward Blackwood Castle.

"Let's do that." Harry led his horse.

"There oughtn't to be any trouble about your visiting with him, Mr. Challenge," said the doctor. "Mr. Mariott, after all, isn't a prisoner."

* * * *

Tubbs sneezed. Twice.

"Cease that grumbling," advised McMillion.

"I were sneezin', guy. Due, in good part, to bein' up to me bloomin' fundament in the dust of hantiquity."

"I do believe, old fellow, that I've unearthed something of considerable interest."

"Hunearthed is right. They oughter bury hall this musty—"

"Yes, this will come in deuced handy when we explore the castle."

The two of them were in one of the dim, dusty storerooms far below the Dunkelstein town hall.

"Was we hanticipatin' the exploration of some bloody old castle, guy?" Tubbs was at rest atop a knee-high stack of fat, ancient record books.

"We must have a look-see inside Blackwood Castle." The handsome journalist spread out the large architectural drawing he'd located in one of the venerable strongboxes. "This looks to be the original floor plan of the castle, showing—Hello, this is jolly interesting." He pointed to the margin.

"A plop of fly manure, is hit?"

"It happens to be an inscription, no doubt written in 1693 shortly after the castle was completed."

"Ham I safe in concludin' hit don't contain such news as'll cheer me up?"

"Apparently the architect, one Christian Steinbrunner, went stark raving mad just before the castle was completed."

"One of me cousins is married to a stonemason an' there's a bloke could drive you bonkers if you was to work side by side with 'im for more n' a—"

"What sent poor Steinbrunner round the bend is described as 'certain things that came up out of the unhallowed ground upon which the cursed castle is built.' Villagers found him late one rainy evening running about in the woods and gibbering like a monkey. His hair had turned quite white."

"Can good times such as that still be hobtained in the vicinity? Sounds like hit'd put the bloomin' Crystal Palace ter shame."

McMillion was moving his gloved finger over the dusty plans. "Ah, yes. Yes, one could quite probably enter here...or even here, unobserved. Then we'd make our way through the crypt until—"

"Crypt? 'At's where they store the defunct members of the 'ouse'old, hain't it?"

"My, just look at this." He chuckled, moving his finger along a zigzag path. "A series of secret passages that will allow one to travel to all levels of the castle unseen."

Tubbs stood up and scratched at his groin. "Hain't it likely the doc knows hall them nooks an' crannies an' secret passways hin that pile?"

Rolling the drawing up carefully, McMillion then concealed it beneath his jacket. "Perhaps he does," he replied. "Yet that merely makes this even more challenging."

Chapter 17

"Couple of damn fools."

"They're quite concerned over you."

"Over my money, son."

Harry was sitting in an arbor at the south side of the castle grounds. Flowering vines climbed and twisted all up and over the white latticework surrounding him and the tea merchant.

The amiable Dr. Mistley had brought them together ten minutes ago, then discreetly withdrawn. Glancing around the green lawns beyond the arbor, Harry said, "There's nobody around, Mariott. You can level with me."

"What the hell's that supposed to mean?" He was a thickset man of middle height. This morning he wore a lightweight cotton suit.

Harry had to admit to himself that the millionaire was looking healthier than he had in any of his recent photographs. "You're not being kept here against your will?"

"Where'd you get a tomfool idea like that, son?"

"Both your niece and nephew feel that—"

"My niece and nephew, you'll excuse my pointing out, Challenge, are a pair of ninnies. In fact, I strongly suspect Jack is—"

"Why did you refuse to see them when they were here?"

"I didn't wish to." He leaned forward in his wicker chair, rested a hand on his knee. "See here, son, I'll be honest with you. Boston is one of the most boring spots on the face of the earth. And those two mooncalves are about as dull as a bowl of cold porridge."

Several bees were buzzing around the blossoms of the arbor. Idly Harry watched them flickering through the warm air. "Just how long do you intend to remain here?"

"That's nobody's business but my own, son."

"Still Jack and Amy might feel better were you to set a specific…"

"A specific what, young man?"

"Date," said Harry casually, trying not to look directly at the bee who'd alighted on Mariott's thick neck. "If they knew exactly when you intended to come home they—"

"It's not beyond the realm of possibility, son, that I shall never return to Boston. When you consider how many wonderful romantic cities there are in the world, you—Just what are you gawking at, Challenge?"

Harry glanced away. "I was intent on catching your every word." The bee, Harry was damn sure, had stung the tea millionaire smack on the neck and then gone buzzing off. But Mariott hadn't even noticed.

That must be because he wasn't Mariott.

Nope, he was another of Dr. Mayerling's automatons. An even better one than any of those at the Pavilion of Automatons. Good enough to fool Harry, certainly.

Probably, though, they hadn't wanted to risk letting his close relatives get a look just yet. That's why Jack and Amy were turned away.

"Was there anything else, son?" asked the Mariott automaton impatiently.

Harry took out a cigar, cut off the end, lit it. "I do believe, sir, your kin would be relieved if you were to allow them to visit you and witness for themselves how well you're doing." He stood up.

"You ought to cease smoking," advised the automaton as he rose. "It can kill you."

"There are a hell of a lot of things on the list ahead of smoking," said Harry, taking another slow puff.

Dr. Mistley stopped beside a heavy wooden door in the cool stone corridor. "If you have a moment before departing, Mr. Challenge, I'd like very much to show you something," he said. "In my office."

"Sure, go ahead."

Smiling, the young doctor turned the brass knob and the door creaked open. "I trust your visit with Mr. Mariott was satisfactory."

"Certainly took a load off my mind."

The office was large, beam-ceilinged. The late morning light coming in through the three high narrow windows didn't quite rid it of its chill.

Crossing to a neatly kept desk, Mistley seated himself. "I understand you're a close personal friend of an excellent illusionist named the Great Lorenzo." His left hand rested on a glazed skull that served as a bookend.

"Yep, we're pals. Why?"

The young doctor picked up a small crystal sphere about the size of a baseball. "I suppose it's a foolish hobby for a man of science, yet I enjoy dabbling in parlor magic."

"A good place for it."

"Please don't let me bore you or take up too much of your valuable time." He hefted the crystal, which was cloudy now. "I did, however, very much want to show you this new trick I've just mastered."

"Proceed," invited Harry. Surely they weren't going to make another try at hypnotizing him? The crystal grew cloudier. Smiling, Dr. Mistley threw it into the air. "Watch the crystal."

The globe remained floating, about four feet from the floor. Pulsing, glowing with a faint yellowish light, it drifted close to Harry.

"No strings?" he said.

"You ought to be seeing something about now." Harry did.

Inside the crystal was an image of Jennie Barr. Her auburn

hair was down and there was a dark bruise across her cheek. He saw only her head against a background of gray stone wall.

Slowly Harry got to his feet. "Where is she?" The image left the crystal ball; the ball dropped to the rug.

"In a safe place," replied Dr. Mistley, smiling. "The moment you leave Orlandia, the young woman will be released." He stood to face Harry. "It won't be necessary, you see, to arrange for a meeting with Dr. Mayerling at all. You have forty-eight hours to consider. After that—"

"Nothing's going to happen to her."

"Oh, really?"

"Because if it does," Harry promised him, "something'll happen to you."

Chapter 18

Wearing a fluffy white chef's hat, white jacket and flowing white apron, the Great Lorenzo came hurrying along the Mariahilferstrasse just at dusk. He was carrying a small pig over his left shoulder.

From the Exposition grounds, merry waltz music wafted on the darkening air.

"I cut quite a figure on the dance- floor in my youth," he confided to the pig. "Nimble was but one of the many glowing terms used to describe me. Adonis was—Ah, but we have arrived."

He stopped before the rear gate of the palace grounds. Through the wrought-iron bars he could see across the cobble-stone yard to the brightly lit windows of the kitchens.

"Let's have some expediency," he boomed out. "I can't wait all the blessed night out here." He agitated the bellpull while kicking at the bars.

"Here, here, this is the palace." A uniformed guard came running up to the gate.

"I should hope so," said the magician, "since I'd feel foolish delivering this porker to the Kunsthistorisches Museum."

"We aren't expecting a pig."

"You aren't, the kitchen staff certainly is," the Great Lorenzo informed him. "The royal physician, not an hour ago, telephoned Dinglehoofer's Grand Prix Butchery to order this very piglet." He lowered his voice. "It is hoped some pork chops will perk up His Majesty."

"They think so? Why, when I'm under the weather a greasy pork chop is the last item I'd—"

"Ah, but then you aren't a king," the magician reminded. "Now you'd best let me in, lest we both get in deep trouble."

The guard hesitated, gazing at the pig for several thoughtful seconds. "Very well. I don't want to interfere with His Majesty's health, poor fellow."

"Precisely, my boy." As soon as the gates swung a few feet open, the Great Lorenzo insinuated himself onto the palace grounds. "Now I must continue on my errand of mercy."

He trotted across the cobblestones while the twilight deepened all around.

Once inside the hallway connecting the kitchens, he stepped through the first open doorway.

A husky red-faced woman in white was standing by a wooden table, tossing salad in an immense copper bowl. "What?" she inquired, glowering at him.

"I've come with the pig."

"So I see."

Grunting, the Great Lorenzo placed the small pinkish creature down on the hardwood floor.

The interesting thing about this particular porker is—"

"Who are you? Why have you intruded into the royal kitchen?"

"The interesting thing about this pig," resumed the magician, "is that he isn't dead. Nay, merely hypnotized into a trancelike state. When I snap my fingers thusly—Voila! He awakens."

The little pig blinked, glanced around the huge room. Scrambling to his feet, he commenced to squeal loudly and run around the floor in anxious circles.

"Oh! Oh!" exclaimed the head cook. "That horrible thing. Ugh! Get him out of here." She began screaming, waving a wooden salad spoon in the air.

"I leave that chore to you, dear lady." Bowing out, he continued along the corridor.

Various other members of the culinary staff were emerging from various other doorways, curious.

"Terrible accident," the magician told one and all, pointing back. "Bloodshed, horror. Pigs running amok. Hurry."

They did and he raced off in the opposite direction. "I do believe," the Great Lorenzo said to himself, "I've created a splendid diversion."

* * * *

"Such trash," muttered the Great Lorenzo.

He was searching the ornate claw-footed bureau in the suite of rooms Baron Otto Van Horn had been occupying the past few weeks. The third stack of yellow-backed French novels in as many drawers had brought forth his critical comment.

"Does no one read of Deadwood Dick anymore?"

The magician was rummaging through Dark Otto's impressive collection of silk underwear, in search of something that would provide details on what had been done with the missing Wolfgang Spangler, when he heard approaching footfalls in the palace corridor outside.

Easing the drawer shut, he hurried to a closet. He crouched amid the highly polished riding boots, leaving the heavy door open a few inches.

Seconds later Dark Otto entered the suite, accompanied by someone else.

"Your performance this evening is faulty," the baron said, clicking on the electric lamp by his bedside. "One of the physicians went so far as to eye you curiously."

Some of the light came seeping into the closet, almost touching the hunkered magician.

"We've had far too much damp weather lately," replied the pleasant voice of Princess Alicia. "That always affects me, Otto."

"Yet that swine Spangler assured us you would not have such problems," complained Van Horn. "The king can't possibly live much more than a few days longer. When the old fool does expire, you must be able to assume the throne."

The princess had a very lovely laugh. "Don't fret so," she told the baron. "Was I not born to rule?"

* * * *

Duchess Hofnung gave the Great Lorenzo an enthusiastic farewell hug. "My brave and courageous Renzo," she said, "you must promise to return safely to me."

"I fully intend to survive this venture, m'love."

They, with Helga Spangler close by, were on the platform at the Zevenburg rail station. The nine o'clock express to Dunkelstein was due to depart in six minutes.

"Do you really believe?" asked Helga, "that my father is a prisoner at Blackwood Castle?"

Nodding, the magician extricated himself from the grasp of the affectionate duchess. "So I learned, dear child, from my eavesdropping earlier in the evening."

"I still don't understand why they—"

"'Twould take far more time than I can presently spare to explain this conspiracy to you now." Stooping, he gathered up his portmanteau and a long, thin package wrapped in butcher paper.

"Won't you at least tell us, Renzo, what's in that strange parcel?" asked the petite Duchess Hofnung, following him as he hurried toward his first-class compartment.

"A curio that I'm most anxious to deliver to Harry Challenge."

"Did you borrow it from the Lusitanian Pavilion at the Exposition, love? Is that the reason we had to stop there in our mad rush to—"

"Dear ladies." He opened the door of his compartment with

a sweeping gesture. "Before many more days have passed into oblivion all will be made clear, crystal clear, to you." He carefully deposited his bag and his package inside.

From out of the night air he plucked two gardenias. He bestowed one on the duchess, one on Helga.

"Renzo, promise you won't try anything danger—"

"Farewell, adieu." After kissing his fingertips at both of them, the Great Lorenzo stepped into his compartment, shut the door and drew the shade.

Chapter 19

Harry kicked the door open.

"I thought so." He went striding into the room.

Seated at the small desk near the window was Peter Starr McMillion. He was wearing a silken smoking jacket with scarlet dragons embroidered on its back, and he had an architectural drawing spread out before him.

"Ah, hello there, Challenge. I was just thinking of going out for a spot of lunch," he said, smiling handsomely. "Care to join me for—"

"It's three in the afternoon."

"Is it really? Jove, how—"

"When I got back from Blackwood Castle yesterday, I had another talk with Professor Staub." Harry stopped in the center of the room. "He and—"

"I sent my man Tubbs out to invite you to dine with me last evening," said McMillion.

"We might have, had you accepted my invitation rather than punching Tubbs in the face, compared notes." He gestured at the door to an adjoining room. "Poor chap's lying in yonder room with an icebag on his eye, cursing you and—"

"After Staub and I talked to Jennie's other contacts in town," Harry continued, "I came to the conclusion I'm going to have to sneak inside that damn castle, take care of Mayerling and then rescue Jennie."

The journalist chuckled. "Well, there, you see? You and I, old boy, have arrived at the same—"

"The problem is, and I didn't find this out until I'd spent six hours in the bowels of the town hall today, that you swiped the only existing copy of the—"

"So that's where you've been, eh, old boy? Wasn't going to comment on how dusty you look, but since you—"

"I want those plans." He crossed the room.

Pushing back in his chair, McMillian stood to face him. "Pause a moment, Challenge, and reflect," he suggested. "Granted you're a brave chap, capable of facing all sorts of hazards. Yet Dr. Mayerling is a formidable foe, ensconced in a fortress to boot."

"That I already know."

"Then accept my offer of assistance," said McMillion. "I've certainly proven myself a handy fellow in a tight spot. Surely you've read of my—"

"All your exploits are written up by you."

"Even so, I happen to be as honest and truthful as…as Henry Mayhew was in writing of the wretched poor of London. Why, I—"

"I don't need help."

"See here, Challenge, we all of us slip up now and then. Should you make a mistake now, it will jeopardize not only you but Jennie as well," he said. "I am correct in assuming that your primary motive in assaulting Blackwood Castle is to rescue Jennie Barr from therein?"

"She's in there, yes. I saw her yesterday."

"Saw her, did you? Jove, how is she faring under—"

"What I saw—" Harry glanced around, feeling a sudden weariness. He walked to an armchair and sat. "Okay, McMillion, I'll accept your offer. But after I tell you what's really going on out there at the castle, you may not want to join in."

Throwing his shoulders back, McMillion assured him, "I've faced worse dangers than this and not flinched."

"I don't think so," said Harry.

Harry was in the courtyard of the inn that evening, smoking an after-dinner cigar, when the Great Lorenzo arrived. It was a clear, cool night and the sky was rich with stars.

Harry had been gazing upward, wondering what it might feel like to be three-hundred-some years old.

The carriage came rattling in under the archway. The magician and a tourist couple emerged. Both the man and the woman, middle-aged Italians, were carrying armfuls of roses and had puzzled expressions. The Great Lorenzo had obviously been entertaining them on the ride from the Dunkelstein station.

"Ah, Harry, my boy," exclaimed the magician when he caught sight of his friend. "You are the very object of my breathless pilgrimage." He handed him a long skinny package. "Carry this; I'll manage my portmanteau."

"Ow." Harry discovered he'd been given something with a blade. "What the hell is—"

"The Sacred Silver Sword of San Sebastian—try saying that some time with a lisp." He pushed on into the inn. "We must have a conference at once, lad."

"You planning to take rooms here?"

"I can bunk with you for the nonce."

"This way then." He led him upstairs to his room.

The magician gave the place a swift appraisal. "Better than a room in a Philadelphia hotel," he decided.

"How'd you come by the Sacred Silver Sword of San Sebastian?" He dropped the package on the foot of his bed.

"Swiped it from the Lusitanian display at the Exposition." Shedding his black cape, he draped it over a chair. "Had to hypnotize two guards plus several little pig-tailed lasses and their art teacher. A third guard proved a faulty subject. Him I conked with my cane."

"Aren't you supposed to be putting on a magic show just about now back in Zeven—"

"'What is the basis for all true friendship? I'll tell you. Sacrifice. Greater love than this has no man and so on." The magician sighed, fluffed his side-whiskers. "At this very moment I fear my assistant and sometime understudy, a woefully inept illusionist named J. Randolph Cox is filling in for me. By now, he's already botched the Devil's Buzzsaw illusion and is about to stumble through the Mandarin's Chest Myster—Ah, but no time to lament over the possible complete and total ruin of my show and my treasured reputation. Nay, I turned my back on all that to rush here to this tank town."

"Why exactly?"

"To lend a helping hand to you, why else?"

"Appreciate that," said Harry, sitting on the edge of the bed. "I could use some help, since I'm planning on leading a raid on Blackwood Castle in the hour just before dawn."

Nodding, the Great Lorenzo said, "Yes, and you don't know what I know."

"That's possible."

Settling into an armchair, the magician said, "I have learned much since we parted, Harry."

"Been having more visions?"

"No, not at all. I've been doing detective work. Yes, first-class crackerjack detective work, my boy." He held up a plump forefinger. "Firstly, Dr. Mayer-ling is no mere mortal. Ah, not at all. He is—and be prepared for a stunning surprise—he is a vampire."

"I know."

"You know?" A slightly crestfallen expression came over his face. "I risked life and limb, playing peeping torn within the walls of the Zevenburg Palace itself to learn this and you—"

"Friend of Jennie Barr's told me. See, Lorenzo, Jennie's been grabbed by Mayerling and—"

"That's exactly why I borrowed the silver sword, for use on the doctor. Nothing works better on a vampire than silver and—You and Miss Barr sound to be on a different footing than you were when you departed Zevenburg."

"That I'll fill you in on later. Do you have other reasons for rushing here?"

"I'd learned that Dr. Mayerling was considerably more dangerous than originally advertised. I naturally assumed you'd have need of a fellow who knew his way around in supernatural circles." He tapped his broad chest. "I have also uncovered facts you may not be in possession of, my boy. Do you know who Wolfgang Spangler is?"

Harry shook his head. "Nope. What's he got to do with—"

"Spangler is the key figure in the entire nefarious plot," answered the magician. "He is the premier builder and designer of automatons in all Europe. Dr. Mayerling is in cahoots with none other than Baron Otto Van Horn, also known as Dark Otto. Dr. Mayerling lured Spangler from his hearth and home in Munich. They promised him a lucrative position with the Exposition in the Pavilion of Automatons, with which you are all too familiar. Instead they spirited the man away, putting him to work at fashioning insidiously clever mechanical reproductions of actual people."

"I met one of them yesterday."

The magician eyed him. "Who?"

"They've got an automaton version of old Mariott," answered Harry. "Damn convincing, too, and much better even than the gang in the pavilion."

Exhaling, the magician continued. "Spangler has been a prisoner of Blackwood Castle for several months," he said. "He has built, to my knowledge, at least one other nearly flawless simulacrum."

"Of whom?"

"The Princess Alicia," said the magician.

Chapter 20

"Jove, I knew my disguises would come in handy."

"Would yer move 'at bloomin' fiddle, guy, hit's diggin' inter me fundament."

"Don't thrash about so, Tubbs; you nearly brushed my moustache loose."

"Moustache, is hit? Looks more like a caterpiggle what—"

"Hush."

These voices were coming from within a canvas-covered wagon that was wending its way, with considerable creaking and rattling, along the predawn forest road.

At the reins, with a bold crimson bandanna on his head and a large golden ring dangling from his ear, was the Great Lorenzo.

Beside him, looking no different than usual, sat Harry.

"He isn't," remarked the magician, "a very convincing Gypsy."

"We aren't going to run into all that many people we'll have to convince," said Harry.

"Are you insinuating we don't even need this absolutely authentic Gypsy vehicle which I procured at considerable—"

"It's as good a way as any to get all of us to Blackwood Castle."

Up on some dark, unseen branch an owl hooted mournfully.

"My boy, you're rather gloomy," remarked the Great Lorenzo, his eyes on the swaying backs of the two sturdy horses who were pulling the wagon through the predawn woodlands. "Do you always sulk on the eve of battle?"

"I feel easier when I work alone."

"In this instance you are going to need all the help you can muster, Harry, my lad. In fact, it might have been a wise move to alert the local law so—"

"Sure, Lorenzo. We pop into police headquarters and tell them we'd like some help going up against Mayerling. Seems he's a vampire and—"

"We're not obliged to provide all the details of this venture to—"

"And they better bring along plenty of artillery because there are also probably going to be some mechanical men to overcome. Not to mention a stray werewolf or two plus—"

"Granted most coppers are not excessively imaginative, yet they'd certainly understand kidnapping."

"We can't prove he's kidnapped a single soul."

"You saw the titian-tressed Jennie yourself when—"

"I saw her image in a crystal ball, Lorenzo. That's not exactly admissible evidence."

"What about the Princess Alicia then? She, too, is a prisoner of Blackwood Castle."

"All we have on that is your word."

Tugging at his earring, the magician asserted, "But I heard Dark Otto discussing the whole vile plot while I was lurking amid his excessively large collection of boots. He, working closely with our own Dr. Mayerling, forced Spangler to create a highly convincing mechanical replica of Princess Alicia. Once old King Ulrich kicks off, which sad event may occur any day now, they intend to put that clockwork imitation on the throne. The baron hasn't the nerve to seize power openly, but he yearns to become the gray eminence who—"

"Hearsay," put in Harry. "No law officer, here or in Zevenburg, would believe any of this."

"'Tis true nonetheless."

"And that's why we're going to invade the castle. After we clean things up we can let the law know."

Shrugging, the Great Lorenzo said, "At least you ought to be encouraged about one thing."

"Which?"

"It wasn't the real princess who ordered them to give you the bum's rush at the palace," he replied. "Nor was she behind the attempts on your life. Dark Otto and Dr. Mayerling feared you'd spot a ringer if you got too close to their replica of your true love and thus they—"

"Alicia isn't exactly my true love."

"Ah? Do I detect a shift of your affections to some other quarter?"

Harry said, "We're nearly at Blackwood Castle. Start looking for a spot to ditch this wagon."

* * * *

Tubbs hugged himself, whispering, "Gor, hit's colder nor a witch's jampot."

"I'd prefer, old man, that you suffer in silence."

The journalist and his valet were crouched on a wooded hillside a hundred yards from the rear of the castle wall. Ten minutes earlier Harry and the Great Lorenzo had gone downhill to try to gain entry by way of a hidden passageway in the stone wall.

"Whyn't we get the hinside arf of this bleedin' job, guv? Hit's bound ter be warmer hinside that mausoleum."

"In an operation of this sort, each man must play his assigned role." McMillion patted his flowing black moustache, then touched the handle of the revolver tucked into his yellow sash. "Our job is to back up Challenge and the magician chap."

"I seen 'is show once, hin Bucharest. Punk stuff," commented Tubbs. "Honly interestin' thing ter look hat were a dark-'aired quiff wearin' a frock what barely succeeded hin coverin''er ladyjane an' then this stupid sod kept makin''er disappear."

"He seems a capable fellow, although a bit longwinded."

Hugging himself tighter, Tubbs inquired, "'Ow long do we freeze our fundaments 'ere?"

The sun was rising now, a thin yellow light spreading through the trees.

"We're to wait an hour. Then we go in after them."

"Hif they hain't out in an hour; hit'll mean the gobblings got 'em," the shivering valet pointed out. "Hinstead of puttin' our own tails in the snare, guy, we ought to 'op in that wagon an' depart fer sunnier climes an' scenes."

"One doesn't desert one's comrades."

"Neither of them blokes his me comrades."

"Nevertheless."

"Hin fact, 'Andsome 'Arry the Boy Detective seems fair ter stealin' yer freckled grummett—yer lady reporter—from hunder yer bloomin' nose."

"We'll watch and wait in silence, old man."

Tubbs produced a grumbling sound.

The day grew gradually brighter, but the chill did not depart.

After a few moments Tubbs asked, "Hif yer hain't goin' ter win the wench, guy, what's hin this fer you?"

"A tremendous story," replied McMillion.

* * * *

"We've done admirably thus far," observed the Great Lorenzo.

Harry nodded and held his oil lantern higher.

They were traveling along a narrow stone-walled passageway that snaked beneath Blackwood Castle. The gray stone blocks of the wall were rich with a thick, black, fuzzy mildew, and the damp air was fragrant with the smell of decay.

"Once in San Francisco, that fabled city beside the Golden Gate," said the magician as they moved along the passageway, "I briefly wooed a comely lady whose husband was a mortician by trade. Although she was striking in appearance, she always smelled just about like this tunnel. Thus, with some regret, I severed the—"

"Here's the wooden door."

"So it is." He consulted the notes he'd made after poring over the castle plans with Harry. "Yon portal ought to lead us right into the crypt."

"Which is where, according to Professor Staub, we find Mayerling snoozing in his coffin."

After rubbing his palms together, the magician took hold of the brass handle of the heavy wooden door. "Yes, vampires are noted for creeping back into their coffins once sunup arrives," he said, trying the handle. "And since rosy-fingered dawn was already touching the countryside when we effected our subtle entrance into this stronghold some moments ago, we'll surely find Dr. Mayerling safely tucked away and helpless.

"If the professor's right."

"He ought to be, my boy. Vampires are traditionbound and almost always keep their coffins, spread with a layer of their native soil, in the handiest sepulcher."

"You've had considerable experience with vampires?"

"Some. I've led, as who should know better than you, a colorful—Ah, she's opening."

Amid some creaking and scraping, the door came open toward them.

Harry moved to the dark threshold, shining the lantern light into the musty stone room beyond. "Coffins," he reported.

"So I see."

The room was large and chill. On stone shelves around the shadowy walls rested ancient coffins. Sitting atop the lid of one was a disdainful, well-fed rat.

In the center of the room, with a path to them worn in the dust, rested two newer coffins. Black, gold-trimmed, they sat on low wooden platforms. Both coffins were open.

"Let's have a look." Harry entered the crypt, scattering the dust as he walked to the coffins.

Crouching, he looked down into the nearest of them.

"That is not the good doctor," said the magician as he knelt beside Harry.

"So she's one, too."

Asleep in the satin-lined box, arms folded over her breasts, was Naida Strand.

"Would this be Miss Strand?"

"Yep." Rising, Harry walked around to the other coffin. This one was empty. "He's not here, Lorenzo."

"That's odd. I thought all vampires went to sleep at dawn."

"Not all," said a voice in the shadows.

Chapter 21

From beneath his cloak the Great Lorenzo produced the Sacred Silver Sword of San Sebastian. "This ought to come in handy about now," he suggested as he passed the glittering blade to Harry.

Harry accepted it, setting the lantern down on the chill stone floor.

The figure across the room had stepped free of the shadows. It was Dr. Mayerling, judging from the descriptions Harry had collected. He was a tall, lean man, dark, with his black hair slicked down and parted exactly in the middle. He seemed no more than fifty.

"Ah, the dauntless Harry Challenge," Mayerling said. "I must say, you don't even live up to the dreadfully modest reputation you've earned as a keyhole peeper." He glanced briefly at the magician. "As for your frightfully fat friend..." Chuckling, he rolled his eyes.

Harry said, "If I understand my vampire lore correctly, this silver blade ought to take care of—"

"Don't be so horribly naive, Challenge. You surely don't believe I came to this little encounter totally unprepared." Shedding his own dark cloak, he revealed that he, too, possessed a sword. The lantern light made the filigreed hilt and the blade flash as he held it up. "In the course of a long and frightfully eventful life, I've had the opportunity to become rather an accomplished swordsman. Not that I'd have to be all that marvelous to dispatch a bumpkin such as you."

The Great Lorenzo made a negative sound. Without warning Dr. Mayerling lunged at Harry with the blade.

Harry dodged, backstepped, brought up his own sword.

When Mayerling lunged again, employing as much of a fleche attack as the crypt allowed, Harry parried.

Their blades clacked and clanged against each other.

"I do think it only fair to inform you, dear boy," said Mayerling as their blades met again, "that I was laying out fellows a good deal more skilled than you in Berlin as far back as the late 1780s."

"Here's a lad with three whole centuries of dull anecdotes to dump on us," remarked the Great Lorenzo, who'd drifted off into the shadows somewhere.

Harry parried again, got in under the doctor's flashing blade and almost scored a touch.

The shadows of the two dueling figures were projected on the stone wall, long and distorted, by the lantern sitting on the floor.

All at once something came whizzing out of the darkness. It hit the doctor's head, hard, producing an unexpected bonging.

Mayerling's legs wobbled, buckled, then spread like a broken wishbone.

He fell over, hit the floor, lay still.

The Great Lorenzo stepped back into the light, retrieved the stone funeral urn he'd used on the doctor's skull. "I assumed you weren't especially committed to a fair fight."

"Not especially, no." Frowning some, he was gazing down at the sprawled doctor. "That pot made an unusual noise when it connected."

"Rather a Chinese gong effect, wasn't it? Yes, I noticed." He set the urn aside. "The doctor also sounded rather like a gunnysack of plumbing supplies falling off a wagon when he came to rest, too."

"Damn it, not another ringer." Down on one knee, Harry tugged at the doctor's sleek black hair.

Three pulls and the hair and scalp came free, revealing a metal skull beneath.

The magician observed, "Apparently Herr Doctor Mayerling does abide by vampire tradition and sleep days."

"But where?"

"'Tis a large and roomy castle."

Harry rested his sword across the open coffin, the one holding the dark Naida. He hefted up the urn, used it as a hammer to ruin the automaton's head. "Least we can incapacitate this decoy."

Shuddering once, the Great Lorenzo said, "I should wallow in all this mixing of illusion and reality, yet this little set-to has unsettled me some. I'd have sworn this was the real article."

"If the Alicia automaton is this good, she'll make a damn convincing queen." Harry stood.

"Ought we, do you think, render Miss Strand harmless?" He coughed into his hand, rubbing his foot across the stone floor.

"With the silver sword in her heart, you mean?"

"Merely a suggestion. We were planning to do as much for Dr. Mayerling when we—"

"She won't awaken until nightfall," said Harry, picking up his sword. "We'll leave her here for now."

"Just as well," said the magician, sighing with relief. "Shall we Seek Dr. Mayerling elsewhere?"

"If he's asleep, too, I'd rather concentrate on Jennie and the rest. We've used up too much time already just tangling with substitutes."

"Then I'll lead on to a secret passage that'll take us to an upper level of the castle."

"Let's go," said Harry.

* * * *

They hadn't taken away Jennie's notebook. Perched on the window seat of her room high in the left wing of the castle, legs tucked under her, she was writing out an account of all that had befallen her since leaving Zevenburg. Scribner's ought to be interested, or maybe McClure's or The Century.

From her barred window she could see down across several miles of green forest. Two silky black carrion crows were circling in the morning air.

The handsome Harry Challenge...

"No, that's rather too trite," decided the reporter. The manly, open-faced Harry Challenge... "Now he sounds like a sandwich."

Speaking of Harry, where the heck was he? He must've realized by now that she was a prisoner here.

"Suppose he's already tried to storm this place and—"

She'd never been able to warn him about Dr. Mayerling's true nature. Harry might've barged in, not expecting to meet up with a vampire.

"But he's smart. When I turned up missing, he'd have gone to Willie Staub."

Certainly, and the leonine professor would've—

Jennie flipped back over her last few pages, finding that, as she'd suddenly suspected, she'd used "leonine" twice to describe Professor Staub.

She chewed at the end of her pencil, gazing out the leaded windowpanes. The crows were swooping down toward the woodlands.

Maybe Harry had dismissed her from his mind. If he knew, as she now did, that the real Princess Alicia was also a prisoner here in Blackwood Castle, he might be concentrating solely on rescuing the princess.

"How can a man as bright and perceptive as Harry see anything in that insipid blond with—"

Not that Jennie had met the princess since becoming a fellow prisoner. All she knew about her was what she'd gathered from young Dr. Mistley when he dropped in now and then for a chat.

"Darn, I ought to be able to charm him into letting me go," she told herself. "Or at least into telling me if they've hurt Harry."

That was one of the things she hadn't been able to worm out of Dr. Mistley.

He was a bit strange, though, and maybe that was why she wasn't succeeding as much as she wanted. There was something a bit...unearthly about him. He wasn't a vampire, because she'd seen him more than once during the daylight hours. He wasn't a werewolf either. No, he'd sat right here in this room last evening, with a full moon out there in the misty night sky, and he hadn't even sprouted stubble.

Whatever Mistley was, though, he wasn't anywhere near as strange as Dr. Mayerling.

Mayerling had visited her only once. He'd given her goose-flesh. He was...decadent. Much like that young illustrator she'd interviewed in London last summer. The fellow who wouldn't openly deny the rumor that he slept with a skeleton most evenings.

The manly, good-natured Harry Challenge shared my journey from...

"Harry isn't exactly good-natured, either," she reminded herself, and crossed out the line.

A tapping came on the door.

"Yes?"

It had to be Dr. Mistley, who was so polite he knocked on the door even though it was locked and he had the key.

The key sounded in the lock, the door opened. Mistley came marching in, stiff-legged, smiling tensely.

Jennie hopped to the floor. "Bit early for a chat, isn't—Harry!"

Just behind the blond doctor came Harry. "Good to see you again," he said, grinning.

She noticed, as she hurried closer, he had his Colt .38 pointed at young Mistley's back.

"Same here. I was fearful they might have killed you or worse."

"I've been attempting to assure Mr. Challenge," put in Dr. Mistley, "that you've been treated with the utmost consideration and—"

"Well, it's better than Devil's Island," she acknowledged, rubbing at the welt on her cheek.

"You were struck by mistake, believe me. The automaton had been specifically instructed to use a hypodermic syringe on you rather than—"

"Enough," mentioned Harry, shutting the door with his foot. "Any idea where Mayerling is, Jennie?"

"He sleeps by day."

"We haven't been able to determine where."

She indicated Mistley, jabbing her pencil in his direction. "He knows."

"Haven't been able to persuade him to confide, though."

"My loyalty to my employer, to say nothing of my physician's oath, makes it next to—"

"Tie him and gag him, can you, Jennie?"

She took down the gilded cords that held the drapes. "These ought to do the job," she said, setting about the task. "You alone?"

"Lorenzo's here, and your chum McMillian is backing us up

outside."

"Oh, him? Whyever did you—"

"There was no need for any of this violence," cut in Dr. Mistley. "Knocking out the sanitarium staff, disabling our costly automatons. A calm and rational conversation could—"

Jennie thrust a pillowcase into his open mouth, tied it in place with another. "The princess is here, too," she said, frowning. "I feel obliged to inform you of the fact, in case you wish to desert me and rush off to—"

"Get to her next," said Harry, putting his gun back in his shoulder holster. "Lorenzo and I, using what he describes as impressive stealth and cunning, have pretty much crippled the crew here. People and mechanical men. There were seven of the former and three of the latter. Been a busy morning."

She guided Dr. Mistley over to the bed, tipped him over on top of it. "He's got keys to all the rooms."

"I have those now." Harry tapped his coat pocket and it jingled. "I kept him this long to make sure I found you."

"Well, you've found me, so now you can get to the princess. Don't let me keep—"

"Lorenzo's going to set Spangler loose."

"Yes, he's the one who's been making, against his will, all these lethal and highly believable mechanical people," she said. "Oh, and Mariott is two doors down from me. I can turn him free if you want.

"For a prisoner, you've been learning a lot."

"People, especially Dr. Mistley here, like to confide in me," she said. "I have a comfortable face."

"That you do." Harry came over and kissed her.

Chapter 22

McMillion consulted his watch, which he was keeping in a pocket of his colorful Gypsy vest. "Exactly an hour has passed by, old man," he announced.

"So hit 'as, an' what a gala, fun-filled hour hit's been." Tubbs was sitting with his back to the trunk of a mighty oak.

"One of us ought to venture forth into the castle, don't you know. Only sporting, since we promised to extricate Challenge should—"

"One! I 'ad the himpression we was contemplatin' a team effort, guv."

Readjusting his head scarf, the journalist said, "While reflecting on our original plan, I've come to the conclusion it would be far wiser for just one of us to enter Blackwood Castle at this juncture, Tubbs. Should anything be seriously wrong within, then I—that is, the chap remaining outside—could ride like the wind to Dunkelstein for succor."

"Yer can't heven ride like a gentle breeze on either of them bloomin' plow 'arses what come with the wagon."

"I'd do my best."

Nodding sourly, the valet got to his feet. "I feel hit's me bloomin' duty ter volunteer for this 'azardous mission, guv."

"Jolly. That's the spirit that has made the British Empire great."

"'At's the same spirit what's caused many a bloke to get 'is diddlywhacker lopped off in some 'eathen land, too."

"Here's a lantern." McMillion hung it over Tubbs's elbow. "And here, old fellow, is that pistol I picked up in Dunkelstein. It fires silver bullets, as you may recall."

"Waste of money. Lead works just as—"

"Not on some of the creatures you may encounter inside the dark halls of Blackwood Castle." He pressed the weapon into Tubbs's hand. "To be on the safe side, use this on anyone you so much as suspect of being a vampire, a werewolf, witch, warlock—"

"Suppose I just pot hanythin' what moves. 'Ow'll that be?"

"Splendid. Spoken like a true warrior."

"I'll be gettin' on with it then." Saluting with the hand that held the gun, Tubbs turned and began making his way down through the morning forest.

* * * *

"Permit me to introduce myself," said the Great Lorenzo, stepping into the long, beam-ceilinged workshop. "I am none other than the Great—"

"Who are you?" A broad-shouldered man of fifty-five, wearing a leather cobbler's apron over his clothes, jumped up from behind the cluttered workbench at the center of the room.

"I happen to be, since you apparently don't recognize my world-renowned face, the Great—"

"How'd you get in here? Only Dr. Mayerling and—"

"A lock like this is mere child's play for—"

"I'm doing the best I can trying to finish this job. Interrupting me like this isn't going—"

"Sir, I've come to rescue you."

The other man set down the soldering iron he'd been using. Stretched out upon the table was the metal skeleton of a man-size automaton. Propped against a jug at the side was what looked to be the head of a prosperous middle-aged gentleman.

"Rescue me? I don't—"

"You are Wolfgang Spangler, are you not?"

"Yes, of course. Do I know you?"

"All the world knows the Great Lorenzo." He strolled over to the worktable to pick up the wax head and scrutinize it. "This is Sir Robert Briney, is it not?"

"Yes, and such trouble I've had with the speech mechanism you wouldn't believe," sighed Spangler. "Sir Robert is forever saying, 'Harumph, harumph... Gad, sir. Harumph... I meant to say... Harumph.'" He shook his head. "Try building that into a clockwork speaking device."

Setting the head aside, the magician surveyed the room.

Two other mechanical men, complete save for their heads, rested in armchairs against the far wall. There were bits of wire, scraps of metal and glass scattered all across the hardwood flooring.

"By the way," said the Great Lorenzo, "I bring you greetings from your daughter Helga."

"Helga. She is well?"

"Doing splendidly, sir, for a lass who's been pining away for her missing father."

"They wouldn't allow me to write or—"

"All such tribulations are in the past." He gestured toward the open doorway. "We can depart."

"I won't even have to finish Sir Robert?"

"That," the magician told him, "is but one of the many blessings of freedom."

* * * *

She was standing by a large stained-glass window, and the morning sun tinted her long golden hair a delicate pink. Her gown was a floor-length one of white satin, high-waisted and simple in design.

She recognized him at once.

"Harry," she said, smiling a bit sadly, "are you a prisoner of this awful man, too?"

"Nope." Pocketing the borrowed keys, he came into her tower room. "Nobody's a prisoner anymore."

She frowned briefly before moving gracefully to him. "You mean you've rescued me?"

Harry nodded. "Along with the others."

Princess Alicia laughed gently and stepped close to put her arms around him. "I should have known, Harry," she said, pressing her lovely cheek against his chest, "that no matter where you were in the world, as soon as you heard I was in trouble, you'd come to save me."

Very carefully he put his hands on her slim shoulders and pushed her to arm's length from him. She was as pretty as ever. "That's not exactly how it was, Alicia."

Her bright blue eyes opened wider. "Then you didn't fight your way into Blackwood Castle for me?"

"You were part of it, certainly. Thing is, I don't want you getting the notion—"

Shrugging, he let go of her and turned away. None of this was what he'd planned to do or say when he finally reached the princess.

Behind him she asked, "What of my father?"

"He's still alive."

"Yet no better?"

"No."

"You'll take me back to Zevenburg?"

He faced her. "Sure, soon as we clear things up here."

"I must be in the palace during—"

"There's going to be a problem at the palace," he told her. "How much do you know about why Mayerling's been holding you here?"

"Nothing. He's only spoken to me twice since I was kidnapped and brought here."

"There's another Alicia in the palace."

"How can that be?" She pressed one hand to her breast. "A girl who looks something like me?"

"A dead ringer, Alicia."

"But how—"

"She's an automaton, a mechanical replica who—"

"No one would be taken in by such a creature."

"Right now, with an assist from Dark Otto, she's fooling just about the whole damn country."

"Otto," said the princess. "Yes, I see. He's behind this."

"He and Dr. Mayerling. The idea is to put this fake on the throne after your father dies. The power behind the throne'll be Baron Otto Van Horn."

"And they kept me alive in case anything went wrong," she said. "Once this…replica is crowned, they'd have no need for me."

"None of that'll happen now."

She said, "I shall have a fight on my hands when I return to the capital."

"A hell of a fight, yes."

"You'll help me?"

Harry put a hand in his trouser pocket. "Sure, because I don't consider this business is finished until all the loose ends are tied up."

"Good, then I am confident all will go well," she said, smiling at him. "And, Harry..."

"Yes?"

She touched his arm. "What happened between us a year and more ago," she said quietly. "That really is over and done, isn't it?"

"It is," he answered, just now realizing that it was.

Chapter 23

Sir Robert Briney was saying, "Gad, sir... Harumph, harumph... What's the meaning of all this, what?"

Spangler nudged the Great Lorenzo. "See what I mean?"

They were gathered in the tapestried great hail of the castle, all the freed patients and other prisoners as well as the captive members of the sanitarium staff.

"Son, I suggest we make immediate plans to vacate," Jonah Mariott told the magician.

"Just as soon as Harry Challenge returns with the fair Princess Alicia we shall—"

"Malarkey." Jennie, notebook in hand, had been interviewing as many people as she could. "Harry and that blond are probably smooching up in the tower and won't be down here for hours yet."

"Ah, the proverbial green-eyed monster rears its—"

"Gad, now what, eh? Harumph, harumph... Are we to be invaded, I mean to say, by Gypsies and fuzzywuzzys, what?"

Peter Starr McMillion had just entered, somewhat cautiously, through the wide open front door. "Hello there, Jennie." Smiling handsomely, he came striding toward her with hand outstretched. "This is a jolly reunion, isn't it? It certainly appears, yes, as though our rescue efforts have been most fruitful."

"Your moustache is drooping," the reporter informed him. "Better patch it up."

"It's supposed to droop, don't you know. Yes, Gypsy moustaches are notoriously droopy." He was glancing around the vast hall. "I say, you haven't chanced to see my man, have you?"

"The loathsome Tubbs? Nope."

"Strange, since I dispatched the fellow into this place quite a—Mr. Lorenzo, sir, have you noticed Tubbs about?"

"No, I..." The magician hesitated, then pressed his side.

Jennie hurried over to him. "Are you ill?"

He shook his head. "No, child, merely suffering from an uninvited vision." He snapped his pudgy fingers at McMillion. "Come along with me, my boy, and we'll retrieve the loyal Tubbs. Jennie, tell Harry we'll return shortly."

"Where are we off to?" inquired McMillion.

"Below," replied the Great Lorenzo.

* * * *

The magician moved once more along the rear wall of Dr. Mayerling's deserted office. "Ought to be just about here," he murmured. "Trouble with these visions of mine is they don't always come in perfect crystal-clear focus."

"What precisely are we seeking?"

"A slight navelesque depression is what I saw in Aha, this must be it." He pushed against a spot on the stone wall.

A low rumbling commenced. The stone wall shivered, the doctor's collection of framed diplomas rattled. Then a door-size section of wall swung open.

"I say, there was no mention of this on the plans."

"We overlooked the obvious fact that the good doctor must have made more recent additions to his store of hidden passages and secret rooms."

"And your vision tells you that Tubbs is to be found beyond there somewhere?"

The Great Lorenzo picked up the lantern he'd set on the doctor's heavy wooden desk. "Let us see." He ventured into the corridor on the other side of the secret door. "Very little dust underfoot, indicating frequent and recent use."

"One notices a rather unpleasant odor." McMillion, carefully, followed him.

"That'd be Dr. Mayerling."

"The blackguard is down here, is he?"

"He was." The passageway was taking them down and down.

"I find your conversation a bit cryptic at times, old man."

The magician trotted down a short flight of stone steps to stop before a wooden door. "Hold this." He passed the lantern back to his companion.

Crouching, he fished a lockpick from an inner pocket and set to work. The task took little more than three minutes.

Hand on the knob, he called out, "It's us, my dear Tubbs." Then he opened the door.

Tubbs, the silver bullet pistol on his lap, was slouched in an armchair. "Gor, 'ad I but known 'e'd reek so, I'd never of shot the beggar."

The room they entered was much like a bedchamber, except instead of a bed there was a coffin at its center.

Jerking the kerchief off his head and pressing it over his nose and mouth, McMillion approached the open coffin. "Jove, what a sight. A putrefying corpse I once encountered in Calcutta looked hale and hearty by comparison to this."

"The late Dr. Mayerling, if rumor is to be credited, lived a long full life," said the Great Lorenzo, glancing into the coffin. "But three hundred years of hard living has a way of catching up with you. Used silver bullets on him, did you, Tubbs?"

"That was hall I 'ad, guv." He stood, gesturing vaguely with the gun. "I stumbled in 'ere by purest haccident. I was explorin' hup habove an' paused ter strike a bloomin' match an'—well, I muster brushed hagainst a brass dingus on the wall. Next thing I knows, I'm fallin' through the floor and landin' on me fundament right smack next to this casket."

The Great Lorenzo squinted up at the ceiling. "And then the trapdoor shut fast after you."

"Right yer are, guv. Trappin' me in this 'ole," said Tubbs. "Well, yer may not credit this next, but this bloke sits right hup in his casket and glares hat me somethin' fierce." He shrugged. "I shot 'im."

"Good work, old man." McMillion clapped him on the back. "You've rid the world of a prime scoundrel."

"I weren't hexpectin' 'e'd smell so foul afterwards. An' me stuck 'ere for all heternity maybe."

"We can leave now." The Great Lorenzo shut the lid of the coffin.

Chapter 24

The Great Lorenzo hummed as he walked. "This reminds me of a parade I once led through the thoroughfares of Youngstown, Ohio," he said. "Although we don't have Rollo the Ferocious Wild Man of Sulu along this time."

"And we're bringing up the rear of this one and not leading," added Harry.

He and the magician were at the tail end of a procession consisting of their Gypsy wagon, two borrowed farm carts and whatever released patients couldn't fit in the horse-drawn vehicles. Tubbs was driving the wagon.

"Although we've overcome Dr. Mayerling," said the magician as they made their way through the afternoon forest, "we still can't consider ourselves safe in port."

"Not with that spurious Alicia still extant, no." Harry had both his hands in his trouser pockets.

"We must work out a strategy to cope with the situation."

Harry said, "Hell, we'll just walk into the palace and confront Dark Otto and his automaton."

"Force, as well as cunning, may be needed to gain entry."

"We've got the real Princess Alicia; that ought to get us through the damn gates."

Bending, the Great Lorenzo picked a fallen oak leaf from

the roadway. "Speaking of the true and authentic princess, my boy," he said while crumbling the leaf in his palms, "do I detect a certain coolness twixt you twain?"

"Probably so."

"Alas." He opened his hands and a yellow finch flew out and away. "I've been considering yours one of the great romances of the decade."

"Dime novel stuff," said Harry.

After humming to himself for a few moments, the magician said, "Still and all, Harry, if you hadn't tried to pay that call on the princess and gotten thrown out on your ear, why, this whole conspiracy might well have succeeded. A great many people would've been hurt."

"Remind me," said Harry, "to ask Princess Alicia to give me a medal."

* * * *

The rain began while they were still a half mile outside of Dunkelstein. It was a slow chill rain that made the dust of the road smoke.

They heard the bells then, too, tolling mournfully from the town's three churches and the town hall tower as well.

"I fear," said the Great Lorenzo, "this means bad news."

"Yep, the king must've died," said Harry, "and word's reached here."

"We can't get back to Zevenburg until tomorrow night. By then Dark Otto's clockwork princess will be queen of the whole country."

"Maybe not." Harry ran through the rain to the Gypsy wagon.

He hopped up on the back step, let himself in through the rear door.

The princess was riding inside, sharing the wagon with Jennie and three of the female patients.

Jennie had her open notebook on her lap. "What's wrong, Harry?"

"The bells," he said.

The golden-haired princess was sitting on a folded blanket. "My father is dead," she said quietly. "That is why the bells are ringing."

"This changes things some," Harry told her. "When we get back to Zevenburg this ringer'll be queen."

Jennie said, "They have to crown her first."

"Hey, that's right," remembered Harry. "And they won't hold the coronation until after the funeral. So maybe we have enough time to—"

"There is some precedent," said Alicia with a sad shake of her head, "for having the coronation while the last monarch lies in state. Not every new ruler has done that, but Dark Otto certainly will."

"How soon could they crown the automaton."

"As soon as tomorrow perhaps."

Harry said, "Here in Dunkelstein they probably don't know Princess Alicia is supposed to be residing in the capital at this very moment. We're going to the train station, Alicia, and you're going to order us a special express train."

"Yes, but that may only gain us a few hours, Harry."

"A few hours may be enough," he said.

* * * *

The head conductor found Harry in the smoking car of the special express that was speeding through the rainy night toward Zevenburg. "You are certain, Herr Challenge, that Her Highness is satisfied with the accommodations?"

"Everything's fine," Harry- assured him. He'd been sitting alone, smoking one of his thin cigars.

Taking off his gold-braided hat, the small plump conductor wiped his forehead. "We usually have on the line a much more luxurious car than the one the princess is traveling in," he explained. "Unfortunately, some rowdies derailed it a few nights ago and it lies, badly damaged, at the bottom of the Wohnzimmer Ravine. When we pass I'll point it out to you, although in the rain and dark you probably—"

"No need." Harry exhaled smoke. "Although I should think you'd be more careful about whom you allow to use that private car."

"Oh, the gentleman who rented our splendid car is not the one who shoved it off the tracks, no. He is, so I am given to understand, an author of faultless reputation. Englishman." The conductor returned his hat to his head. "It was, we believe, Gypsies who caused the accident. Or possibly anarchists."

"Or both."

"That well may be." He bowed. "If there is anything further the railroad can do, Herr Challenge, you have but to—"

"Thanks."

When the conductor was gone, Harry stretched up out of his chair and stepped out on the observation platform. Night was closing in, rain was hitting hard on the metal awning that protected the observation area.

Harry took a final puff of his cigar before flinging it out into the wet darkness.

"It's only me," announced Jennie, stepping out to join him.

"So I noticed."

"Didn't want you to think I was a lycanthrope or an automaton."

"Very few freckled werewolves in the world."

She shrugged. "I've never seen any figures on the matter." Jennie was wearing the jacket of her tray suit over her shoulders and she adjusted it now, shiv ering once as she glanced out at the rain. "You've been, I can't help noticing, very glum since we le the castle."

"You know how it is when a vacation's over." She sat on one of the two metal chairs. "Oops, this is damp."

"Not surprising."

"Off the record, Harry. Did you and the princess have a falling out?"

"Nope."

"Then your romance is still on?"

He shook his head. "No."

She pulled her jacket tighter around her. "Of course, we still have quite a few hurdles to overcome when we reach Zevenburg tomorrow afternoon. Just about everyone believes that insipid automaton is the real thing," she said. "So if we don't play our cards just right, we could be executed for treason or thrown in prison. Dark Otto isn't an admirable person. Well, he couldn't be and have a nickname like that, could he? And if you're brooding about what the outcome of everything is going to be, why, I guess that's a good enough reason for your being glum and sour-faced, and it hasn't a thing to do with whether the princess and you...whether the queen and you are in love or not."

Harry laughed. He sat down in the other chair. "When I got into this damn mess it was because I thought I was in love with the princess," he said. "There were all sorts of handicaps and odds against it and barricades. I'd worried about all that, which was one of the reasons I stayed away from Orlandia for a year or more. When I came back, though, I figured maybe I'd be able to work something out in spite of all the difficulties."

"Now you believe you can't?"

"Now I believe, Jennie, that I'm not in love with Alicia."

"Well, that's surely a good reason for being down in the mouth. You have an ideal, a goal and then it all..." She gestured at the rainy night. "...fades away on the wind."

"I'm gloomy, if I am gloomy, because I think I'm hooked on somebody else," he said. "And this girl is an even worse bet. She's as independent and feisty as I am. She roams the world like I do, a real loner most of the time, and she's not at all demure and ladylike. She's a damn good investigator, and a fair shot. We more than likely wouldn't get on together at all. She has freckles."

After a silence of several seconds, Jennie stood up. "Oh," she said quietly, and went away.

Chapter 25

Duchess Hofnung came hurrying along the afternoon train platform. "My darling Renzo," she cried, arms outspread. "I rushed here as soon as I received your wire." She hugged him. "I am so glad you survived."

"I share your sentiments, m'love," he said. "But what of the coronation?"

"It is going on even as we speak, dear. I don't quite understand why—my heavens!" She'd caught sight of the true princess alighting from the express on Harry's arm. "Oughtn't she to be at St. Norbert's Cathedral?"

"She ought, yes," agreed the magician. "We'll borrow your estimable carriage and deliver her."

"Haven't you time, Renzo, for a small snack and a bottle of—"

"Duty calls, my pet."

Harry and the princess joined them. "Is it on?" he asked.

"Right now." The Great Lorenzo paused, took in the gratifying scene of Helga Spangler reunited with her father, then started trotting toward an exit. "The dear duchess has kindly offered us her swift carriage."

"Let's go then."

All along the platform the rescued patients of the Blackwood Castle sanitarium were disembarking from the special train. Some still wore looks of bewilderment.

"What about the ladies and gentlemen of the press?" asked the Great Lorenzo as he spotted the duchess's carriage at the curb.

"Let them get their own transportation," said Harry.

"Are you and the charming Miss Barr no longer chums, my boy?"

Harry helped Princess Alicia into the carriage. "I think maybe I frightened her last night," he told the magician.

"We'll discuss the matter at some length after we put the royal house in order."- He climbed up beside the uniformed driver. "To the coronation, my lad."

Harry had to fight one more duel.

Their carriage couldn't get closer than two blocks to the cathedral, then the crowds were too thick to move through. Abandoning it, Harry, Princess Alicia and the Great Lorenzo started along the Singerstrasse on foot.

"Make way, make way," ordered the magician in a booming voice. "Can't have a coronation without a princess."

"Mother of mercy! It's Princess Alicia!"

"Can't be. She just went into the cathedral."

"Don't I know the princess when I see her, dumbhead?"

"Who's a dumbhead?"

"The princess!"

"It's she! It's Princess Alicia!"

"Three cheers for the queen!"

"Long live the queen!"

On the wide marble steps of the towering Gothic-style cathedral three uniformed guards stepped forward to keep them out.

"No one is allowed in—Oops." The guard blinked. "Forgive me, Your Highness."

"Urn..." said another of the guards timidly. "Didn't you already enter once, Your Royal Highness?"

"She did indeed," explained the Great Lorenzo, "yet she was so impressed by the showing you lads made, she had to slip out for another look. She's quite pleased with you all. Now, step aside so—"

"Yes, to be sure." All three clicked their booted heels and saluted.

The interior of the lofty cathedral was packed with people—dignitaries, officials, royalty. Altar boys in scarlet cassocks and crisp white surplices, dozens of yellow-haired, bright-faced tykes, lined the wide center aisle. The scent of sharp incense and hundreds of burning candles was thick in the air. A huge unseen organ was roaring out a majestic hymn.

Up on the scarlet-carpeted altar, amid the myriad candles and gilded candelabras, stood the Bishop of Zevenburg himself, a doddering gentleman of ninety-one, weighted down by the gold and crimson robes and miter. He held a bejeweled gold crown in his quivering old hands.

Kneeling before him was the Alicia automaton, lovely in a flowing gown of white silk.

Baron Otto Van Horn, in a uniform of crimson, gold and silver, stood stiffly nearby.

"...in the eyes of God and in the eyes of man," the bishop was intoning in his thin reedy voice, "you, beloved and divinely chosen Princess...Princess...um...what is her dratted name?"

"Alicia," whispered one of the brightly robed priests who shared the wide altar area with him. "Eh?"

"Princess Alicia!"

"Of course, of course...um...where was I?"

"'Beloved and divinely chosen...'"

"To be sure, to be sure... Ahum... Beloved and divinely— Eh? What's this? A commotion in the very main aisle of the St. Norbert's Cathedral?" The old bishop gasped, staring at the determined approach of the trio.

"Before you continue," said Harry, "you'd better take notice that this is the true princess."

"Get this crazed swine out of here!" ordered Dark Otto, glaring. "The man's a known assassin who—"

"Wait, wait," said the perplexed bishop as he squinted beyond the automaton at the real princess. "This seems most unusual. In all my years of officiating at such sacred ceremonies, never have I had two candidates for—"

"Seize them!" The baron, face flushed with anger, was waving and pointing.

The Great Lorenzo stepped casually up beside the still-kneeling automaton replica of the princess. "Your Excellency," he said to the bishop, "please watch my hands closely."

Swiftly and unexpectedly, the magician snatched at the mechanical woman's golden locks. The wig came off and he flung it aside.

"Behold. A metal dome beneath." The Great Lorenzo knocked on the naked skull, producing a metallic bong.

"You idiot!" said the bald automaton, rising and backing

away from him.

"It's your fault, Challenge," accused Dark Otto. "You intruded into my affairs! Ruined months of hard work and cunning preparation. You...you swine!" From the gilded scabbard at his side he jerked out a wicked sword. "Even though my scheme has vanished like the wind, yet I mean to have satisfaction. I'll gut you like the pig you are!"

"Fellow's obsessed with porkers." The Great Lorenzo reached under his dark cloak. "You'll need this trinket again, Harry my boy." He produced the Sacred Silver Sword of San Sebastian and tossed it down to his friend.

Harry caught it, grinned and nodded at Dark Otto. "You were saying?"

"Swine!" The baron charged down the carpeted altar steps at Harry.

"Stop," gasped the shivering bishop. "You cannot fight in this sacred place." He scowled at the magician. "And you, sir, what are you doing with a priceless relic that has recently been reported stolen?"

Harry and the baron faced each other on the scarlet-carpeted center aisle of the great cathedral.

Most of those who'd come to witness the coronation were on their feet now, talking, shouting, muttering. The organ continued to play from the loft far above.

Dark Otto lunged.

Harry parried.

"Five pfennigs the American wins," said one of the cherubic altar boys to the next one in line. "Taken. Dark Otto'll finish him in a trice."

The baron had an aggressive style, greatly favoring a running attack. He was very angry now, though, taking risks.

Harry, patiently and calmly, parried his every thrust.

The organ, wheezing enormously, ceased playing. The spectators fell silent. The clash of the sword blades echoed through the vaulted cathedral.

Dark Otto made a misstep, was off balance for an instant.

Harry slipped in under his guard, his blade cutting into the baron's side.

Staggering, cursing, Dark Otto stumbled back. Harry struck again, slashing the weapon out of his opponent's grip.

The baron's sword spun through the air, landed at the bishop's feet.

Glaring at Harry, Dark Otto spread his arms wide. "Go ahead, swine. Finish me off."

Harry eyed him for several long silent seconds. Then he grinned. "Hell, you're not worth the trouble."

He handed his sword to the Great Lorenzo. Turning on his heel, Harry went striding out of the cathedral.

Chapter 26

The Great Lorenzo was sitting opposite Harry in the train compartment, gazing out at the activity on the twilight platform. "You're making a rather abrupt departure, my boy," he remarked. "A mere three days after the fair Alicia is crowned queen, you hop on a crack train heading out of the country. Think of the various benefits that might shower on a brave and courageous chap such as yourself. Why, you're something of a national hero, and that, if exploited just right, should be worth several thousand—"

"You're the real hero of the piece," Harry told him, lighting his cigar. "Getting us to the church on time, providing me with a weapon to use against Dark Otto."

"True," admitted the magician modestly. "And you ought to see how my new notoriety is beefing up the box office. I am seriously thinking of extending my engagement another month and adding several more matinees per week."

"Well, I wasn't in the mood to linger in Zevenburg anyway," said Harry. He took a cablegram out of his coat pocket and passed it to the magician. "On top of which—"

"Ah, I sense the kindly hand of your warm-hearted old dad."

Dear son:

You've cleaned up that mess, so quit sitting around on your duff. Get to Paris quick. We've got a new client who thinks maybe his Egyptian mummy has been taking walks of an evening. Sounds like moonshine, but he's got a stewpot of money to spend.

Your loving father, the Challenge International Detective Agency.

Refolding the cable, the Great Lorenzo returned it to Harry. "Did you and Queen Alicia part friends?"

"We'll always be pals."

"Looks like Dark Otto will be exiled rather than made to languish in a dank cell."

"That's one of the advantages of being royalty."

The magician said, "Did you chance to see a copy of today's edition of the European version of the London Graphic?"

"Isn't it there among the stuff you materialized for my trip?"

After searching through the scatter of fruit baskets, flowers, newspapers and magazines on the seat beside him, the Great Lorenzo shook his head. "Seems I neglected to provide one. At any rate, our recent comrade-in-arms, Peter Starr McMillion, penned a true account of the Dark Otto—Dr. Mayerling affair for the sheet. You may be surprised to learn that it was Pete and not we who masterminded the raid on Blackwood Castle as well as the showdown at the cathedral. He does, almost as a footnote to his stirring autobiographical account, mention he had some small bit of help from 'a little-known American private inquiry agent and a music hall entertainer.' Music hall!"

"Doesn't sound like anything you'll want to paste in your scrapbook."

"They even ran a drawing of him in that Gypsy outfit." Sighing, the magician rose to his feet. "Have a pleasant journey, my boy. I must return to the theater and prepare to astound my early show audience."

Harry held out his hand. "Thanks, Lorenzo."

Shaking hands, the Great Lorenzo said, "We'll meet again. I'm certain we will, since I had a vision about it only this morning. Won't give you any details now, so as not to spoil the surprise of it. Adieu."

He stepped out onto the platform and went walking away into the twilight.

* * * *

The train crossed the border at a few minutes before midnight.

Harry was sitting in his compartment, reading at one of the novels the Great Lorenzo had given him. The story had to do with a murder and other foul deeds at a vast, gloomy English countryhouse. The detective on the case wasn't particularly bright.

Someone tapped on his door.

Shutting the novel without bothering to insert a bookmark, Harry said, "Yes?"

The door opened and Jennie Barr's freckled face looked in. "I heard there was an American detective on board," she said, "so I decided to take a peek. See if it was anyone I knew."

"C'mon in," he invited.

"Somewhat late."

"Even so."

She entered, closed the door carefully behind her and sat facing him. "You're leaving Orlandia?"

"Seem to be. You?"

Jennie smiled. "My editor was so pleased with the stories I wired him, he told to take two weeks off. With pay."

"And you're going where?"

"Paris. I always like Paris, especially in the spring," she replied. "Where are you traveling to?"

"Paris. A new case."

"Isn't that an amazing coincid—Well, actually it isn't, Harry."

"Lorenzo told you I was taking this train and where I was bound for."

"Matter of fact, he did."

Nodding, Harry said, "He didn't mention you at all during our farewell chat. I figured that was the reason."

She reached into her shoulder bag. "He presented me with this," she said, extracting a bottle of brandy. "From Duchess Hofnung's own cellar, although she may not know it."

"There are a couple of glasses in that picnic hamper, next to the hard-boiled eggs," said Harry.

"You open this then." She handed him the bottle. "I'll find the—yes, here they are."

"Okay, the bottle's opened."

Jennie smiled and moved across the compartment to sit beside him.

THE CURSE OF THE OBELISK

Chapter 1

Paris in the spring of 1897 was a city of gaiety, light and movement, pervaded with an air of joyous living. An immense city, full of broad handsome streets, magnificent buildings, grand open spaces with fountains and statues, great public gardens and parks, miles and miles of stores and shops filled with the most beautiful and interesting things that are made or found in any part of the world.

Harry Challenge didn't much want to be there.

As he went striding along the twilight Boulevard Saint Germain, unlit cigar clenched in his teeth, he made a list of places he'd rather be.

A lean man of middle height, Harry was dark haired and clean shaven. His tan, weather-beaten face tended to give people the impression he was a few years older than his thirty-one years. He wore, as he usually did, a dark suit. His hat was soft brimmed, and in his snug shoulder holster rested a Colt .38 revolver.

"Fool's errand," Harry muttered to himself. Not for the first time.

An open carriage rolled by, the horses' hooves clacking on the smooth pavement. The satin-clad woman in the carriage glanced approvingly at Harry, and the light of a street lamp made the diamonds in her tiara and on the collar of her little white Maltese dog sparkle. Scowling, the dog yapped at Harry.

He tipped his hat to both of them and hurried on.

The street was crowded. People strolling, people sitting at the little tables in front of cafés, workmen in blue blouses and wooden shoes heading homeward, even a priest in long black clothes and a broad felt hat taking the air.

Absently Harry patted the pocket of his vest that contained a folded copy of the latest cable from his father in New York. The message had been waiting for him when he checked into his far too fancy Paris hotel this afternoon. What it said was:

Dear son:

Get off your rump. Go see our half-wit client. Name is Maurice Allegre. He runs the Musée des Antiquités on Rue Balbec. If you ask me he's got bats in his bonnet, but his money's good. You find out what's really going on. I doubt his museum is haunted.

Your loving father, the Challenge International Detective Agency.

An earlier message, which had reached Harry while he was finishing up a case in the capital city of the small sovereign nation of Orlandia had mentioned a mummy that roamed the museum by night.

Harry'd handled several supernatural cases of late, too many in fact, and he was hoping M. Allegre would turn out to be, as his father implied, suffering from hallucinations.

He passed the Café de Flor, dropped a few centimes in the dented copper cup of the ragged blind man standing just beyond its bright Art Nouveau facade and turned onto the Rue Balbec.

The dusk was deepening. From a sharply slanting tile roof a clutter of sparrows rose up into the oncoming night. Someone was playing a mournful tune on a rusty violin in a lamplit parlor up in a thin building on his left.

Cutting across the cobblestoned street, Harry started through a public garden. A greened brass plate on the stone column at its entrance proclaimed it the Jardin Réve.

According to his red-bound Baedeker, the museum he sought was on the opposite side of this shadowy, block-square little park.

The light was fading faster. Darkness and quiet came closing in on Harry. He seemed to be the only person walking through the Jardin Réve. Yet Harry was commencing to feel a shade uneasy, wondering if he really wasn't alone.

The white gravel path wound through a thick grove of trees. In among them lurked pale white figures that Harry decided, after reaching into his coat for his .38 revolver and then thinking better of it, were statues.

He recognized, quickening his pace, a pudgy Venus and a muscle-bound Hercules.

Through the dark trees ahead he spotted now the two glowing electric lamps that framed the arched doorway of the Musee des Antiquites.

From behind him came a rustling sound.

Halting, he spun around. He drew his Colt and stared into the darkness behind him.

Harry had the impression something large and dark had settled into the high branches of one of the big trees a few hundred yards away.

He stood still, eyes narrowed and gun ready, watching.

The shape he thought he'd noticed wasn't there. Or if it was, the new night masked it.

He waited nearly a full minute before holstering his gun and continuing on his way.

Not quite ten seconds after that a young woman screamed. Two pistol shots rang out.

Harry dived to the ground, rolled across the grass and came to a squatting position behind a wide tree trunk. His Colt was once again in his right hand.

"Well, damn," he remarked aloud.

Rising up above the treetops was an immense birdlike creature. Its body was nearly man-size and it had bat wings that creaked and made bellows sounds as it flapped them.

Harry sprinted back to the gravel path for a better look. Down out of the night sky fell a drop of something hot and sticky. It splashed him on the cheek.

"Serves me right." He yanked out his pocket handkerchief, wiped at his face and stuffed the cloth away.

The giant bird or bat or whatever it was was flying away over the rooftops of Paris. The glow of street lamps and window lights illuminated it until the creature rose too high. Darkness swallowed it.

Putting away his gun, Harry went trotting back the way he'd come. "Now where the hell's the lady who hollered?"

She was slumped on a wrought iron bench, a derringer lying in the grass at her feet. A slim and very pretty young woman she was, her hair a pale reddish gold. It had tumbled down from under the checkered cap she was wearing. The cap matched the man's Norfolk jacket and tweedy knickers she had herself decked out in.

"Jennie Barr." Harry's tone was not especially cordial. "You were too busy to have dinner with me tonight. You had to get to work immediately on your story for the New York Daily Inquirer. You lied to me."

Taking a deep breath, Jennie sat up straighter and tucked her hair back up under the cap. "Well, I suppose I did fib some, yes."

"We travel all the way from Zevenburg to Paris together," he continued, angry. "I even, behaving like what my father would classify as a nincompoop, declare that I'm fond of you. I entertain the half-wit notion that I can trust you not to be a newspaper reporter above all else. But you were just conning me, Jennie, so you could—"

"Fond of me? What you did on the Zevenburg-Paris Express, Harry, was tell me you loved me."

"Okay, I do love you," he admitted. "Fact is, I was in the process of telling you that again just a few hours ago. But you told me you had to get right to work on your assignment. No time for romance, no time for the gaiety, light and movement of Paris. So it turns out this damn story of yours has to do with my private—"

"Hey, I just saved your life."

"Thanks," he said. "Now tell me why you're dressed like a guy and tailing me."

Jennie grinned. "Did pretty darn well, didn't I? I followed you all the way from the Hotel Grand-Luxe and you never even tumbled."

"You did, huh?" He made a face and shook his head. "There's one thing my father's right about. Getting involved with a woman dulls your—"

"Your father, if you'll forgive my reminding you of the fact, is a sour ball, Harry," the reporter put in. "One of the things that scares the heck out of me is the possibility you'll grow more like him as you get older. Spending my declining years with a curmudgeon isn't my idea of—"

"You won't even spend the rest of the damn evening with me unless you explain what's going on."

Reaching up, she took hold of his arm and pulled herself to her feet. "Take me to a nearby café and over coffee I'll tell all," Jennie promised.

"I'm on my way to see a client. Don't have time for—"

"Let me give you some advice." She bent, grimacing, scooped up her tiny gun and tucked it away under her jacket. "Don't pout that way. You don't have the face for it. I think it's an attractive face, albeit a mite beat-up and—"

"Okay, I'll take you someplace." When they started to walk, he noticed the red-haired young woman was limping. "Did that critter hurt you?"

"Nope, but I twisted my ankle while I was running and shooting at it. That's why I fell and dropped my gun."

"You can't faze a gigantic bird with a dinky gun like that anyway."

"Wasn't a gigantic bird," she assured Harry. "It was a gigantic bat."

Jennie poked at her raspberry ice with her spoon. "It is, you have to admit, the sort of story I do well." She'd taken off the cap and the faint night breeze brushed at her hair.

Across the small outdoor table from her Harry lit his cigar. "A curse?" He blew smoke at the marble tabletop.

"Three weeks ago the noted French archaeologist Reynard Courdaud met a strange end at his villa near Nice," said the reporter. "Then five days ago Sir Munson Bellhouse died in a fall while hunting in Scotland."

"A death in Nice, another in Scotland. Why does that prompt the Daily Inquirer to send you here to Paris?"

After savoring a spoonful of the ice, she answered, "You haven't done, Harry, sufficient research into this affair."

The light spilling out through the stained glass window of the sidewalk café gave a pale golden glow to her face. Harry looked away for a moment, toward a plump German tourist who was sipping a solitary absinthe. "Was Bellhouse an archaeologist, too?"

Jennie nodded. "He was one of the five men who headed the expedition to the Valley of Jackals in 1895," she said. "They found considerable treasures, including the dornick that's been dubbed the Osiris Obelisk."

"Is it anything like the one in Central Park or the one right here in town at the Place de la Concorde?"

"This is a miniature version, only about six feet high. Thing is, one of the inscriptions started the rumor that—"

"Wait now. Is there a curse on the thing?"

"There was a lot of talk to that effect, back when the Courdaud expedition first broke into the tomb it was standing in front of. My editors believe there's a—"

"Awful slow for a curse. Don't they work faster than that?" He rested his elbows on the tabletop, watching her faintly freckled face. "Waiting two years before striking isn't my idea of—"

"Let me give you a few details about Reynard Courdaud's death." She set her spoon aside. "His valet swears that Courdaud was attacked on his terrace at dusk by a giant bat. That's one reason I hollered and started shooting when I saw that thing tonight lurking over your—"

"A giant bat?" Harry sat up.

"Your elbow." Jennie pointed. "You've got something sticky on it."

"Coffee." Fishing out his handkerchief, he wiped at his coat. "This seems to be my night for...hum."

"What is it?"

He'd brought the stained square of linen up to his nose and was sniffing at it. "While I'm not an expert on bat lore, I'll bet their droppings don't smell like machine oil."

She reached across and took the handkerchief. "That's oil sure enough. What makes you think—"

"While that thing was flying away directly overhead, I looked up."

Crumpling the handkerchief, Jennie said, "This is commencing to look like one of the oddest curses I've ever investigated."

"This guy in Scotland..."

"Sir Munson Bellhouse, one of the most respected archaeologists in Britain. Haven't you ever heard of—"

"What caused his fall?"

"A gamekeeper from the estate where they were shooting swore he saw a giant bird circling the spot where Sir Munson did his brodie. He wasn't believed."

"Okay, and where do I tie in?" asked Harry. "Was that damn bat planning to make me the next victim of the curse of the obelisk? And if so, why?"

"Don't you know where the Osiris Obelisk is?"

Harry ground his cigar out in the pewter ashtray. "At the Musée des Antiquités?"

"For five more days," she replied. "Then it's being shipped to the capital of Urbania. The museum's sold it to a private collector. The whole business has caused quite a stir."

Harry said, "You were trailing me because you figure the troubles at the museum are linked with this curse."

"Seems likely, doesn't it?" There was a mixture of contriteness and excitement in her voice. "Honestly, Harry, I don't like to trade on our friendship, but so far nobody else knows the Challenge International Detective Agency has been called in on this case. That exclusive angle'll make my series of articles for the Daily Inquirer much more—"

"I'll make you a deal."

"You sound sort of grim."

"Instead of putting on half-wit disguises and skulking around, you can come along to the museum with me," he said. "After I meet with M. Allegre, in private, I'll see if he'll let you interview him."

"Well, that'd be fine, I guess. But you're scowling at me as though—"

"We've known each other for quite a spell. Back in New York and—"

"Known and liked. Even though sometimes—"

"When our paths crossed in Orlandia and it turned out we were both interested in the prisoner of Blackwood Castle, I initially tried to ditch you."

"Harry, I do…well, love you. And you can trust me," she assured him in a quiet voice. "It's just that I'm a reporter, and a darn good one, and so sometimes—"

"We'll forget what happened on the train from Orlandia to Paris." Harry stood and signaled the gaunt, aproned waiter. "It never took place. We'll go back to being rivals, friendly rivals."

"But, Harry, something did happen. We can't just—"

"I'm late for the meeting with my client. You coming along?"

She hesitated, then smiled tentatively. "Yes," she replied.

Chapter 2

After rubbing at his nose, Maurice Allegre tapped the drawing in the newspaper open upon his desk. "My reputation is in shreds already, M. Challenge," he said, wringing his small hands. "Just this past Monday here in Le Figaro no less a formidable penman than Caran d'Ache depicted me as a grave robber. You see?"

Harry leaned forward in his heavy wooden chair. "Doesn't resemble you that much."

"Ah, but all Paris knows at whom this barb is aimed," said the forlorn museum director. "Even though he's seen fit to give me an extremely large Hebraic nose. It is sad enough to be blamed for selling that accursed obelisk without being branded a Dreyfusard as well. If the outside world were to learn of my latest sorrows..." He sighed.

"Suppose you detail your problem to me."

The office was shadowy, the furniture heavy and dark, the carpets and drapes the color of deep autumn. Hovering in the dim corners that the light from the faintly hissing gas lamps didn't reach were coffins, mummy cases and at least one suit of Oriental armor.

Allegre patted at the part in his slick dark hair. "My two regular watchmen had let me down," he said, taking another disheartened glance at the cartoon attacking him. "After all, M. Challenge, I do not own this Musée des Antiquités. Nay, I am but an employee. When the directors, you understand, agreed to sell the obelisk to Baron Groll in Urbania, I could only, meekly, go along with them." He poked a delicate finger at the cartoon. "This is, after all, a private institution and not a public one. They can sell whatever they wish and to whomsoever they wish. Therefore, when this Caran d'Ache shows me looting tombs and selling the treasures of France to foreigners, he errs in—"

"You told my father your museum was haunted."

Allegre said, "Your father, at least in his cablegrams, strikes one as a highly intelligent man. I was halfway expecting that he himself would journey here to Paris to handle the—"

"He rarely travels these days," said Harry. "Do you have ghosts?"

Allegre shrugged with both his shoulders and both hands. "Ah, but I myself have seen not a one," he replied. "My addlepated watchmen, on the other hand, insist that on several occasions some unusual incidents have taken place."

"Such as?"

"Most, if not all, of this outré activity has allegedly occurred in our Antiquités Égyptiennes Wing, M. Challenge," said the director. "Both Gaspar and Albert have insisted they heard many strange sounds and, furthermore, that they saw with their own eyes..." He shrugged once again. "They saw one of the mummified corpses leave its resting place and walk."

"When did these incidents begin?"

Allegre answered, "Approximately three weeks ago. Fortunately, I have been able, thus far, to keep it quiet. I fear that—"

"I'd like to talk to Gaspar and Albert."

"Ah, but alas, monsieur, that is not possible," explained Allegre. "They are no longer employed here. Albert, in point of fact, ran screaming from this place three midnights ago. Though Gaspar made a less flamboyant exit, he too is gone."

"Is midnight when the ghostly happenings usually happen?"

"Not every midnight, but far too many, yes," answered the museum director. "You also cannot, I fear, interrogate either Gerard or Paul."

"The new watchmen?"

"Exactly, monsieur." He sighed his deepest sigh thus far. "Gerard and Paul lasted but a single night. Thus, you have indeed arrived at a most fortunate juncture in the affairs of our plagued institution."

Harry eyed him for a few sconds. "You want me to act as watchman tonight?"

"Are you not ideally suited for such a task? A stalwart and manly fellow, well versed in the handling of such unusual situations," said Allegre. "You know how to deport yourself when faced with dangers of an unusual sort, and you are not superstitious like Gaspar, Albert, Gerard and Paul."

"Have you ever spent a night here?"

The director shuddered. "I am, you understand, not a brave man,' he confided. "Were I to run screaming from the premises in the dead of night it might lead to further scandal, providing fodder for yet another unflattering caricature in Le Figaro and other vicious publications. Besides, M. Challenge, since we are paying you such an enormous fee, it is only fair that—"

"Substantial," corrected Harry, "not enormous. Okay, I'll stay here tonight. That'll give me a chance to go over the Egyptian wing and the rest of the museum."

"I appreciate that," said Allegre, allowing himself a small, sad smile. "Will your quite charming young assistant who waits in the foyer be sharing your nocturnal duties, monsieur?"

Harry grinned. "Yes, I seldom go anywhere without her."

* * * *

The ceiling of the vast room was lost in shadows. The air was chill, scented faintly with sandalwood and ancient dust.

"This particular chest is one of my favorites," Allegre was saying. "The framework is of ebony, the inner panels of beautifully carved redwood. Here we see the bronze and ivory blended to produce…"

Jennie whispered to Harry, "You're a rat."

He assumed a beatific expression and ignored her. "Passing me off as an operative in your dim-witted detective agency after promising me a chance to interview this guy." She delivered a disappointed nudge to his ribs.

"He loathes the press. Now hush."

"…the king, you see, is offering Omnophris a pot of perfume and a lamp. Omnophris is, of course, but another guise of Osiris, who guards the…"

"I'm not some pushy French news hound," persisted Jennie in an annoyed whisper. "And if you don't tell him who I really am, then I myself will."

"Listen, didn't I arrange for you to spend the whole damn night inside this place? When the mummy does his jig, you'll be the only reporter on hand."

"Yes, but—"

"You go telling him who you really are and you'll get nothing but the old heave-ho."

"Ah, but I must be boring you by riding my hobbyhorse so vehemently." The director turned away from the glass case that housed the chest.

"I'd like to see the case the mummy climbs out of at midnight," Harry told him.

"But certainly, monsieur." Bowing slightly, Allegre led them past more ornate chests, an alabaster casket, a case filled with glittering bracelets and bangles.

In an alcove, illuminated by a single hanging lamp, a carved coffin with a lid of gold, turquoise and crimson rested on a low platform.

Noticing something stuck to a nail on the platform, Harry bent and took it. "Little hunk of linen," he said, passing it under his nose. "Doesn't smell especially ancient."

The museum director blinked. "May I inspect that, monsieur?"

"I don't think it came from the mummy in that case."

"No, certainly not. This bit of cloth is of recent manufacture." He was rubbing it between his fingers. "Superficially like that used to wrap the bodies of our Egyptian friends, yet not the real thing. How, do you think, did this come to be here?"

Retrieving the patch, Harry tucked it into the watch pocket of his vest. "We'll try to find that out tonight."

Allegre gestured at the coffin. "This is made of wood. Over the lid was placed first a layer of plaster and then one of gold. After which the—"

"Does the lid lift off easily?" inquired Jennie.

"It is not too difficult to remove, Mlle. Barr." Smiling, he demonstrated.

Harry took a look inside. "This fellow can't do much walking around, not with his legs wrapped together that way."

"Precisely what I tried to explain to those fools, Gaspar and Albert." He nodded toward Jennie. "Would you care for a glimpse of King Baydmadroub II?"

"Pass," she said.

"Now I'd like," requested Harry, "to see the obelisk."

After returning the inlaid coffin lid to its place, Allegre said, "It's really not that impressive, monsieur. A very small and stunted thing that is no match for the so-called Cleopatra's Needle that—"

"Even so."

The director sighed, shrugged, patted his hair. "Very well. If you will but follow me."

Slowly he led them through the big room, along a dimly lit corridor and into a smaller room.

Mounted upright on a wooden stand was the miniature obelisk, a tapering shaft of red granite profusely covered with carved hieroglyphs. Two small gas lamps, one on each side of the room, provided the only light.

Allegre hunched his shoulders. "A paltry example, hardly worth making a fuss about," he observed, stroking his nose. "It stands approximately six foot eight in height, which makes it roughly one tenth the size of the obelisk to be found in your country."

Jennie edged closer. "Do these inscriptions spell out the curse?"

"Among other things." Reluctantly he joined her near the obelisk. "Those lower rows there, near the base, provide the phrases that give the obelisk its unsavory reputation."

Harry strolled over. "What do they say exactly?"

Impatiently Allegre translated. "'By the awesome power of Osiris, who holds the secret of eternal life, cursed be those who disturb this tomb. Death, not life, shall be their sure and swift reward.' And so forth and so on. A standard and not especially imaginative curse, as ancient curses go. Yet sufficient, because of the idiocies practiced by the disgraceful press to—"

"Some reporters," put forth Jennie, "are highly reputable."

"I am astounded to hear you express such sentiments, Mlle. Barr, since America's newspapers are, one is told, even more vile than—"

"Is Osiris usually associated with the secret of eternal life?"

asked Harry.

"He is the king and the judge of the dead," answered Allegre. "One doesn't often find him addressed in exactly these terms, yet the association is—"

"Take the New York Daily Inquirer. There's an honest and well written paper," said Jennie. "Why, some of the reporters on its staff are—"

"We'd best get on with your inspection tour, Operative Barr." Harry slipped an arm around her slim waist and gave her an unobtrusive prod in the ribs. "You and M. Allegre can chat about journalism some other time. I want to check all the entrances before he leaves us."

"Ah, yes," said the director after consulting his gold pocket watch, "the hour does indeed grow late. I would like to be far from here before midnight strikes." He started out of the room.

After kicking Harry in the shin, Jennie followed.

Chapter 3

Jennie placed the tray on the floor near a case that held a gilded leopard mask. "The coffee isn't too bad," she said, sitting down cross-legged on a sofa cushion she'd appropriated from the long departed director's office, "considering I had to brew it over a spirit lamp. Have some, it'll keep you awake."

"I am awake." He was hunkered on the floor of the Egyptian wing, back against the buff wall. "Never go to sleep on a job."

"I thought that was the Pinkerton slogan." She passed him a delicate china cup. "The petits fours I can't vouch for. They may be a mite stale since I found them in a tin in a bottom drawer of his desk."

Harry sipped the coffee and declined the tiny cakes.

"What about that little piece of cloth you found?" she asked him. "You got a whiff of something off it."

"Greasepaint."

"That must mean—"

"Could mean several things." He looked away from her, toward the corridor leading to the obelisk.

After a moment Jennie asked, "Are you still miffed at me?"

"Miffed isn't exactly the word I'd use."

Out in the Paris night a bell began to toll midnight.

Jennie tried one of the petits fours, wrinkled her nose, then went on chewing. "You still don't realize, Harry, how difficult it is for me to balance things. My career requires my traveling all over the world for stories and that means I can't have a settled way of life. I have a sort of rule not to let myself get too involved with anybody anywhere. But then I bumped into you again and...well, it makes things rough."

"I know, torn between love and duty," he said. "Saw a heartrending painting on the subject once in a saloon in Elko, Nevada."

She gave him a polite snort. "Mother O'Malley! You're the most—"

"Quiet a minute." He put a hand on her arm.

"You hear something?"

Slowly and silently Harry eased to his feet. "Key turning in a lock somewhere."

The auburn-haired reporter stood, watchful and listening. A door creaked. The sound came drifting to them across the big, chill room.

Harry reached under his coat. "Get back against the wall."

"I want to see what's—"

"Back." He pushed her into the shadows.

Moving away from Jennie, he started for an arched doorway.

"Beware," moaned an echoing voice, "the graves of the sacred dead had been defiled."

Harry drew his Colt .38. "Speaks pretty fair French for an Egyptian ghost."

"Be careful, Harry."

Through the archway a linen-wrapped figure came limping. It looked somewhat like a mummy, with its head wizened and nearly skeletal. One arm hung stiff at the figure's side and its limp grew more pronounced as it took a few more faltering steps into the Antiquités Ègyptiennes Wing.

"Flee, O despoiler of tombs," the mummy intoned.

Harry grinned. "If you're already dead, friend, a bullet won't bother you," he told the mummy. "But if you're some down-and-out actor dressed up to throw a scare into us, then you'll be joining the sacred dead right soon."

The creature took one more faltering step. "A moment, monsieur," it said. "You are obviously more sophisticated than the other watchmen. Therefore, let me suggest a—"

"Not open to suggestions," Harry told him. "Raise your hands up high and then walk over here."

"There's no reason why we can't agree on—"

Two shots sounded. They both hit the mummy in the chest. It brought up a bandage-wrapped hand to clutch at the bloody spots that were swiftly spreading.

"But, monsieur, I thought we…"

Its left knee hit the floor, then the other. There was blood staining the bandages all down the torso. Gasping, swaying, the mummy suddenly died. It fell over on its ancient face, twitching.

In the corridor it had emerged from there was the sound of at least two pairs of booted feet running. A door opened, then slammed.

Harry didn't give chase. Nor did he cross to the dead man.

He turned, his gun still in his hand, to stare at Jennie. "Why the hell did you shoot him?" he asked her.

The young woman's face had gone pale, the freckles stood out. She was shivering hard, teeth chattering. Her frightened eyes went from Harry to the derringer in her hand and back to Harry. "I don't know," she said. "I don't know."

Harry turned up the flame on the wall gas lamp. "Feeling better?"

"Not especially, no." Jennie, hugging herself and still shivering slightly, was sitting in an armchair in the museum foyer.

"Fairly soon now I'm going to have to telephone the police," he said. "We ought to be able to convince them it's self-defense.

But just for myself, I'd like to know why you killed the guy."

She shook her head sadly. "I really don't have any idea, Harry."

"Maybe you were rattled. You assumed the mummy was going to attack me and—"

"C'mon, I don't rattle under pressure. You know darn well I can keep my nerve under just about any circumstances," she said. "If I could stand being locked up for a week on Blackwell's Island for a story or face an escaped lunatic in the wilds of—"

"Okay, I was just trying to suggest a reason."

"I don't have one," Jennie said. "I was as anxious as you were to get him to talk. An exclusive interview with a mummy, even a fake one, would've been marvelous for my newspaper story. All of a sudden, though, I had this overwhelming impulse to gun him down."

Harry rested a hip on the arm of her tufted chair and touched her shoulder. "Like a cup of coffee?"

"Hemlock would be more—"

An exuberant knocking had begun on the street door of the museum.

Standing, Harry said, "Can't be the police."

"What ho within!" boomed a deep voice.

Jennie brightened. "That sounds like—"

"The Great Lorenzo." Harry sprinted across the thick Oriental carpeting, unlocked the heavy oaken door and yanked it open.

The portly magician stepped in out of the night. He was clad in a suit of evening clothes, a jauntily tilted top hat and a flowing, scarlet-lined cloak. The buttons of his silky waistcoat glittered almost as brightly as real diamonds. "Ah, you're not dead, my boy." He chuckled with relief and gave his greying muttonchop whiskers a fluff.

"Was I supposed to be?"

The Great Lorenzo noticed Jennie, who was standing beside the maroon armchair. Doffing his hat, he bowed in her direction. "Good evening, young lady," he said. "You don't look as pert as when last we met in Orlandia."

Harry shut the door. "You were supposed to be en route to Urbania by now, you and your entire magic show."

"Indeed I was." He placed his topper on a claw-footed table. "You and I, Harry, have been chums for lo! these many years. I, modestly, tend to think of myself as a second father to—"

"I like you better than that."

"Ah, yes, I forgot for the moment that your dear papa lacks many of the warm and lovable traits that I am blessed with." He fluffed his ample sideburns once again. "As I was saying, dear lad, I have never professed to be anything more than a humble stage illusionist—the best professional magician in the world if one believes the critics and an idolatrous and adoring public— simply a man with nary a true supernatural gift. And yet..."

"You had one of your visions?"

He was gazing across the foyer at Jennie. "You're extremely peaked, my child," he observed. "What was I saying, Harry?"

"You had another of your mystical hunches."

"Indeed I did." He rubbed at his broad chest. "Most inconvenient it was, too, striking as it did whilst I happened to be sharing the opulently furnished private railroad car of an impressively amorous countess and demonstrating my fabled manual dexterity." He paused to cough into his gloved hand. "Of a sudden I was taken over with a most unsettling vision, my boy. What I saw was none other than yourself stretched out in what appeared to be a gaudy Egyptian sarcophagus, all swaddled with linen wrappings. The wrappings in question were splattered with blood and you, alas, appeared to be singularly defunct."

"As sometimes happens, Lorenzo, you got your facts slightly garbled. But even so I—"

"This strange and awesome power, if indeed I do possess it— and I make no claims—doesn't always work with the accuracy and dependability of the telegraph," said the plump magician. "Included in the trance image was the address of this benighted institution, today's date and the warning that the traditional hour of midnight was the crucial one. I made arrangements to disembark from the Orlandia-Urbania Express and hastened here. An unfortunate altercation with my cabdriver over the sanitary habits of one of his steeds caused me to arrive a few moments beyond the witching hour. Yet I am pleased to observe that no serious harm has as yet befallen anyone."

Harry took hold of his plump arm. "Step into the Egyptian wing," he invited. "Will you be okay for a few minutes, Jennie?"

"As well as can be expected." She sank back into the chair.

Frowning, the magician allowed Harry to escort him down a corridor and into the large room where the dead man was sprawled. "Ah, there is an approximation of the very bloody corpse I saw in my vision. Except it isn't you, Harry."

"This guy's been sneaking in here evenings to scare off the watchmen."

Puffing some and grunting, the Great Lorenzo knelt beside the mummy. "What precisely was his motivation?"

"Never had the chance to ask him."

"You were forced to shoot him to prevent his doing you and the fair Jennie bodily harm, eh? Well, that's understand—"

"Jennie shot him."

The magician's knees made small crackling noises as he got up. "I fail to detect a note of gratitude."

"He was about to give himself up."

The Great Lorenzo made a slow thoughtful circuit of the body. "There's something familiar about this lad," he muttered.

"Know him?"

"Not as a bosom friend, no. Yet I have the feeling I've encountered him sometime in the past," he replied. "Most likely during one of my many triumphal engagements here in this dazzling and wordly city."

"Somebody connected with the theater maybe."

"Yes, that sounds..." The magician grimaced suddenly, clutched at his middle.

"What's wrong?"

"Jennie." He pivoted, starting trotting toward the foyer.

Harry ran faster, reaching the young woman ahead of the

magician. "You seem to be all right," he told her, puzzled.

"No worse that I was a few minutes ago when you dragged Lorenzo off to view my handiwork." She was looking up into his face. "What were you expecting to find?"

"He gave me the impression you were in danger."

"She is, my boy." Panting, the Great Lorenzo halted beside the tufted armchair.

"From the police you mean?"

He bent and took both her hands in his. "Sometime within the last dozen hours, dear child," he informed her, "you were hypnotized. And for an evil purpose."

"By whom?" asked Harry.

"Alas, my latest vision failed to include that helpful kernel of information."

Chapter 4

The sky began to lighten. In the thin blueness of dawn Harry saw the Eiffel Tower take shape in the distance, a dark skeleton rising up into the pale morning.

He turned away from the paneled windows of his hotel suite parlor. The room was mostly shades of brown, with touches of mauve and gold.

Seated comfortably on a candy-striped loveseat was the Great Lorenzo. He'd removed his gloves and was fingering a large silver coin. "The procedure, I assure you, is completely and utterly painless."

Jennie, who was now wearing a full-length dark skirt and a puff-sleeved white blouse, was pacing the ochre and mauve carpet. "Well, it'll be just about the first thing that is since I hit Paris this morning."

Harry stationed himself in front of a wall covered with vertically striped purple and chocolate wallpaper. "You don't remember running into anyone unusual after you ditched me in the lobby?"

"I didn't exactly ditch you," she said. "I really was sent here to cover this obelisk story, though. Those cablegrams I showed Inspector Swann prove that.... Thanks, by the way, Harry, for vouching for me and telling the police I was more or less assisting you on this case."

"Swann knows my father and, for some reason, admires him," said Harry. "So he seems to have nothing but respect for the Challenge International Detective Agency and all its investigators."

"Your papa," remarked the Great Lorenzo, "may be a cantankerous old goat, yet he's a sterling sleuth for all that. You're perhaps too young to recall in full the details of such cases of his as the affair of the Yonkers Trunk Slayer back in '77 or—"

"Can you counteract whatever's been done to Jennie?"

The coin was spinning from plump finger to plump finger, catching the light of the electric chandelier overhead. "A trifling task, my boy. Fear not."

Jennie took a slow deep breath, then exhaled. "Well, let's get started."

The portly magician gestured at the lyre-backed wooden chair near the small empty fireplace. "If you will but seat yourself, dear child."

Jennie complied. "I think, Harry, I really was planning to follow you on the sly," Jennie confessed as she smoothed her skirt. "But, honestly, I'm not even sure of that."

"Don't fret. Lorenzo'll get you back shipshape."

"This is a silver dollar," the magician told her. "On one side we notice Liberty and on the other an eagle. Watch now... Liberty...eagle... Liberty...eagle..."

Her hazel eyes were already taking on a glazed look.

"The eagle seems to be...flapping his wings...flapping them...not rapidly...but slowly...slowly..."

Jennie made a small whimpering sound and slumped sideways in her chair.

Harry moved to help her up, but the Great Lorenzo waved him off.

"You're asleep now, dear child," the magician informed her. "A very pleasant sleep, very relaxing. You can hear me as you blissfully slumber and, what is more, you will be able to speak. Isn't that right?"

"It is, yes." Her voice was faint and childlike.

"Not a thing can hurt you, nothing can harm you," the Great Lorenzo assured her. "No matter what you have been told earlier. Is that clear?"

Her hands clenched into fists. "Yes…"

"Sometime today, after you arrived in Paris, you were hypnotized. Is that so?"

She shuddered. "I must not…ever say…"

"No, no, child. You simply misunderstood the original instructions. I am in control now. The Great Lorenzo is in charge and what I tell you, and only that, is true."

The shuddering grew more severe. Jennie shut her eyes tight, hitting her fists together. "If I ever speak…terrible things…"

"That was an error. A false bit of news sent to you. I am the only one you need listen to. The Great Lorenzo. Listen to me now, Jennie, listen. Whatever was told to you by another hypnotist, whatever warnings you were given, whatever orders…they are no more. Your mind is yours again; it belongs to none other. And you will remember all that happened."

She shivered even more violently. "But I must obey…the…" Leaping to her feet, she held her arms out and cried, "Harry, Harry! Help me."

He bounded to her, put his arms around her. "Easy now. It's all right."

She hugged him hard, beginning to sob against his chest. "It was like…like being attacked by… Oh, Harry, just hold on to me. Please."

The Great Lorenzo flipped the silver dollar into the air. It vanished up near the cocoa ceiling. "I suggest we adjourn for a bit of breakfast before delving into the question of the identity of the scoundrel who did this."

* * * *

The restaurant's main dining room was covered over with a high dome of steel and glass. There was a flourishing potted palm next to their white-covered table and the Great Lorenzo, after brushing the last of the croissant crumbs from his dimpled chin, plucked two lighted cigars from it and passed one to Harry. "I am, dear friends, glad I made this side trip to Paris," he told them, puffing contentedly on his cigar. "I only regret I must journey onward in but a few days in order to reach the fabled Spielzeug Theater in Urbania's glittering capital in time for the initial performance of my magical extravaganza."

"Damn good thing you did stop," Harry said. "Otherwise we wouldn't have known what had happened to Jennie."

For the past several minutes Jennie had been writing in a stenographer's notebook with a stub of a pencil. Sipping now and then at her coffee, she paid no attention to Harry, the Great Lorenzo or the other patrons in the as yet uncrowded restaurant. "Well, I think I remember just about everything now," she announced, dropping the pencil on the crisp white tablecloth. "It's pretty darn strange…and frightening."

Harry asked, "Are you up to talking about it?"

"Yes. Thanks to Lorenzo, I feel I've got my mind back." She touched the magician's pudgy hand for an instant, smiling at him. "You really are a wizard, you know."

"I have never laid claim to any true magical powers," he reminded. "But one can't help but be aware that a few of my little knacks do seem a trifle supernatural."

Jennie flipped back a few pages in her notebook. "You have some serious opposition, Harry," she said. "Have you ever heard of an Englishman named Max Orchardson?"

"A true mountebank," murmured the magician.

Harry exhaled smoke. "Sure, he's been called the most decadent man in Europe," he said.

"He supposedly pals around with the Yellow Book crowd— Oscar Wilde, Aubrey Beardsley and such—and also dabbles in black magic. Though that last could be only an affectation."

"It isn't," she said. "I wrote a series of articles on Orchardson last year while I was in London for my paper."

Harry frowned. "Don't recall seeing those."

"That's because they never ran," Jennie explained. "My editors decided we might be risking libel charges after...well, I'd had signed statements from several witnesses. One evening all of them suddenly burst into flames while sitting on my desk in the hotel room. Next, two of my best witnesses got in touch with me and claimed they'd lied. A third dived into the Thames one foggy night and never surfaced."

"Typical of the way Orchardson operates," commented the Great Lorenzo.

"The guy is really a magician?"

"The man seemingly does have true powers," he acknowledged. "He also has a great deal of money, earned in India long ago by kin less aesthetic than he. And, like Wilde, he is a master showman."

"I had a sworn account of devil worship and at least one instance of human sacrifice," said Jennie.

Harry asked her, "Is Orchardson here in Paris? Is he the one who hypnotized you?"

She nodded. "He was waiting in my hotel room," she said, shivering once. "He's an obese man, puffy and pale as death. He...even though I tried to fight against it...hypnotized me. Using an opal medallion he wears around his fat neck."

"Nowhere near as effective as a coin," said the magician.

"What were you supposed to do?"

She lowered her head, picked up the pencil and tapped at the tablecloth with its blunt tip. "Follow you, report to him all that you did while in Paris."

"He knows why I'm here?"

"Seemed to. At least he knew you were going to the museum and when. I was instructed to follow you."

"Why?"

"He's interested in the Osiris Obelisk."

Harry said, "What about shooting the mummy?"

She turned to the next page of the notes. "I was told to destroy anyone who tried to get near it."

"Including me?"

"No, no. I was only to keep close to you and report regularly to him."

"What about that giant bat?"

The Great Lorenzo coughed. "There's a striking detail no one has bothered to share with—"

"Fill you in later." Harry promised.

"I don't know anything about the bat," answered Jennie. "Apparently when I shot and scared the darn thing off, I was acting on my own."

"How were you supposed to report to Orchardson?"

"He's staying in a villa in a suburb of Paris, Neuillysur-Seine."

"When do you report?"

"Three this afternoon."

Harry nodded at the magician. "Is your afternoon free?"

"I had intended to rekindle a touching relationship with a countess who is, except for a cork leg, the quintessence of middle-aged charm and beauty," he replied. "However, I'll give up that pleasure to put myself entirely at your disposal, my boy."

"Good. We'll pay a call on Max Orchardison."

"Harry," warned Jennie, "he's dangerous."

"So am I."

Chapter 5

The Great Lorenzo swung his cane vigorously as he hurried along the late morning sidewalk. He wore a suit of an impressive green shade, an embroidered waistcoat and a silk cravat whose bright color scheme rivaled that of a rainbow. With his tongue placed behind his upper teeth, he was whistling a music hall tune having to do with a gentleman known as Burlington

Bertie.

Dodging a family of strolling American tourists, he turned down a side street off the Avenue Montaigne. The shop he was seeking sat squeezed between a brownstone office building and a dark-fronted bistro.

Inscribed in gilt on the narrow shop window was the single name Grandville. Tumbled together on the other side of the dusty glass were domino masks, curly blond wigs, lace-trimmed fans, shaggy dark beards, straw hats and pairs of tinted spectacles.

A tinny bell jangled when the magician pushed the dark wood and stained glass door open. "You haven't changed your window display since I was here last, Grandville," he announced to the long shadowy room. "My little lecture on American methods of merchandising and advertising had no effect, alas."

Shelves lined the walls and were piled with hatboxes, shoe boxes and bundles of clothes. Manikins dressed in the costumes of other climes and other times stood patiently all around.

In a high-backed wicker chair at the rear of the long, narrow shop sat a small, dark man of fifty some years. He had both his hands resting on the ivory handle of a stout cane. "Ah, it has to be Lorenzo," he said, wheezing and struggling to his feet. "Who else speaks in a voice substantial enough to shatter glass."

"I hear there's a new tenor with the La Scala company whose vocal prowess comes near to equaling mine. The magician went striding toward the proprietor. "I trust I find you in good health, old friend."

Grandville's laugh was raspy and wheezy. "I am no worse," he replied. "But why are you in Paris, Lorenzo? I read you had been relegated to putting on your magic show in such backwaters as Zevenburg and Kaltzonburg."

"Old chum, I don't mind your addressing me as plain Lorenzo rather than the more acceptable Great Lorenzo," he informed him. "When you, however, allude to my world renowned festival of magical artistry as a mere magic show, I, sir, bristle."

Grandville laughed yet again. "You are appearing, then, in Paris?"

Leaning closer, the Great Lorenzo addressed the owner of the costume and makeup shop in a confiding tone. "I have taken time out from a very crowded schedule to put on a limited performance for a small, select audience."

"A command performance, eh?"

"One might say that, although I am not at liberty to divulge any details," he said. "In fact, I would appreciate it if you'd keep this visit of mine a secret."

"That should not be too difficult, for few of my friends or customers even know who you are," said Grandville.

"Except for Goncourt the tailor who continues to complain that you owe him in the neighborhood of two hundred francs for some garments he ran up for you back in 1894 and for which you have not as—"

"Nonsense. I've never draped myself in his shabby work," the magician said.

"Now, dear friend, let us return to the purpose of my call. I have need of two of your excellent costumes, plus the false whiskers and makeup that goes with them. One to fit my own manly frame, the other for a younger chap of medium height and more slender build."

Grandville rubbed thumb and forefinger together. "A cash deposit is required for all costume rentals, Lorenzo."

Giving him a disdainful look, the Great Lorenzo reached up into the musty air above the man's head and plucked a fistful of paper money. "Here, old friend. I trust this will soothe your greedy heart and allow us to—"

"This is German currency. Marks and—"

"Ah, forgive me, my mind is wandering." He grabbed the wad of bills back, crumpled it even further and flung it away from him. The bills vanished before reaching the dusty wooden floor. "I would like to see what you have in the way of costumes for—"

"My money."

"Eh?" The magician had wandered over to study one of the faded theatrical posters decorating the wall of the shop.

"The francs with which you intend to pay for the rental of the costumes and sundries you need."

Brow furrowed, the Great Lorenzo leaned to study the poster more closely. "Ah, that's the name I was trying to remember," he muttered. "The fellow wrapped in bandages last evening." He tapped the poster with a plump forefinger. "Whatever became of LePlaut, who used to appear in this poor man's Grand Guignol of M. Slepyan's?"

"Ah, there is a sad tale," answered Grandville with a sympathetic wheeze. "After the company failed, LePlaut fell in with evil companions. When last I heard he was working as a dishwasher in a low dive in Montmartre."

"Do you perhaps recall the name of the place?"

"I believe it was called Le Demon des Glaces."

"Well, enough of this pleasant chitcat about days gone by and vanished friends." The Great Lorenzo rubbed his hands together and turned away from the poster. "Let me see the costumes I need."

* * * *

Whistling, and not a franc poorer, the magician exited the costume shop some twenty minutes later. He carried a large parcel wrapped in green paper under his arm.

He had covered a little more than a half block when a closed carriage, pulled by a handsome black steed, rolled up alongside him. When the window shade was raised and an extremely pretty blonde woman of no more than thirty-five smiled out at him, the Great Lorenzo nodded and tipped his bowler hat.

The door opened and the blonde, who wore a dress of satin and lace and a white fur stole, called out to him in a sweet voice. "Is that all you have for such an old and dear friend as Yvonne Turek? No more than a flick of your hat, dear Lorenzo?"

The carriage stopped and so did the magician. "Ah, forgive me, dear lady, I was woolgathering."

She pouted attractively. "Ah, only a few scant years ago, my dear dumpling, and you could not tear yourself from my side.

My name was on your adorable lips from noon till night."

Easing closer to the carriage, he scrutinized its lovely occupant. "One can well believe that, for you are a most attractive creature, Yvonne."

Extending a gloved hand, she tugged delicately at his sleeve. "Why not, for the sake of old times, ride at least a short way with me?"

"Don't mind if I do." Shifting the package, grunting and huffing, he scrambled into the dark interior.

Reaching around him, Yvonne shut the door. "Is this not wonderful?"

The carriage was thick with the scent of jasmine. As soon as the door had closed, it resumed clacking along the street.

"It is more than wonderful, dear lady," the magician told her, "since you have never in your entire life met me before."

She sighed and reached into the beaded white purse. "I feared this ruse might not work," she said, producing a pearl-handled .32 revolver and pressing it into his portly side.

Chapter 6

Jennie sat, hands in her lap, gazing out the window of her small hotel room. The midday sky was growing increasingly grey. "My room is quite a bit smaller than yours," she mentioned. "Must be difficult for you, since you're in the mood to pace."

"I don't enjoy posh hotels and ritzy suites. That's my father's idea, says it keeps up the image and reputation of the Challenge International Detective Agency." Skirting her brass bed, Harry paced along the edge of the Persian rug. "Wish I had Lorenzo's gift of second sight, then I'd know where the hell he is." He tugged out his pocket watch again.

"He really does have some sort of unusual power," said the reporter. "I've exposed a lot of bunco artists and fake mediums, but he's authentic. Coming to the museum the way he did last night, simply getting off his train and rushing to Paris."

"Sure, he's got a gift." Harry frowned at his watch before returning it to his pocket. "He's also fairly shrewd. Sometimes he can con you into thinking a lucky guess is a mystical message from beyond."

The sky continued to darken; a wind rattled the windows.

Jennie said, "This plan you've worked out for getting inside Max Orchardson's lair is—"

"We've worked out," he corrected. "You were in on the—"

"As a bystander mostly. You and Lorenzo outvoted me every time I attempted to express a little reasonable doubt as—"

"That's the essence of democracy. The will of the majority is—"

"Well, this representative of the minority is going to be just as dead as you two hooligans should this crack-brained—"

"Audacious. Our scheme is audacious, not crack-brained."

Standing, she faced him. "I don't want any of us to get hurt. No newspaper story is that important, no detective investigation either."

"This is a different Jennie Barr," he said, grinning. "You were claiming only yesterday that getting the story for the New York Daily Inquirer was more important than—"

"Could you let up a hit, Harry. I wasn't exactly myself yesterday and I'm feeling low enough without your—"

"Okay, sorry." He crossed to her and put his hands on her shoulders. "We'll all come out of this all right."

"You're concerned about Lorenzo already, though, aren't you? Because he's late."

"He's only..." Harry let go of her to pull out his watch. "Damn, nearly a half hour late."

"Keep in mind he's a very romantic soul. This is spring and we're in Paris."

"I suppose he might've made a stop to see that lady with the cork leg." He glanced at the door. "He usually doesn't daily when he's helping out on something like this, though."

"Where was he going to pick up the costumes and all?"

"Shop of an old friend of his."

"You know where it is?"

"Just off the Avenue Montaigne," Harry answered. "We'll give him maybe another half hour, then go over there to…" He put his finger to his lips, hunched slightly and ran over to yank the room door open.

The dark brown corridor was empty, but a pale blue envelope lay on the flowered carpeting.

Bending, Harry picked it up. "Addressed to me in Lorenzo's handwriting." After shutting the door, he opened the message. "'My dear colleagues, There have been several new and illuminating developments. Thus a small change of plans is called for. Meet me by no later than two at the address below. And, Harry my boy, be absolutely certain you aren't followed. Ever yours, the Great Lorenzo.'"

Jennie frowned. "This could be a trap."

"It could," he agreed. "But we'll have to go over there to make sure."

* * * *

Looping his arm around the stone chimney, Harry used his free hand to pull Jennie up the slanting slate roof.

The rain, light thus far, had begun to fall just as they'd leaped over to this rooftop from the three story pension next door.

Slowly and carefully Jennie worked her way up through the maze of chimney pots and stovepipes to Harry's side. She was wearing her Norfolk suit and cap. "The balcony of number 104 Rue Brindavoine ought to be directly below the apex of this dam roof."

"Yep, so I'll lower you down and then join you."

"Be careful on this slate; rain's making it slippery."

"I've had quite a lot of experience climbing roofs." He took hold of her arm and pulled her down into a crouch with him. "By the way, how do you go about buying a man's suit?"

"I got this in the Boy's Department of Estling's Universal Emporium in London last year." She kept close to him as he progressed toward the front edge of the apartment building roof.

"Told them it was actually for my nephew Harry, an unattractive and rather dim lad whom I was nonetheless attached to."

"You didn't try it on then?"

"No, but it fits just fine. You really are very provincial, Harry."

"Little baggy in the seat."

"No, it isn't. I'm certain of that because only last evening I was pinched on the Rue—"

"Hush for now." He was flat out on the tilting roof, the afternoon rain pelting lightly down on him.

Harry tugged himself until he was out over the edge and could get a glimpse of the wrought iron balcony below.

There was someone standing on it now, under the shelter of a pink parasol.

The parasol started to spin and after a half dozen turns was lowered to one side.

The Great Lorenzo was beaming up at him. "I'm greatly impressed by your acrobatic entrance, my boy," he said. "Yet since time is important, it would have been better to have availed yourselves of the doorway downstairs."

* * * *

The Great Lorenzo was using the rolled up parasol as a pointer. Aiming it at the blonde woman who sat stiffly in the cane-bottom chair, he announced, "This charming damsel is Yvonne Turek—or rather that's the name she assumed for her part in this intrigue. In reality she is Yvette Tardi, a gifted yet, sadly, unemployed actress."

"And who's the gent dozing on the floor yonder?" asked Harry.

"He is Manuel Bulcão, an import from Lisbon," said the magician as he pointed the ferrule of the parasol at him. "He's not in a hypnotic trance, as is the fair Yvonne. Him I conked on the noggin and trussed up, using some of the impressive knots I learned during a recent cruise of the Mediterranean."

"Who are those folks exactly?" Jennie was standing near the crackling fire in the small marble fireplace. "Do they work for

Max Orchardson?"

"On the contrary," the Great Lorenzo said. "They are in the employ of the opposition.

Harry settled into an armchair next to a marble-top table. He drummed his fingertips on the base of the hurricane lamp for a few seconds. "Opposed to us or to Orchardson?"

"Both." He took a few steps away from the entranced blonde, shoes clicking on the black and white mosaic tiles of the parlor floor. "You have both no doubt heard of a gentleman named Anwar Zaytoon."

"The Merchant of Death," said Harry.

"Just about the most powerful arms dealer in the world," added Jennie as she held her cap to the fireplace. "I tried to interview him once in Constantinople and three of his toadies came dam close to tossing me in a public fountain. A very mysterious, not at all cordial man."

Harry asked, "Is Zaytoon interested in the obelisk?"

"Very much so." The Great Lorenzo nodded at the blonde actress. "She was hired to entice me here and make me an offer of ten thousand francs to double-cross you and become an informant for Zaytoon."

"You're worth more than that."

"Twice at least," agreed the magician. "Apparently our death merchant is aware you're in Paris, Harry. He's had your hotel watched and your movements scrutinized. Which is how they became aware of my advent upon the scene and why I warned you to shake off any tails before venturing here to share in the fair Yvonne's reluctant hospitality."

"Why," asked Jennie, "is everyone so interested in the Osiris Obelisk?"

"Yvonne is—forgive me for stating this so bluntly, dear lady—only an underling who knows little of the motives of the sinister Mr. Zaytoon."

"He's in Paris now?"

"Nearby."

Getting up, Harry went to the window they'd recently

climbed in through and looked down at the rain-swept street. A mournful black carriage was rolling by. "What about the mummy—who was he working for?"

"Zaytoon. I determined, only moments before Yvonne put her ill-fated plan to lure me into a life of espionage and trickery into effect, that he was a seedy actor named LePlaut. The lady confirmed that."

"They wanted to scare off all the guards," said Harry, "and then steal the obelisk?"

"That's it exactly."

Jennie said, "It's sort of ugly and squatty, not worth anywhere near as much as some of the other artifacts at the museum."

"Ah, my child, but it apparently holds some secret," the magician told her. "A secret worth killing for, a secret even worth trying to corrupt a man of my sterling character for."

Chapter 7

Every few feet a thin tree grew up from a small plot of ground surrounded by sidewalk. The narrow trunk of each was guarded by a circular fence of wrought iron. The rain hit hard at the trees and made them shiver.

The carriage, borrowed from the unprotesting Yvonne, had been left around the corner, the dark horse tethered to one of the frail trees.

Held high above the heads of the three of them was an immense black umbrella the Great Lorenzo had found in a compartment under the driver's seat of the carriage he'd driven here to the suburb of Neuilly-sur-Seine.

"Don't fret should you get splashed by the elements, my boy," the magician told Harry, shifting his grip on the ebony umbrella handle. "The makeup I've expertly applied to our visages is one hundred percent waterproof."

"I wasn't worrying about that." Harry reached up to adjust the crimson fez he was wearing. "Instead, I was wondering if

Orchardson will fall for this."

The Great Lorenzo brushed at the striped kaftan he was wearing. "You forget he is extremely eager to obtain the obelisk," he reminded. "He covets the thing, despite its cursed nature.

He will be, therefore, anxious to believe the yarn we're going to spin. We are two high-placed Egyptian officials, extremely close to his Highness the Khedive. On our handsome persons we carry authentic documents proving beyond a shadow of a doubt that the obelisk in question doesn't rightly belong to the Musée des Antiquités at all. Orchardson will dote on us, never fear, and be elated at what looks like a chance to purchase the object he seeks."

They'd reached an iron-barred gate in a high wall of pale brownish stone.

Jennie swallowed hard. "This is it, Max Orchardson's villa," she said. "I'm supposed to yank this bellpull three times."

"Go ahead and do it," said Harry.

"I don't think I like you with a beard."

"Neither do I. Ring."

"Once we're inside," said the Great Lorenzo, "I'll use my superior hypnotic powers on the fellow and we'll find out all we want to know. Ring, child."

Shrugging, Jennie tugged the dangling black chain.

Through the gates they could see a half acre of grounds covered with hedges long untrimmed, high grass and tall shaggy pines. Beyond that loomed a sprawling stone house, turreted, that was the exact shade of the rainy afternoon.

Before the third tug of the bellpull a dog was barking, a deep gruff bark that seemed to be coming from a large hollow room.

"Let's hope," said Harry, "we can convince the dog we're Egyptian officials."

"Hounds are no problem," the magician assured him. "In my vanished youth I toured the States in the company of, among others, Professor Swaim and his Educated Canines. He imparted to me the tricks of the... Ah, this must be the butler."

A huge black man in a frock coat and striped trousers was

walking methodically down a grey gravel path toward them. He carried no umbrella and appeared to be oblivious of the rain.

Halting a few yards from the locked gate, he gave Jennie an inquiring stare. "What is the meaning of this, missy?"

"I was told to come here," she answered. "Today. At three."

"Alone," the butler said.

"Well, I intended to be, but these gentlemen approached me at the museum last evening and insisted on tagging along. They claim to have a proposition."

"It is?"

"We are in a position to sell your employer the Osiris Obelisk," said the Great Lorenzo. "Assuming that he, whoever he may be, is interested."

"Who," asked the black man in his deep rumbling voice, "might you be, sir?"

Tugging impatiently at his beard, the magician said, "Ah, but of course, my fame does not extend to foreign climes such as this. I am, my good man, Mohammed Ali Pasha." He bowed. "My young associate is Cherif Pasha. We both represent the Khedive of Egypt and come equipped with papers proving the obelisk in question is rightfully ours."

"It is," added Harry, "our wish to sell it to the highest bidder."

Stepping forward, the butler unlocked the heavy gate. "Please to enter."

"To hear is to obey." The Great Lorenzo bowed once more before stepping through the open gateway.

The black man waited until all three of them were on the villa grounds and then relocked the gate. From beneath his frock coat he brought forth a .45 revolver. "If you'll step inside the house, Mr. Challenge, Mr. Lorenzo and Miss Barr," he suggested, "I'm certain Mr. Orchardson will be quite pleased to see you all."

The living room was on the top floor of the villa. Vast, high-ceilinged, with peach-colored walls. There was little furniture and all of it was huddled in the room's center around a white potbellied stove. Except for a worn Oriental carpet on which rested a divan, two mauve armchairs, a claw-footed table and a bust of Voltaire, the hardwood floors were bare.

"Come in, come in, you three," invited Max Orchardson. "Like most recluses I simply can't stand to be alone."

He was lounging on the maroon divan, a three-hundredpound man who seemed to be made of partially risen bread dough. His face was puffy and dead white, his close-cropped hair the color of driven snow. An enormous silken smoking jacket was wrapped around him, a pattern of exploding orchids decorating the taut silk.

"You've lost a bit of weight, Orchardson." Harry scratched at his thick false beard. "Judging from the last society page portrait of you I saw."

"Yes, I do believe I'm wasting away from worry," he said. "Those of us who loathe life as much as I do have a terrible fear of death. It might turn out to be even more boring."

The black butler cleared his throat with a sedate rumble. "Shall I fetch the hot coals and the pokers, sir?"

"Not yet, Logo." The languid fat man stretched and plucked a green carnation from the lacquered vase on the table. "Suppose, Challenge, you tell me what you have in mind with this delightful masquerade."

Harry moved across the hardwood floor to the edge of the rug. "We're all interested in the obelisk. We wanted to find out how much you knew about it."

"There was no need to dress up like a pair of road-show Othellos to do that, dear boy," Orchardson pointed out, brushing at his puffy cheek with the green flower. "No, you intended to take me unawares."

"I'm not too happy over what you did to Jennie." Harry scratched at his false whiskers once again. "These damn things are starting to itch."

"The price of duplicity." Orchardson pushed himself to a sitting position and the divan gave a protesting moan. "If I catch your drift, Challenge, you had in mind to find out all that I was up to and perhaps give me a sound thrashing as well."

"I still may."

Orchardson blinked. Then he started laughing, a whooping, gasping noise. "Forgive me," he apologized after a moment, "I fear my grief expresses itself in odd ways. I even laughed at my mother's funeral."

"He's grieving for you," explained the large Logo, "because you'll soon be dead."

After giving his fez an adjusting shove, the Great Lorenzo went striding over to the center of the room. "What say we get down to business," he said. "You don't want to kill us because then you won't have a chance at the obelisk. Nor will you be able to find out what sort of a deal we're contemplating with your chief rival."

Orchardson's colorless eyebrows climbed. "Who might that be?"

"Let us refer to him merely as the Merchant of Death."

"A colorful name." Orchardson poked the stem of the emerald-dyed carnation into his doughy chin as he glanced toward the wide windows at the front of the room. The rain was pelting the thick panes. "Not one that means anything to me."

"He's certainly aware of you. In fact, this very day he offered us, via an emissary, a considerable sum to arrange for the delivery of the obelisk into his hands." The Great Lorenzo pushed his fez to a more jaunty angle. "We'll, of course, entertain a higher offer."

Orchardson waved the green carnation at Logo. "You'd best start bringing in the torture implements," he said. "This polite social intercourse has stared to be quite tedious." His pale lips seemed to disappear into his flesh as he smiled. "We'll begin with the lady, since I have never gone along with the rather antiquated dictum that young people should be seen and not heard."

"The iron boot, sir?"

"To start." Orchardson plucked a few petals from the flaring pink spots of color decorated his pudgy cheeks as he rocked back and forth on the creaking divan. "Ah, I do wish I could express my deep sorrow for Miss Barr in a more seemly fashion." He flung the smashed petals to the rug.

"You do anything to her," warned Harry, "and you'll never get the secret of eternal life."

Orchardson suddenly stiffened, his three hundred pounds freezing. Finally he asked, "Whatever are you talking about, dear boy?"

Grinning, Harry nodded at the Great Lorenzo and then started scratching at his beard. "Now," he said.

The portly magician threw himself to the left, snatching off his fez as he headed for the floor. Concealed in the hat was a pearl-handled .32 revolver. He shot Logo twice in his gun arm before the black man could swing his own weapon around to fire.

Jennie, meantime, had dropped flat out on the hardwood. And Harry had yanked out the derringer that had been taped under his bushy Egyptian beard.

He pointed the gun at the seated Orchardson.

The fat man did a sudden and unexpected thing. He executed a perfect, graceful backward somersault off the divan. Landing on his slippered feet, Orchardson ran surprisingly rapidly toward the high, wide windows. Not even pausing to open one, he went crashing through it and out.

"Holy Christ!" Harry sprinted to the shattered window.

He was about to look down for a glimpse of the fat man's broken body on the grounds far below, when two shots came whistling in at him from out in the rainy afternoon.

Harry hit the floor, rolled out of range.

Looking out, he saw another of the giant bats flying away through the rain-swept sky. Clutched in its talons was a laughing Orchardson.

* * * *

The black butler was sitting on the floor. "Forgive me, gentlemen and lady." He slapped his good hand to his mouth, swallowed. "You shan't have the opportunity to question me." His eyes snapped shut and he fell over backwards on the bare floor.

Harry lunged, tried to pry the man's mouth open. "Damn it."

"Is he dead?" asked Jennie.

"Nope, looks like some kind of trance."

Squatting, the Great Lorenzo sniffed at the comatose butler. "It's maracuya, an obscure herbal drug used by certain mean-minded tribes of the upper Amazon," he concluded. "Friend Logo will be dead to the world for weeks to come."

Jennie had wandered over near the divan. "Here's something." She lifted up the vase of green carnations. "A little wooden panel full of buttons. That must be how Orchardson summoned that bat and had it hovering outside the window."

"Bats are notoriously difficult to train, child." The magician huffed to an upright position. "I seriously doubt one could be induced to come running every time a buzzer sounded."

"This isn't a regular everyday bat." Harry joined Jennie to examine the control panel. "Fact is, Lorenzo, it's probably a flying mechanism of some sort."

"Impossible. Successful flight is years off, its secret yet to be revealed to mortal man."

Jennie perched on the divan edge: "Speaking of secrets, Harry, why did you taunt Orchardson by saying you were on to the secret of eternal life?"

He grinned. "That's got to be what's behind all this interest in the obelisk," he told her. "Remember that odd inscription Allegre translated for us? Orchardson is ailing and Zaytoon, from what I've heard, is up near ninety. Both of them are especially interested in immortality and they must have the notion that somehow the obelisk can give that to them."

"Though still in my prime and in tip-top shape, I must admit that I, too, have entertained the idea of living beyond my allotted time," admitted the Great Lorenzo. "Not for selfish reasons, mind you, but because of my exceptional gifts. It seems unfair to keep generations as yet unborn from enjoying an evening of my magical entertainments. My fabled Floating Lady illusion, for instance, belongs to the ages. Even the Japanese Diving—"

"Hey." Harry tugged out a small drawer that had been

concealed beneath the marble top of the small table. "Some letters and a few pages torn out of a magazine."

"Those pages are from The Journal of Advanced Technology, published in England," recognized Jennie.

"Dated April 1892. Article's entitled 'The "Flying Machine" of Professor G. P. R. Stowe Successfully Tested.' Goes on to describe the flights of a steam-powered craft Stowe calls an aerodrome."

"Oh, I interviewed him three or four years ago when he was in New York trying to raise funds." Jennie shook her head and wrinkled her freckled nose. "He struck me as an eccentric and probably a charlatan."

"This aerodrome, though, would look quite a bit like a giant bat with a few modifications," said Harry.

Taking the tearsheets from him, she studied the steel-engraved drawings. "Maybe you're right at that. Orchardson might have Professor Stowe working for him."

"One way or the other."

"Ah, listen to this." The magician was thumbing through the letters. "These missives are from various physicians in Great Britain and the continent. The general medical opinion is that unless Orchardson suspends his decadent style of living only a miracle can keep him alive more than a few months."

"A good motive for going after immortality," said Harry. "I'm wondering, though, why everybody waited until now to make a try for the obelisk. It's been sitting in the damn museum for months."

"Let's search the villa," said Jennie. "The answer may be here someplace."

For the rest of the rainy afternoon, until twilight took over, they went through the rented villa. But they found nothing more of interest.

Chapter 8

The horse-drawn omnibus made an unscheduled stop directly in front of the Musée des Antiquités. On the open upper level the Great Lorenzo stood up, adjusted his Inverness cape and started for the metal stairway. To the scattering of perplexed open-air passengers he said, "I hope, dear friends, you'll be able to avail yourselves of the free passes to the Great Lorenzo's magical extravaganza. I hear he's tops and well worth a twenty-six-hour journey to nearby Urbania."

He paused by a pretty nursemaid who had a chubby little boy in a sailor suit in her care. "And for the little admiral..." From the mid-morning air he plucked a bottle containing a model of a full-rigged clipper ship.

"Where's the crew?" inquired the sour-faced little fellow as he accepted the gift with sticky hands.

"For you, dear lady..." A bouquet of yellow roses appeared in his gloved hand. Bowing, he presented them to her.

"Oh, monsieur. I am quite...taken aback."

"And well you should be, dear Albertine. Adieu for now."

"Oh, but how did you know my name?"

He tipped his bowler, which was the color of green tree moss. "It is my business to know things." Bowing again, he then went hurrying and clanging down the stairs.

The uniformed conductor helped him to the sidewalk and handed him his plump portmanteau. "A pleasure to have served such an important official, Inspector Swann."

"Your duty to France will not go unrewarded, Gallimard." The Great Lorenzo saluted him briskly and then grabbed up his suitcase.

The pair of sturdy horses began moving again and the omnibus with its nonplussed passengers rolled away down the street.

Ascending the museum steps two at a time, the Great Lorenzo tried the brass doorknob.

The heavy door was locked.

He started knocking on it enthusiastically with his fist. "I have a train to catch."

After a moment the door was opened a fraction and a lean, moustached man who was obviously a plainclothes police detective peered out. "The museum is not open to the public at this time, monsieur."

"I know that, which is why I've been standing out here for untold minutes rapping on the door." The Great Lorenzo thrust a well-shod foot into the opening. "Were you as perceptive as one in your profession ought well to be, my friend, you would have noticed that I am far from being a member of the public. Nay, I happen to be a confidential operative for the prestigious Challenge International Detective Agency."

"Ah, yes. M. Challenge, accompanied by a very charming young lady, is within this institution at this very moment."

"That fact, my colleague, accounts for my being upon your doorstep."

"Come in then, M....I fear I don't know your name."

"I am the Great Lorenzo."

"Indeed? An unusual name for a private investigator, is it not?"

The magician pushed his way into the museum. "I happen to be an unorthodox sleuth." He went striding along the corridor toward the director's private office.

"Yes, your very attire gave me a clue to that fact." The policeman remained at the entrance.

Knocking twice, the Great Lorenzo let himself in to Maurice Allegre's office. "Excuse my intrusion, one and all," he said, taking off his hat and dropping it on the edge of a large alabaster casket. "I also request there be no tears and handwringing when I make my sad announcement."

Allegre had hopped to his feet. "Who in the world is this uncouth—"

"One of my operatives." Harry rose from his chair. "What's happening, Lorenzo?"

"You sound very dire," observed Jennie from the other chair in front of the desk.

"I must, alas, take the very next train to Urbania's fun-filled capital of Kaltzonburg," he announced ruefully. "It seems the madcap heir to the throne, Prince Rudolph, has insisted on a special command performance of my entire magical evening. The manager of the Spielzeug Theater wired me at the crack of dawn. Therefore, I needs must cut short my stay in this magnificient city and rush across field and fen to Urbania. Prince Rudy is not a fellow one offends or disappoints, especially when one intends to play three, possibly four, weeks in his domain."

"As it turns out," Harry told him, "I'll be leaving Paris for Urbania in a couple of days myself."

"We' ll be leaving," modified Jennie.

"Oh, so? That's splendid news and goes far toward explaining the vision I was visited with as the new day's rosy fingers touched at my eyelids," said the Great Lorenzo. "For I saw the three of us—you were excluded, M. Allegre—Yes, I saw you and I, Harry my boy, along with you, dear Jennie, together in Urbania and languishing in... Ah, but the setting is of no import."

"What was it?"

"Well, a dungeon. But you know these images, these portents of the future, are rarely one hundred percent accurate." After smiling at them all, he put his hat back on. "Until we meet again, dear friends."

"Bon voyage." Jennie got to her feet and kissed him on the cheek.

"By the way, Harry," he said as they shook hands, "my hotel is still being watched by somebody's toadies. I had to duck down several quaint Paris byways and then commandeer an omnibus to throw them off the scent. Farewell for now, no tears." He gathered up his heavy portmanteau and took his leave.

Allegre sank back into his desk chair. "An omnibus?"

"Merely a figure of speech," Harry assured him. "Let's get back to business."

"There is but little more to discuss, M. Challenge," he said. "As I was explaining before your corpulent associate burst in, Baron Felix Groll has decided, because of certain unfortunate incidents here at the museum, that he wants the Osiris Obelisk shipped to him even earlier than planned. It will be crated and ready to travel, by way of a special train, two days hence. You, as well as two of Inspector Swann's best men, shall travel with it. And, let me add, I wish you luck."

The restaurant floated leisurely along the darkening Seine. Its upper deck was ringed with softly glowing paper lanterns. At the cluster of small tables sat gentlemen in dark suits and top hats, women in stylish frocks and hats. On the small platform at the stern of the riverboat was a trio of hefty young men in straw hats and tight, striped blazers. They were playing exuberantly romantic music on concertina, guitar and violin.

The lights along the banks of the river were coming on, reflected yellow and gold in the water.

Harry had an elbow resting on their small checkered table-cloth. "You've fallen silent," he mentioned.

Jennie stroked the stem of her wineglass idly. "I dislike using trite phrases," she said, "and so I've been sitting here trying to come up with a fresh, brand-new way of saying how wonderful this all is."

He grinned. "We're both off duty."

"Very well, then it's a wonderful evening and I'm very fond of you," she told him. "The dinner was lovely and I wish we didn't have to leave Paris for Urbania day after tomorrow."

"We'd have to, even if I didn't have to guard the obelisk and you didn't have to write about it," he said. "Lorenzo gave us a pair of free passes to his show."

"As much as I admire his showmanship, I doubt I'd travel hundreds of miles by rail to see him. Although he is... What's the matter, Harry?"

"Nothing."

She started to turn to look in the direction he'd been looking. "You saw something that—"

"Keep your eyes on me." He put his hand over hers. "What is it I'm not staring at?"

"Couple husky fellows wearing Zouave uniforms and sitting at a table near the opposite railing."

"I hadn't noticed them."

"Only came up from the saloon below about ten minutes ago."

"Why are they causing you to scowl?"

"For one thing they've been, very unobtrusively they think, keeping an eye on us since they got up here," he said. "For another, their uniforms aren't quite authentic. Costume shop stuff."

"There's certainly been a lot of dressing up going on lately."

"I didn't spot these boys following us earlier, so maybe they're only interested in pretty red-haired lady reporters."

"Auburn," she corrected. "My hair isn't red."

"Should they make a move, just, duck under our table and let me—"

"Like heck I will. I've been a newspaper reporter for eight years. A couple of louts in fezes and pantaloons don't scare—"

"Relax, they may not have anything to do with the obelisk."

"Seems like just about everybody in Paris does," she said. "Max Orchardson, Anwar Zaytoon and lord knows who else. Do you think that hunk of granite really does contain the secret of eternal life?"

"Doesn't matter what I think," answered Harry. "Orchardson and Zaytoon are obviously convinced—and I'd like to know who or what convinced them all this time after the thing was hauled here from Egypt."

"I've been looking into that angle." She reached into her purse for her notebook. "After we parted company this afternoon I called on a few people I know in Paris."

"You were supposed to stay in your room."

"C'mon, it's unlikely Orchardson'll try to hypnotize me twice. And most other threats I can cope with."

Harry shrugged. "Who'd you talk to and what'd you find out?"

"About four months ago, and this initial information I got from Allegre himself, a onetime professor from the University of Graustark spent a week at the Musée des Antiquités," she said as she opened her notebook. "He devoted a good deal of his time to photographing and measuring the Osiris Obelisk. He got, according to Allegre, quite excited on his last day there. Left abruptly at midday, never to return. His name is Alexander Fodorsky."

"You talked to some of your contacts about Fodorsky?"

"I did, and it turns out his reputation of late has beep sort of unsavory," the auburn-haired reporter replied. "He'd been a reputable scholar up until two years ago, which is why Allegre let him hang around. His special fields are Egyptology and Orientology. More recently, however, he's grown interested in sorcery and the black arts."

"Any links between him and Orchardson?"

"Fodorsky is rumored to have been a house guest of his in London last winter."

Harry leaned back, glancing up at the deepening night overhead. "Fodorsky must've found out something about the obelisk, something Courdard and his colleagues may not've been aware of. He passed the news on to Orchardson."

"And somehow Zaytoon got wind of the secret, too."

Harry said, "Why is Orchardson killing off everybody who was on the expedition?"

"He can't be certain they don't know something about the secret. So he eliminates them." She shut her notebook. "In a way I'm disappointed there really isn't a curse. With a good ancient curse my paper's guaranteed syndication of my articles all over the—"

"Our Zouaves," cut in Harry, "are making a move." Casually she looked over. "They do seem to be, don't they?"

The two husky men, decked out in fezes, short blue jackets loaded with glittering medals, baggy red trousers and white leggings, were coming toward them as rapidly as they could across the crowded restaurant deck. Each was holding a wicked-looking dagger in his teeth.

"Sure you don't want to hide under the—"

"Hooey."

The larger Zouave arrived first. "I am insulted," he snarled around the knife handle. "I can stand no more. You, monsieur, have been making snide faces and wicked gestures at myself and my companion for far too long."

"The honor of the regiment is at stake." His broad-shouldered companion took his knife from his teeth to his hand.

"Fellows," said Harry, grinning amiably up at them, "I suggest you forget about the honor of your alleged regiment and go quietly back to your table before you find yourselves picking your backsides up off the deck."

"Gar! He insults us further." The bigger of the two grabbed his knife from between his jagged teeth.

"I'll take this one," Harry said across the table.

He unexpectedly brought up his foot and kicked the Zouave resoundingly in the groin.

The tassle of the man's fez stood up straight. He yowled, doubled up and clutched at himself.

Harry kicked him in the knee. He then stood, grabbed the belligerent Zouave by his thick neck and, seemingly with little effort, tossed him clean over the railing.

A paper lantern got tangled with the Zouave and it fell, shedding sparks, down to the dark Seine with him.

Jennie had worked less flamboyantly. She'd punched her surprised Zouave hard in the midsection, whacked him across the shin with a spare chair. Before he fully recovered from that, Jennie shoved him against the railing, booted him in the backside and then tipped him over into the river below.

"Very deft," said Harry just after the second splash.

Smiling, she rested her elbows on the railing and watched their two bedraggled attackers go swimming toward a stone quay. "I suppose, Harry, we really should've kept at least one of those louts to ask questions of and all."

"Maybe," he admitted. "Thing is, whenever I get into a brawl alongside a body of water, the temptation to toss everybody in is too much."

Smiling, she straightened up the things atop their table and seated herself again. "Do you want to explain this incident to the waiter who's running over here now? Or shall I?"

"I'll handle it," he offered. "Least I can do."

Chapter 9

On the morning the obelisk was to leave Paris Harry awoke an hour ahead of daybreak.

He hopped free of his brass bed, grabbed his Colt .38 from the bedside table and sprinted to the door.

Yanking it open, he got ready to dodge.

"I say, those are rather smashing underdrawers, Mr. Challenge. Jove, you Americans do have a flair for that sort of—"

"Who the hell are you?"

The young man was wearing a tweedy traveling suit and a deerstalker cap. His face was long, lean and deeply tanned and there was a monocle shielding his left eye. "One is rather impressed, don't you know, by the acuity of your hearing," he said. "I mean to say, I was approaching on tiptoe so as not to awaken any of your fellow guests in this jolly hotel and yet—"

Who," repeated Harry, pointing the revolver at his visitor's breastbone, "are you?"

"Ah, deuced rude of me, old Man." He smiled a toothy smile. "Name is Albert Melville Pennoyer. Just about everyone, from the mater on down, calls me Bertie. Rather a chummy sort of name I—"

"Why are you pussyfooting outside my door at this ungodly hour?"

"Is beastly early, ain't it?" Pennoyer shrugged his narrow shoulders. "Yet if one wants to catch a ride on this deuced secret train, one had best be up and doing with the proverbial cock, eh?"

Taking a step back, Harry asked, "What secret train?"

"What? Oh, I see, yes." He put his gloved right hand over

his mouth before chuckling. "Very clever of you, old bean, pretending to know nothing of the Osiris Obelisk. Admirable example of the sort of cunning and duplicity one expects from the Challenge International Detective Agency."

Frowning, Harry said, "Bertie Pennoyer. Wait now, you're one of the five who led the expedition."

"Very good. Mind like a steel trap. Good show. Spotted me right off." He hid another appreciative chuckle. "When I inform you I've fair got the wind up, Challenge old chap, you'll understand why."

"You figure you may go the way of Reynard Courdaud and Sir Munson Bellhouse."

"Rightho, not to mention Emil Koontzman."

"Did something happen to him?"

"Just yesterday in the Bavarian Alps... I say, might I come inside, old man. Confessing cowardice in a public hallway is deuced awkward."

"Sure, come on." Harry stood aside. "What's that stuck to your shoe?"

"Rather imagine it's a cablegram from your dear pater." Bending from the waist, Pennoyer detached the flimsy envelope from the sole of his shoe and passed it to Harry. "Saw the thing, don't you know, when I was girding up the proverbial loins to knock upon your portal. Stepped in some muck while sightseeing in Montmartre last evening, you know. Thought I'd succeeded in scraping it all off. Sorry."

"How'd you know my father'd be cabling me?" After elbowing the door shut, he tore the envelope open. "Well, old man, I rather hoped he would. Since we exchanged wires yesterday. Soon as I heard of poor Emil's fate."

The message from Harry's father said:

Dear Son:
    A brainless ninny named Bertie Pennoyer wants a bodyguard to see him safely to Urbania. Loaded with dough. Bundle him up on that special train you told me

about.

Your loving father, the Challenge International Detective Agency.

Refolding the message, Harry tossed it on his rumpled bed. "What happened to Dr. Koontzman?"

"According to preliminary reports, the poor blighter was attacked by vampire bats while mountaineering," answered the nervous young man. "Odd place for such creatures, one would think. Much too cold."

"How did you find out about the train?"

Pennoyer let his monocle pop free and caught it in his palm. "Simple, old thing. Visited Maurice Allegre yesterday and he—"

"That nitwit wasn't supposed to tell anyone about—"

"But, I say, Challenge. I am not just anyone, eh?" He began polishing the lens on his silk pocket handkerchief. "I mean to say, I'm a highly esteemed amateur archaeologist. I did, afterall, finance the whole bloody, you'll forgive my coarse lingo, expedition to the Valley of Jackals. Continually doing that sort of thing, don't you know. Entire Pennoyer clan filthy rich. Great grandfather made a pile out in India. By exploiting the wogs and the fuzzywuzzies, so family tradition has it."

"Has there been an attempt on your life?"

"Not that one is aware of, no. Haven't noticed huge vampire bats flapping about one's digs and all that."

Setting his gun back on the table, Harry started getting dressed. "As of now there's only you and—"

"I say, shall I turn my back, old chap? Some blokes crave a bit of privacy while—"

"Up to you." Harry tugged his trousers on. "Only you and Lady Jane Bedlumm are still alive, of the five who headed up the expedition."

Pennoyer shuddered. "All this beastly talk of death makes one deuced aware of one's mortality, don't you know," he said. "Lady Jane's a formidable old girl. In Tibet somewhere at last report. Seeking spiritual enlightment from some silly sounding bloke called the Ringding Gelong Lama. Doubt the rascals'll find the old girl there."

"Any notion who wants you dead?"

"Not the foggiest."

"Or why?"

"Supposed to be a curse on the obelisk. Never believed that rot before. But now."

Harry buttoned his shirt. "Know Max Orchardson?"

"By reputation. Believe he was asked to leave one of my London clubs a few years ago. Never met the fellow. Wouldn't want to. Why do you ask?"

"He's interested in the obelisk."

"Suppose he would be. Goes in for a lot of magical nonsense. Not a gentleman, you know."

Sitting on the edge of his bed, Harry pulled on a sock. "What about Anwar Zaytoon?"

"The Merchant of Death chap?" He masked a small chuckle. "Never met the bloke personally, but did see a rather amusing cartoon of him in one of the weeklies not long ago. Artist— clever chaps these artists, how they do it beats me—this artist, I say, depicted old Zaytoon as a vulture, don't you know, feeding on a fat corpse that was labeled Ungodly Munitions Profits. Awfully droll. Has the old boy been paying attention to the obelisk also?"

"Some, yes."

"Can't, for the life of me, figure out why." He fitted his polished monocle back into his eye. "Not much of an obelisk as obelisks go. I mean to say, the blooming one they've got right here in Paris beats it all hollow. Midget by comparison. Truth to tell, Challenge old man, I'd just as soon we'd left the thing there in the sand. Others insisted." He shook his head. "Understand Baron Groll paid a pretty penny for it and, which I ought to be grateful for, he's invited me to spend a few weeks at his estate in Urbania. Wants to jaw about the obelisk, Egypt and all that sort of thing."

"Which is why you want to tag along on this jaunt?"

"Once again, old thing, you've hit the nail on the proverbial head," said young Pennoyer admiringly. "Safe as houses, traveling with you and a trainload of French bobbies. That's how I see it."

"I suppose so, but—"

"Already chatted with Inspector Swann. Last evening. Have a jolly nice note from him giving me the old boy's blessing. Where'd I put the blasted thing?" He began searching his pockets. "Jove, here's that one hundred pounds. Your pater suggested I offer you this as a bonus should you show any reluctance to undertake the job. Are you?"

Harry took the money from his hand. "Not yet, but I might at any moment."

An hour after the special train pulled out of Paris the rain began. A heavy rain, hitting hard at the windows of Harry's compartment.

"Cozy," observed Jennie. She was seated opposite him, next to a basket full of food and wine she'd packed for the journey.

He was watching the new rain fall on the French countryside. "Hum?"

"I was remarking about how cozy I felt," the pretty reporter said. "Our own little five car train. You and I together in a comfortable carriage. Two plainclothes and ten uniformed police along as chaperones. The obelisk all crated up and resting in a burglarproof baggage car. Cozy."

"About that obelisk, Jennie..."

"Don't tell me you're starting to believe it's really got a curse on it. That silly ass Bertie Pennoyer seems to...something you want to tell me, Harry?"

He hesitated, then shook his head. "Nope, not really," he said finally. "Well, I am a mite dubious about Bertie Pennoyer and that's what I've been sitting here thinking about. Seems hard to believe anybody can actually be as dim-witted and fatuous as he pretends to be."

Jennie laughed. "There are numbers of the very best people

in Merry England who'd refute you, Harry," she said. "Bertie Pennoyer is simply not very bright. He is, because of the impressive Pennoyer wealth, very popular in British society. Nobody, though, has ever accused him of having much in the way of brains."

Harry took out a cigar, glanced at Jennie and put it away again. "So far on this damn case I've encountered quite a few people who have pretended to be what they weren't," he said. "From that guy LePlaut who was trying to pose as a mummy to those imitation Zouaves the other night."

"You include me on the list? Heartless reporter pretending to love you so she can get her story."

He grinned. "You're still on the list, but your name's only in pencil."

"We're always going to have a complicated time of it." She rested her hands on her knees. "Because just about every time I run into you I'm interested in the same case you are. That was true of the Blackwood Castle affair and the Electric Man business in London last year and—"

There was a knock on the door.

Harry said, "What?"

The door opened and a bent old man in a farmer's smock nodded at them. "Well, monsieur?"

Harry scanned the bearded old man. "Not bad, Pastoral."

"Ah," said Pastoral, "but you knew me."

"Well, I know you here, but in a different context—in a small village, for instance, you'd fool me for sure."

"You agree, Miss Barr?"

"Absolutely, Jean-Pierre."

"Good, good."

"No problems thus far?" asked Harry.

"Not a one." He shut the door.

"Likes to try out his disguises on me," explained Harry. "So I assumed."

"Otherwise he's a pretty good police detective."

"Going to put him on your list?"

"Nope. But I still think maybe I ought to add Pennoyer's name."

Chapter 10

At one A.M., nearly a half hour after they'd crossed the border and entered Urbania, Harry was sitting alone in his compartment. The shade on the outside door was still up and he was watching the black hill country roll by.

Thunder and lightning had commenced at midnight and in the sizzling blue flashes he caught glimpses of thick forest and sharply slanting ground.

"Maybe I should've told her the truth," he said to himself. "But the fewer people who—"

A faint tapping sounded on the corridor door.

"What?"

"Having a devil of a time getting to sleep amid all this impressive natural phenomenon." Pennoyer opened the door and smiled a toothy smile in at him. "Thought if you were still up we might have a bit of a powwow."

"Sure." Harry took out his pocket watch. "I was going to check on you soon anyway. Come on in."

Pennoyer crossed the threshold, chuckling behind his hand. "All part of the thorough Challenge International Detective Agency service."

"Then at 2:00 A.M. I have to go through the whole train."

Sitting opposite him, the young man said, "Been a very uneventful trip so far. Thanks to you and all these efficient frog chaps."

"We're still not in Kaltzonburg."

"You actually believe, old man, that someone might try to snatch the ruddy obelisk right off this train?"

"Yep, that's one possibility."

"Thing weighs quite a bit. I mean to say, it's no match for Cleo's Needle, but one can't tote it around over one's shoulder."

"Even so."

Casually Pennoyer turned toward the window. When lightning next flashed, he gasped. His monocle fell from his eye and he gasped. "Jove, it's a giant bat!"

Harry swung his head around. "Where?"

It was exactly then that Pennoyer hit him behind the ear, very expertly and very hard with a blackjack.

Harry tumbled from the seat and slumped against the door.

The young man hit him again. "Dreadfully sorry, old man, but we can't have any ace sleuthhounds aboard from this point on."

The door opened and Harry was given a strong push.

He felt as though he were flying clear of the roaring train. He sailed across the blackness, the rain hitting at him as he soared.

Then he hit the ground. Shoulder, ribs, thigh smashing into the slanting hillside.

He heard distant thunder and passed into unconsciousness.

* * * *

Jennie hadn't undressed. She'd been sitting in her compartment reading a Tauchnitz paper-covered edition of Rider Haggard's The Wizard and, soon after the special train had halted at the rain-swept border station, had fallen asleep in her seat.

When the train came to a sudden stop at 2:00 A.M., the novel fell from her lap and hit the carpeted floor with a thud.

She sat up. "What the heck's going on?" She reached to pull up the shade.

"Don't do that, old girl. The fewer of our blokes you get a gander at the better."

Pennoyer had come into her compartment unannounced and uninvited. He held a .32 revolver pointed at the reporter.

"So Harry was right about you."

"Did the chap suspect I was a rotter from the start?"

"He figured no one could be as big an idiot as you appear to be."

Pennoyer chuckled behind his free hand. "Very perceptive bloke," he said. "Proving yet again how wise I was to get rid of him."

She inhaled sharply, standing. "If you've killed Harry I'll—"

"Spare me your wrath, old girl. I doubt he's dead."

"What did you—"

"Was very humane, actually. Merely tapped him on the skull and flung him from his compartment."

"He's hurt then. You—"

"Yes, I suppose one doesn't fall from a moving train onto a mountainside without suffering some damage. Still, don't you know, I gave him a fighting chance. Better than the bullet in the head my superiors suggested." He poked at the air between them with the barrel of his gun. "Now gather up your belongings and be quick about it. And don't even consider trying to get the better of me."

"Why are—"

"This train, do you see, is going to vanish. Soon as we get the bloody obelisk unloaded," he explained. "Unless you wish to vanish with it, Miss Barr, you'll allow me to escort you outside."

* * * *

The Great Lorenzo's command performance for Prince Rudolph and an audience of Kaltzonburg's most distinguished citizens had been a triumph. He had astounded and enthralled them with such awesome illusions as the Magic Kettle, the Astral Hand and the Floating Lady. Those he'd followed with his bullet catching act, and for encore he'd introduced his newest trick, the Vanishing Mummy.

Early on the morning after, he sat up abruptly in bed, clutching at his chest. "Harry's been hurt," he said aloud.

The plump, raven-haired lady beneath the silken sheets with him stirred. "Is something troubling you, my adored one?"

"He's lying in the woods beside the railroad tracks...six miles outside of... Is there a town named Schamgefuhl in this delightful country of yours, Countess Irene, my pet?"

The middle-aged countess rolled over on her ample back. "Whatever are you chattering about, dearest Lobo?"

Swinging free of the wide fourposter, he hurried to the purple ottoman on which he'd neatly stacked his clothes the night before. "Schamgefuhl...I see a sign bearing that melodious name. Is there such a place?"

"Well, yes, Lolo, but no one goes there anymore," she answered. "The spa is quite out of fashion and the only people who'd be seen—"

"Where is it, my pudding?"

"A good three hundred miles to the south, Lobo, not far from the border. Why are you—"

"I must use your telephone at once."

"To call someone in Schamgefuhl? I doubt they have the telephone service in such a backward—"

"No, to contact my dear friend and generous patron, Prince Rudy." He was nearly dressed, struggling with his final shirt stud. "He's going to have to convince the police and the railroad officials that I'm not a lunatic and that my vision is anything more than a hallucination. Yes, I am going to need considerable cooperation to get to Harry."

"Who is this Harry person?"

"An old friend."

"He is in trouble in, of all places, Schamgefuhl?"

"I'm not getting a perfectly clear picture. It's possible he's broken his neck."

When she sighed the pale blue sheets shivered and whispered. "Such loyalty you display, Lobo, such touching samaritanism. Yet another reason why I am so passionately fond of you," she said, smiling over the top of the sheet at him, "If, however, this dear friend of yours already has broken his neck, there may not be all that much need to rush."

"I am hoping, dear one, part of my vision is in error." Fastening his cloak around his shoulders, the Great Lorenzo went striding from the early morning bedchamber.

Chapter 11

Harry opened his eyes.

He was flat on his back in the middle of an off-white hospital room.

The early afternoon sun showed over the rooftops of the buildings outside his high window.

"Okay," he told himself, "I'm not in the woods any longer."

His ribs, the ones on his right side, hurt. A fine, intense sort of pain it was. And his side was tightly bandaged.

When he reached to scratch at the bandages, he discovered that his right wrist and part of his right hand were encased in a heavy cast.

The off-white door opened and a very young doctor came shyly in. "Good afternoon, Herr Challenge," he said in his pale voice. "We are awake, I see."

"Apparently."

"I will," said the lean, fair-haired doctor, "explain to you where you are and what has happened, should you be anxious to know."

"That would liven things up, yes."

"First, however," he said as he approached the bed, "allow me to ask you if a cablegram from your loving father would unduly upset you?"

"It wouldn't."

"I have such here." From a lumpy pocket of his white smock he took a tongue depressor, a bottle of yellow pills and an envelope. "I may open it for you, since your hand is not able?"

"Appreciate that."

"I am, by the way, Herr Doctor Hauser." He placed the message, carefully, in Harry's bruised left hand. His father said:

Dear Son:
 Quit malingering. We have another case. Scatterbrained young woman named Stowe will contact you in Kaltzonburg. Claims her crackpot parent is

missing. Big fee. Get up and get cracking.

Your loving father, the Challenge International Detective Agency.

Harry said, "She must be Professor Stowe's daughter."

"Beg pardon?"

"Never mind. Just explain to me what the situation is."

"It is a most unusual case," Dr. Hauser began. "Not from a medical standpoint. There we have nothing very unusual— fractured wrist, three fractured ribs, bruises, abrasions and a mild concussion. Exactly what's to be expected with someone who's been thrown from a moving train."

"You get many patients here who've been tossed off trains?"

"Well, in fact, no. You are my first, but then I am only a full-fledged doctor six and one half months."

"This hospital is...where?"

"You are in Kaltzonburg, as a guest of no less a personage than Prince Rudolph himself."

Using the elbow of his good arm, Harry worked into a sitting position in bed. "The train I was on...did it get through okay?"

The young doctor coughed discreetly. "Everyone is being very secretive," he confided. "It is my impression, though, that this particular train has vanished."

"What do you mean?"

"It never arrived at its destination. There is no trace of it," he replied. "At least, so I hear."

"But Jennie...everyone else on the damn train...what happened to them?"

"They apparently disappeared along with it," said Dr. Hauser. "Let us perhaps change the topic of conversation, since you seem to be getting overly—"

"No, damn it. I have to find out what happened to Jennie." He attempted to get out of bed. "That wasn't even the real obelisk."

"You must not try to—"

The room became all at once smaller and greyer and it closed in on Harry. He passed out.

Fully dressed and fairly wobbly, Harry eased out of his hospital room. He'd been waiting at a crack in the door for the past five minutes, watching. The off-white corridor was empty now.

Unsteady on his feet, he started down the hallway. He'd noticed, while doing his reconnoitering, a door labeled STAIRWAY to his right.

The day had ended and the gaslights along the hall were on. The single narrow window showed him a rectangle of bright-lit public square ringed by shops and cafés far below.

Harry was three paces beyond the window when a hand caught hold of his left arm.

"If you must go for a twilight stroll, my boy, allow me to assist you."

"Lorenzo," said Harry. "How did you manage to sneak—"

"I never sneak," the portly imagician reminded him. "Being highly esteemed in royal circles, I have full access to the Kaltzonburg Memorial Hospital, which was founded by Prince Rudy's great uncle. I was about to peek in on you when—"

"Listen, I have to get the hell out of here," Harry explained. "Jennie's in trouble...someplace."

* * * *

"She and a squad of Paris' finest, plus an obelisk, are missing."

"That's not even the real obelisk."

The Great Lorenzo nodded as he opened the stairwell door. "Yes, I understand you and Inspector Swann worked a variation of my famed Chinese Tomb illusion and switched obelisks."

"The one on the special train was made out of papier-mâché. The real one, with Swann riding shotgun, traveled here in the baggage car of the regular Paris-Kaltzonburg Express in a big crate marked Farm Implements." Harry hesitated at the top of the stairwell. "How many floors?"

"Six. Would you rather I spirit you into a lift. I'm very good at diverting attention from—"

"Nope, I don't want to risk getting stopped."

"Might an old and trusted comrade mention, Harry my lad, that you look godawful."

"Yep, seems to happen every time I get sapped and dumped off a train." He took a deep breath and, with the Great Lorenzo supporting him, began his descent of the metal steps.

"Did the real obelisk get through?"

"Unharmed. The gewgaw was delivered, by the estimable Inspector Swann, to the chateau of Baron Groll. That was two days ago and since then there's been not—"

"Two days?" Harry halted. "No, it couldn't have arrived until this morning because...Christ. I forgot to ask Dr. Hauser how long I've been here."

"This is the eve of your second day, my boy. You were out cold for a good long while." The magician was watching him closely. "Harry, might it not be better to rest at least one more night before—"

"Nope, no." He resumed his downward climb. "Jennie's been missing for two days."

"Inspector Swann is, with the help and cooperation of the Urbanian police, making a thorough and detailed—"

"You sound like a police department handout, Lorenzo. Two days and nothing is what it comes to."

The magician was panting now. "Not that I expected, oh, an illuminated scroll or even a small pewter loving cup," he said. "Yet, after pulling strings, cutting red tape, moving heaven and earth to retrieve your pitiful broken body from the flinders at the side of the—"

"That's how they knew where I was. You had a vision." Harry halted again. "Sorry, I didn't think to ask about that."

"One more proof, lad, that you're not at your usual level of performance," the Great Lorenzo pointed out as they continued their downward course. "An injury to the head can do that. Well do I recall a time in Istanbul when I was conked on the coco by an Indian club being wielded by the irate husband of a voluptuous lady bareback rider who managed to look always graceful even though she weighed in at over—"

"Whatever shape my brain is in," said Harry, "I have to start looking for Jennie. Damn it, I didn't even tell her we were just decoys. She thinks the obelisk is the real thing."

"It has been in my experience that true love—something, alas, I have enjoyed but seldom in my long and colorful life—true love makes for a certain amount of truth telling and confiding, Harry."

"I know." They'd reached the fourth floor of the hospital and he paused for a moment. "The thing is, Lorenzo, I guess I'm still not absolutely sure I can trust Jennie. While we were traveling from Paris to Zevenburg I was certain...then it turned out she was trailing me to get material for her damn newspaper articles."

Tapping his temple, the magician said, "The poor child was under the influence of that most wicked of gentlemen, the infamous Max Orchardson. You can't really blame her for what she did while in a state of—"

"I haven't figured out how much of what she did is due to being hypnotized and how much... Hell, what difference does it make? I have to find her." He started downward.

The music of an accordian drifted out of a sidewalk café across the square. The tune reminded Harry of one he and Jennie had heard on the floating restaurant on the Seine.

"What?"

The Great Lorenzo, who still held Harry's arm while they walked across the parklike square, said, "I was mentioning that a very handsome young woman named Belphoebe Stowe has been to the hospital to try to visit you. On several occasions. She brought a basket of very tasty hothouse plums on her second attempt."

"My father put her on to me." They were passing an empty wrought iron bench. "Think I'd like to sit for a spell."

After helping Harry to do that, the magician settled down beside him. "Perhaps we ought to consult a private physician before you go off on—"

"I'll be okay. A shade shaky is all."

"Miss Stowe is a wholesome British lass, blonde and well formed. A trifle on the slender side for my taste," said the Great Lorenzo. "Reminds me of a lady-in-waiting I once sawed in half while touring Bosnia in the spring of—"

"I don't want any new clients just yet."

"Your dear papa assumes this case has concluded. You have, after all, put an end to the haunting of the musée. You have delivered the authentic obelisk safely to the arms of its new rightful owner. All's well, my boy."

"And where's Jennie?"

"Ah, but being a practical gent with the heart and soul of an accountant, your father doesn't see—"

"I won't take on anything new until I find Jennie." He tried to scratch at his side with the hand that wore the cast. "Damn, I'm going to have trouble even using a gun."

"One more reason for being prudent." The magician poked at the grass with the brightly polished toe of his shoe. "While sharing a plum or two with the handsome and deeply distraught Miss Stowe, I did establish that she is the one and only daughter of the illustrious Professor G. P. R. Stowe."

"Yep, the guy who built that flying machine."

"None other. Seems the scholarly old gentleman disappeared nearly a year ago." He plucked a lit cigarette from the night air, took a single puff and vanished it. "Miss Stowe, whose handsome bosom is filled with anguish and who has an independent income that is most impressive, has reason to believe her long lost parent may be in Urbania."

"What reason?"

"She did not confide that little tidbit in me."

"Right now, even if Professor Stowe is in cahoots with Orchardson, I can't... Hold on." Harry got, not very steadily, to his feet. He started fumbling under his coat with his left hand.

A stocky figure had moved out from behind a dead marble fountain and was crossing the darkness toward them. "It is only I, M. Challenge."

Harry remained standing there. "Have you found out

anything about Jennie Barr, Inspector Swann."

"I was just now on my way to the hospital to consult with you when I noted you and your loyal friend resting here." The French police inspector took off his dark bowler hat and held it with both hands over the middle buttons of his thick overcoat. "You are well enough to be up and about, monsieur?"

"Just about. What have you found out?"

Swann's thick moustache drooped. "We have this very afternoon located the special train," he said. "It had been cleverly switched off onto a disused spur line."

"What about Jennie and the others?"

Swann lowered his head. "The train, monsieur, has been located at the bottom of a deep lake at the end of the tracks," he said slowly. "Until we are able to do some diving, we must assume that all who were aboard are drowned."

Harry did something he'd only done twice before in his life. He fainted.

Chapter 12

Harry circled the rough-hewn wooden table. The table nearly filled the vine covered arbor next to the hillside cottage the Great Lorenzo had brought him to last night.

Spread out atop it were several of the ordinance maps Inspector Swann had loaned him. Resting his sore backside against the table edge, Harry traced his good forefinger along another of the probable routes the hijackers could've taken after running the special train into the lake.

"Lake Knochen." He looked away from the map, out from the arbor. The spires of Kaltzonburg were still blurred with morning mist far downhill. "Jennie's not dead."

"Scat!" came the voice of the Great Lorenzo from within the cottage. "Begone."

Harry sat down on one of the benches, studying a map and absently rubbing his cast.

From around the side of the whitewashed stone cottage came the magician. "Have you ever awakened from an uneasy night's sleep to find an obese calico cat sleeping on your chest?" he inquired.

"Once, in Estonia."

"No wonder I was dreaming I'd become Santa Claus." He wore an impressive dressing gown that was covered with realistic depictions of gigantic orange and black tropical flowers. "You're looking much more chipper this morning, my boy."

"Not quite up to chipper yet, but getting close." From the arbor you would see part of the winding dirt road, a quarter mile off, that climbed their hillside. A leathery old farmer was urging a half dozen shaggy goats downhill. "About my fainting last night. I—"

"Think nothing of it." The Great Lorenzo seated himself on another of the wooden benches. "I've swooned a few times myself. The initial instance I can clearly recall took place during my vanished youth and involved my seeing, in a nearly undraped state, the first tattooed lady I had ever... Are you in the mood for breakfast?"

"Not very hungry."

"Coffee then?"

"That'd be fine."

"Haven't tried this particular magic word for many a moon. Let us see if it's still efficacious." He lifted up one of the big maps and slid a plump hand under it. "Presto!"

The hand reappeared holding a steaming mug of coffee.

Taking it, Harry grinned. "Suppose I had asked for breakfast'?"

"Presto." From beneath the map he produced a china plate holding a fat, many-layered pastry. "Shame to waste this, now I've conjured it up." From behind his left ear he plucked a silver fork. "Enough sugar in your coffee, my boy?"

Harry sampled it and nodded.

The Great Lorenzo concentrated on the pastry, which was rich in various kinds of chocolate filling and topped with thick whipped cream, for the next few minutes. He ate and watched the reluctant goats make their way out of sight around a quirk in the road.

"There are," said Harry finally, tapping the map he'd been studying, "at least two routes they could've taken away from the lake. See here'? Around this way you pick up a good road just over these hills. That eventually takes you to this highway. Or they could've gone back across the railroad tracks right at this point, moved down through the valley here. Beyond that you connect with another fair highway."

"We have to assume they didn't know they weren't going to be stealing the real obelisk." The magician licked a dab of chocolate off his thumb. "The real thing weighs a couple of tons, does it not?"

"Nearer to three."

"You don't simply cry out, 'All right, lads, everyone lift with a will and off we go.' What's needed is a method of draying the thing," he pointed out.

"Right, they had to have a wagon, a damn sturdy one, waiting there at the lake for them."

"Large wagon, pulled by a strong team of horses. That has to leave a trail, even without a granite keepsake aboard."

"Inspector Swann and the local police are supposed to be working on that, looking for wagon tracks and all," Harry said. "First, though, he's concentrating on getting divers down to... Damn it, Lorenzo. She can't be dead." He hit the table with his cast, winced.

"She's not."

Harry frowned across at him. "Have you had some sort of vision about—"

"Alas, no. Merely a hunch." He lifted the map again, peered under it. "Dare I have another pastry? No, only a cruller this time. Presto."

Harry waited until the magician had taken a few appreciative bits of the freshly materialized frosted cruller. "You can't control the visions? Concentrate on Jennie and see—"

"Unfortunately my gift does not work that way, Harry. Over the years I've experimented with varied and sundry ways of trying to..." He grimaced suddenly, his fingers tightening on the cruller until it broke into crumbly pieces. Rocking sideways on his bench, the Great Lorenzo started producing a low moaning.

"Lorenzo?" Harry jumped up, ran around the table.

"I'm fine...stay back..." He pressed both hands to his chest, continuing to moan. "She is...alive... Jennie's alive... I can see...a castle...like a Gothic ruin...same castle I saw before... with all of us in it... Jennie is...locked in a...stone room...young man taunting her...nasty fellow...monocle..."

"Bertie Pennoyer," muttered Harry.

"I see...evil old man...decaying...Zaytoon... It's Anwar Zaytoon... another woman...more dangerous than he...dark and beautiful... Why, it's..." His body jerked, shivered.

Harry carefully sat on the bench beside his friend. He put his good arm around his shoulders. "Easy now."

The Great Lorenzo began to breathe regularly again. "Some of them get rough, like climbing an alp or two." His plump face was blurred with perspiration. He concentrated on breathing in and out for a while.

"So Jennie is okay?"

"Appeared a bit peckish. Also pale and weary. Otherwise alive and not seriously injured."

"And Zaytoon's the one who's got her."

"He is the master of the picturesque castle I saw, yes. Along with this Pennoyer fellow you mentioned."

"Pennoyer is the amiable gent who conked me and treated me like a sack of mail," said Harry. "But you saw someone else at the castle."

The magician took up a fragment of his ruined cruller between thumb and forefinger and contemplated it. "Only a fleeting glimpse I had of the lady," he said. "I am certain, however, she is the one we met before and quite recently."

"Not Naida Strand?"

"'Tis she and none other."

"Damn, we left her at Blackwood Castle in Orlandia, sleeping in her coffin."

"Same as any other true vampire." The Great Lorenzo shrugged. "We both had the opportunity to drive a stake through her black heart. Too sentimental by far we were."

"I don't think I can kill anyone that way. Certainly not a woman."

"Nor I. Whenever I see a sleeping lady, be she vampire and sorceress most foul or sweet-souled maiden, slaying her is the furthest thought from my mind." He spread his hands wide. "Which is why, dear lad, we now have her to contend with as well as the rest of this nest of blackguards."

"Worse, Jennie has to contend with her." Harry tapped the nearest map. "What about the location of Zaytoon's castle?"

"These visions vary." He coughed into his hand. "Sometimes I get the exact location, down to the street address. Other times I don't. This time I didn't. Zaytoon's castle is somewhere in Urbania and that's the closest I can come."

* * * *

From the misty courtyard came the harsh chatter of machine-gun fire.

Jennie Barr was sitting on the cot, her notebook open on her lap.

Zaytoon testing weapons again today, she wrote. Demonstrating to potential customers?

In order to see out the only window in the small grey stone room, Jennie had to stand atop the rickety cot. The view afforded by the effort was not especially inspiring. All she was able to see was another turret of the bleak castle she was imprisoned in and a thin slice of sky. The activities down in the courtyard she had to guess at, assisted by the sounds the various weapons— machine guns, rifles, grenades—made and occasional puffs of smoke that drifted across her portion of sky.

The morning was a pale, overcast one. Jennie'd determined that soon after awakening nearly an hour ago.

She bit on the end of her stubby pencil, glancing up at the slot of a window.

When she began writing again, she put down Is Harry alive?

She'd written that line before, several times since she'd been a prisoner of Anwar Zaytoon, and she hadn't meant to put it on paper again.

"He must be alive and he'll find me sooner or later," she said to herself. "But if he doesn't, I've got to keep working on a way to get myself—"

The thick metal door of her room rattled, made its usual rasping sound and swung open inward.

"Top of the morning, old girl." Bertie Pennoyer came briskly in, a tray in one hand. "One hopes, don't you know, that your appetite's improved. You keep up this ruddy fasting and you'll—"

"I want to see Zaytoon."

Pennoyer kicked the heavy door shut with his heel. "Quite out of the question, as I've been telling you." He set the tray on the stone floor next to her cot.

"He's holding me prisoner and I want to—"

"You're a guest." Pennoyer was wearing a double-breasted navy blue blazer and white trousers. Leaning back against the wall, he popped his monocle and commenced polishing it against his sleeve. "You'll remain our guest, don't you see, until you decide to be talkative."

"I'll talk only to Zaytoon."

"Stubborn, ain't you?" He held the monocle toward the lone window, squinting. "Our jovial host, the guv as I call him, is a bit under the weather still. Only to be expected with a gent as far along in years as the guv is. What strength he's got, he has to reserve for the many business affairs—"

"How old is he exactly?" asked Jennie. "When I dug into his background once, I couldn't find any evidence of when or where he'd been born."

"The guv's quite long in the tooth, but I've never had a gander at his birth certificate." Pennoyer covered his mouth with the hand holding his monocle and chuckled. "Afraid, old girl, I can't give you any facts to scribble in your memory book."

She said, "I came across a rumor once that Zaytoon wasn't born in the nineteenth century at all. They said that by some magical means he's—"

Pennoyer's monocle dropped to the stones and cracked down the middle. "Bally old wives' tale and nothing more." Bending from the waist, he gathered up the pieces. "One hears far too much ridiculous nonsense being nattered about. A reporter of your reputation, one would think, is above believing such poppycock."

"If he is, say, a few hundred years old," persisted Jennie, "then he has a darn good reason for wanting the obelisk and the secret of eternal life. Could be the methods he's been using aren't working any—"

"Who the ruddy devil told you that?" He squared his shoulders and glared at her. "Speaking of the obelisk, which the guv is interested in purely from a collector's point of view—we've been deuced patient with you, don't you know. Now the time has come to be open with us."

"I'll tell Zaytoon himself, face to face."

He came closer. "Thus far, dear girl, the guv's been too busy with other affairs to take a hand in questioning you," he said. "Maybe you haven't realized that this snuggery of yours is deuced close to some of the old torture chambers. If you aren't more forthcoming about where the rascal obelisk has gotten to by nightfall, then you may pay those chambers a bit of a visit."

"I'd be happy to talk to Zaytoon right now."

Pennoyer leaned. "A lovely old friend of yours has joined forces with us recently and is, at this very moment, a guest of the castle," he said. "She tells me she's most anxious to join in questioning you. And she'll, don't you know, be doing that tonight unless you come clean. Her name is Naida Strand."

Jennie blinked. "I thought she perished in Blackwood Castle."

"Far from it. She's very much alive," he assured her. "Well, as alive as a full-fledged vampire can be."

* * * *

Harry spotted the approaching cyclist first. It was less than fifteen minutes after the Great Lorenzo's vision and the magician was hunched, elbows on table, scanning an ordinance map. "Perhaps the name of a town, a river, a lake will trigger something."

Glancing downhill, Harry noted a bright scarlet cycle being peddled energetically in their direction. "What did you say Professor Stowe's daughter looked like?"

"Belphoebe Stowe is a healthy, out-of-doors sort of young lady. Typical product of an upper-class British upbringing and the sort of woman who's helped make the empire great."

"Blonde?"

"Blonde, yes. Tall, close to five foot nine I'd estimate. Tends toward the slim, yet—"

"She's coming up the hill right now. Dressed in a riding habit."

"On horseback?"

"On a bicycle."

The Great Lorenzo finally looked up from the map, narrowing his eyes. "Yes, that's she. Sits a cycle well, doesn't she?"

"How does Belphoebe Stowe happen to know I'm staying in this cottage you borrowed from your duchess?"

"Countess."

"Countess then. How?"

"Inspector Swann is aware of the location, as is Countess Irene." Standing up, he brushed crumbs from his front and retied the orange sash of his dressing gown.

The cyclist disappeared from view, hidden by the cottage itself, and a moment later there was a forceful knocking upon the front door.

"Would you mind scooting around and welcoming the young lady, Harry? I hate to play host when dressed so casually."

"Anybody who greeted me wearing a thing like that'd make a terrific impression." Reluctantly he left the arbor, walked across the tree-filled yard to the front of the place.

Belphoebe Stowe, wearing white riding britches, a black jacket and riding boots, was about to resume knocking when she noticed Harry. "You would be Mr. Harry Challenge?"

"I would," he admitted, "and you're Belphoebe Stowe. Let me save us some time by explaining that—"

"My father has been kidnapped again." She came hurrying along the flagstone path to him.

"Again? I wasn't aware he'd even been—"

"In the first instance, it was a gross and, I suspect, effete, man named Max Orchardson. Most recently Anwar Zaytoon, often alluded to as the Merchant of Death by the more sensation-minded journalists of the day, has abducted him," she explained. "My father, although quite brilliant and inventive in a rather strange and eccentric way, is not an especially admirable nor particularly likeable man. He is, as I find I must keep reminding myself, my only living parent. I, as fate would have it, am his only child. It is my duty, therefore, to rescue him from the clutches of Zaytoon."

"I'd like to be able to—"

"What I shall require from you, Mr. Challenge, is your strong right arm to… Ah, but do forgive me. I note, as I should have at once were I not so preoccupied with my own affairs, your right arm is injured. You will, since you seem a bright and perceptive man, no doubt appreciate the meaning of my metaphor. What I need is a stalwart and fearless champion to come with me to this castle where Zaytoon holds my improvident father. Someone to handle any hand to hand—"

"Whoa," suggested Harry. "By coincidence, we were just talking about the castle. Thing is, we're not certain where it's located. Do you—"

"Well, of course, I know where it is. Have I not been devoting the past week to locating it? Ever since this rather vulgar postcard reached me in my hotel in Rome, after having followed me halfway around the globe. My father, you see, has no idea I have been devoting my waking hours, along with a considerable amount of my own money, to—"

"May I see the postcard?"

"Certainly you can. Being a detective, you will quite naturally wish to examine it thoroughly. I can save you some time by explaining in advance that my father, apparently having to sneak this missive out to me, had no time to put in many specifics." She undid the three top buttons of her silk blouse, dipped in two fingers and extracted the card. "Please ignore the shamelessly underdressed young woman on the front of it. I am giving my father the benefit of the doubt and assuming he, being rushed and in fear of his life, had little choice as to what sort of postcard he could post to me."

The picture side showed a plump young woman in a very thin gown as she rose on her tiptoes to greet the newly risen moon. On the other side, in a crabbed hand, was the message:

> Now Z. has taken me from O. Do try to help. This
> is more than I can stand. I am…must go now. In haste,
> your loving father, GPR Stowe.

Seven weeks ago the card had been posted in the town of Lowen. Harry knew, having spent some time going over maps of most of Urbania, that the town was only twenty miles from here.

"As I mentioned, Mr. Challenge, I have been able, after discreetly making inquiries in Lowen, to locate this castle which Zaytoon and his coterie have rented for the season," said Belphoebe. "While I am an expert shot and excell at most sports, I am still a woman. Thus it was I contacted your father, whose admirable reputation I have long been familiar with, to inquire if he had an able-bodied operative anywhere in this part of Europe. I was pleased, it goes without saying, when I received a cable informing me that his own son was right here in Urbania. Are you, by the way, an only child?"

"I am, yes."

"Then there is something we have in common. I find, and no

doubt you will agree, that some degree of common interest is often a sound basis for a friendship," she told him. "When will you be able to undertake my case?"

He drew out his pocket watch. "I'm ready now."

"I like that," she told him. "No nonsense, right to business. We will get along famously, Mr. Challenge."

"Never doubted it."

Chapter 13

"I wonder," requested Belphoebe, "if you gentlemen might refrain from smoking those odorous cigars."

The Great Lorenzo was sitting opposite her in the plush-lined coach. "Ah, but of course. Forgive me for assaulting your delicate nostrils." He passed his plump hand in front of the smoldering stogie and it vanished.

Harry, who was sharing a seat with the blonde young woman, got rid of his cigar by tossing it out the open window of the borrowed coach that was carrying them through the afternoon to the town of Lowen.

"One's nostrils do not have to be especially sensitive to be offended by such a vile stench."

"Suppose," said Harry, "you give us a few more details about your father."

"My father is a brilliant experimenter in the field of heavier-than-air flight," she said. "He is, as well, a profligate and totally unbridled old reprobate."

Harry nodded, watching the woodlands they were rushing through. "How did Max Orchardson come to kidnap him in the first place?"

"Initially my lamentable father made the acquaintance of Orchardson at some disreputable soiree in some foul backwater of London," she replied. "Father, along with his multitude of other faults and foibles, believes himself to be interested in things occult and supernatural. An interest that is, as you know, shared by the awful Orchardson. He made the mistake of confiding the results of his work with flying machines to that loathsome man. My father really has made incredible strides in the designing and building of such mechanisms. He is far and away ahead of such men as Professor S. P. Langley of your own country."

"These giant bats are really your father's aerodromes?"

"I am afraid they are, Mr. Challenge." She sighed, unbuttoning the lace-trimmed blouse she had changed into before they'd commenced their journey. She reached inside. "If you will but peruse these plans you will note all the modifications called for by Orchardson."

Accepting the three sheets of flimsy paper, Harry unfolded them and spread them out on his knee. "How'd you come by these?"

"They are copies I made unbeknowst to my misguided father," she answered. "Originally, you see, Orchardson pretended he was only interested in financing the building of more aerodromes." She twisted the topmost button of her blouse. "My gullible, and not always sober, father willingly moved into an estate of Orchardson's, a dreary pile in the wilds of Barsetshire. After a few scant months it became all too evident the man had other things in mind."

The Great Lorenzo leaned, scanning the plans upside down. "The demonstration we had, my dear, gave us the impression these mechanical creatures can be controlled."

She nodded. "That is another of my father's inventions," Belphoebe said. "By utilizing an advanced electrical system, one I confess I do not fully understand, he has been able to make an aerodrome do his bidding. Goaded by Orchardson, my detestable father developed a flying machine that could be made to do any number of vile things."

"They can pick up people in their claws? Push them off high places and—"

"All that and more," she confirmed. "When my wayward father showed me the plans you now are studying copies of, Mr.

Challenge, I knew at once that Orchardson was much more than a patron of science."

"You talked your father into quitting?"

"I did, a task that required all my wiles and wits," she said. "Orchardson, however, was not to be so easily thwarted. Once he realized my father had left him and returned to his own home, he dispatched his minions to abduct him. This they succeeded in doing, after rendering me unconscious with a rare Brazilian drug. Upon awakening, two weeks later, I set out to follow what was, by then, a cold trail. Even so, I was able to pick up clues as to where they had taken my father. Orchardson has immense wealth—some say he has found the lost secret of transforming base metal to gold—and thus he has been able to lead me a merry chase from England to Egypt to Ruritania to Albania to Italy. It was while in Rome, where I arrived a few weeks after the wicked Orchardson had again moved his base of operations, that I received the bawdy postcard that led me to call upon your capable father for assistance."

"How did Zaytoon get hold of him?"

"Of that I have no knowledge. Zaytoon and Orchardson are archrivals, which must be why my father has become a pawn in some dread game they are playing."

The Great Lorenzo reached up over his head to pluck an eclair out of the shadows.

"I trust the scent of chocolate will not offend you, Miss Stowe?"

"Not at all," she assured him.

* * * *

The Great Lorenzo came limping into Harry's room at the Lion's Paw Inn. "The dear countess was right," he remarked. "This quaint little town has fallen on sad times."

Harry was at the cracked window, looking out across the tile rooftops toward the wooded hills. "That must be Gewunden Castle up yonder," he said. "Big place with a high stone wall surrounding it."

The portly magician limped over to him. "Yes, my boy, that's the very pile I saw in my recent vision. Jennie is within its gloomy confines at this very moment."

"Why are you still limping?" Harry turned his back on the window, sat on the edge of a sagging Morris chair.

"I am supposedly suffering from the gout, remember?" He pulled a cigar out of the air. "Join me?"

"Think I'll cut down."

"Ah, the prim Miss Stowe has had an effect on your—"

"The gout business is to fool the folks at the inn," Harry pointed out. "To convince one and all you've come to Lowen to take advantage of the hot springs. We're your concerned nephew and niece."

After puffing on the cigar and limping back and forth across the threadbare carpet, the Great Lorenzo said, "A dedicated performer, my boy, never lets down. I am supposed to be suffering with the gout and as long as we're here in this ragtag watering place I intend to limp in a most convincing and pitiable manner."

Harry grinned. "You are convincing," he said. "Brings tears to my eyes just watching you."

"I dropped in, now that we're all settled, to announce that I am going out to hobble through the lanes and alleys of the town," he said. "My task will be to gather in all the information and intelligence I can regarding the Zaytoon household." He limped toward the off-kilter door. "We'll meet, as planned, in the cheerless dining room of this hostelry when twilight descends."

"Yep, that'll give Belphoebe and I time to take a closer look at the castle."

The Great Lorenzo held up a cautionary forefinger. "Be extremely careful while you're in the vicinity of that place, Harry."

"You giving me the benefit of another vision?"

"Merely the benefit of common sense." He bowed, opened the door and limped out into the shabby corridor.

Chapter 14

Belphoebe spread her arms wide and took an enthusiastic deep breath. "This has been quite invigorating thus far," she said happily. "One can see why you so enjoy the detective profession, Mr. Challenge. For it provides both an intellectual challenge and the opportunity for a satisfying amount of healthful outdoor exercise."

Harry wiped his forehead with his pocket handkerchief. "Yes, a ten mile hike up the side of a thickly forested steep hill is great fun," he said. "Sometimes, when I'm between cases, I do this sort of thing for the sheer joy of it."

Smiling, she said, "You have a rather pleasant sense of humor."

He moved ahead through the oak trees until he reached the edge of a small clearing. About a half mile uphill loomed Gewunden Castle. From his coat pocket he took a small pair of opera glasses. "Ugly joint."

The thick stone walls were a good ten feet high, topped with rusty spikes and what looked to be jagged shards of broken bottle glass. The castle itself was a complex cluster of towers and dark tile roofs.

Belphoebe came up beside him. She undid the top buttons of her blouse. "I have brought a sketching pad and a suitable pencil," she told him. "I am quite good at drawing landscapes and buildings, much in the manner of your Joseph Pennell."

"What we could really use is a floor plan of the damn place," he said. "Nobody in town has one, though."

"An accurate rendering of the exterior will enable us to make certain speculations as to what lies within."

"Okay. I want all the gates and doorways marked down," Harry told her. "And a rough sketch of the whole setup."

"That I can assuredly supply," said the blonde Belphoebe. "If I might borrow your glasses for a moment."

"Sure, here."

"I made a few sketches on my earlier visit." She put the

binoculars to her eyes. "Yet I dared not approach anywhere near this close."

Harry frowned, his shoulders hunching slightly. As the young woman began making notes on her sketch pad, he backed away.

They hadn't followed a trail up here, and the trees rose high all around them. Branches thick with new leaves were tangled and intertwined overhead and brush grew high on the mossy ground.

Glancing from side to side, Harry walked back along the way they'd come.

Although sunset was at least a good hour off, the day was already starting to fade.

He had a growing feeling that someone was watching them. Eyes narrowed, he looked to the left and right and then up into the treetops.

"I believe I will get a better view from the clearing just below," called Belphoebe.

Harry turned. "Don't get out in the open."

But she was already leaving the shelter of the trees. He started running.

"Belphoebe, stay here."

From above came a flapping, creaking noise—a harsh whining, and a wheezy coughing.

Then a gigantic mechanical bat swooped down over the clearing.

Belphoebe was aware of it, too, and was trying to get back to the shelter of the woods from the center of the clearing.

The flying machine dived right for her. Two long, clawed arms swung down from its midsection, snatching at her. The second try was successful and the mechanical bat caught her up by the arm and a shoulder.

Its giant wings flapped at an accelerated rate and they both began rising up from the clearing.

Belphoebe cried out, kicking at the dark-painted aerodrome. Her sketchbook fell from her hand, fluttering down to the ground.

Harry had reached the open area and he was running toward them. If he could leap and catch hold of Belphoebe before she rose out of reach, then he could—

The earth opened beneath his feet. Rotted wood, branches, leaves snapped and he found himself plummeting down into a deep hole.

* * * *

At exactly five o'clock the clock high in the tower of the Lowen town hall struck the hour. A lifesize automation representing Hercules emerged from his lair, strode along a catwalk and whacked a bronze gong five times with his club.

Before the last echo had died, the carved wooden doors of the rustic little café across the square from the clock tower swung open. Two large swarthy men in the full military uniform of the far-off Latin American country of Panazuela escorted the Great Lorenzo out into the impending dusk. It was a double-time procession and it ended with the magician being deposited in a bed of tulips at the base of a statue of one of the great Urbanian statesmen of the eighteenth century and his equally praiseworthy horse.

"Do not," advised one of the colonels, "be so unwise, senhor, as to give offense to the senhora again."

"In my country," said the Great Lorenzo as he rose up out of the mangled tulips with considerable dignity, "it is not considered offensive to present a lovely lady with a bouquet of—"

"This is not your country, senhor," mentioned the other colonel, "nor is it ours. The Senhora Picada is here on a most important mission for her beloved husband, General Miguel Picada, an extremely able militarist and a man renowned for his jealousy. Were he here, you would be stretched out upon—"

"Gentlemen," said the magician, "my mission is similar to that of the handsome Mrs. Picada. I, too, find myself most interested in the munitions to be obtained from the esteemed Anwar Zaytoon. Thus, when I chanced to overhear her refer to her similar goal, I bethought me that perhaps a merger of our—"

"The next time you approach her with a handful of paper flowers, senhor, we will not be so gracious."

"Those were real roses," he assured them. "Do you think the Great Lorenzo materializes paper—"

"Adeus, senhor."

Executing an impressive about-face, they marched side by side back inside the café.

The Great Lorenzo fluffed his side-whiskers. "A dozen roses, too," he muttered. "That rarely fails."

"Ah, truly it is written that the monsoon that rips off your roof oft reveals a rainbow in the sky."

"Eh?" The magician did a slow half turn, stepped free of the tulip bed and scrutinized the Chinese gentleman who was sitting on a nearby wooden bench. "Were you razzing me, sir, or passing along a bit of celestial wisdom?"

The man was small and lean, dressed in a frock coat and grey trousers. A top hat rested beside him on the bench. "Wisely it is said that the newly painted barn sometimes fools the homesick cow."

"All well and good, yet... Ha!" He took a few steps toward him. "I didn't—you're absolutely right there—recognize you sans your stage finery, old friend."

Standing, the Chinese bowed. "I am no longer a colleague, Lorenzo."

"You mean you have ceased to be Fengjing the Amazing, Master of Oriental Wizardry?"

Fengjing shook his head. "I have found it more lucrative in the employ of a warlord of my native country."

"A shame, since no one does the Caged Dove illusion as deftly as you."

"True." He bowed more deeply. "What is it that has caused our paths to cross?"

"I suspect," said the Great Lorenzo, approaching the bench, "we share an interest in one Anwar Zaytoon."

"It is written that the vulture and the maggot may feast on the same carrion."

"You are in town to buy arms, are you not?"

"I am to call on the esteemed Anwar Zaytoon, or rather on his trusted servitors, this very evening," replied Fengjing. "There is to be a small reception at his rather dour residence. Should you care to gain entrance, oh friend of my former life, it might be arranged for you to become one of my party."

"That would come in very handy," said the magician. "And, if it's not imposing too much, I'll take the liberty of bringing a young associate of mine along."

Chapter 15

Harry fell approximately eleven feet straight down. He managed to land on his good side. The impression he got, when he banged into the stone floor, was that his taped ribs made a harplike twanging sound. That hand that was in the cast jumped up to whap him across the cheekbone.

A rich assortment of broken branches, splintered planking and tangled brush was beneath him and a bit more came drifting down in his wake to land atop him. Several nettles found their way under his collar.

What little daylight reached the bottom of the pit showed Harry he was sprawled on a flagstone floor. Weeds and spongy moss grew thick between the stones, and they were damp and smelled of raw earth. He pushed himself up to his knees, using his good hand.

The walls were of grey stone, streaked with blackish mildew. In front of him stretched a stone-walled tunnel. After a few yards it was lost in darkness.

Standing, bracing himself against a chill wall, he looked upward. There was no sign of Belphoebe and the mechanical bat in what little of the sky he could see.

"The damn bat works for Orchardson," Harry said to himself. "So what the hell is it doing here?"

And where was it carrying Belphoebe Stowe? To Zaytoon's

castle or off to a hideout of Orchardson's?

There were no footholds in the hole he'd unexpectedly dropped into. Climbing out, even if he had two good hands and all his ribs were in working order, would be damn difficult.

"But if this is an old forgotten passway to the castle, I don't want to get out of here anyway."

He took a last glance at the sky above, then crouched and selected one of the broken old boards from the hatch that had long concealed this hole. Getting out his box of wax matches, Harry struck one with his left hand and set fire to a pile of brush and twigs. He held the end of his three foot scrap of board to the flames. As soon as the board was burning, Harry stamped out the small fire and entered the tunnel.

A thick dampness closed in on him and just beyond the throw of light from his feeble torch he heard the sounds of scurrying.

"Shoo," Harry advised whatever was in his path.

Moving slowly and cautiously along, he started counting off the paces.

By the time he reached fifteen there was darkness in back of him as well as in front.

He was aware of small claws skittering on damp rock, some angry chittering.

Harry kept going, getting the impression he was moving deeper underground as he went ahead.

Fifty paces in.

A hollow dripping off to his left.

A hundred paces.

Something slithered across his foot. He glanced down, but it was gone.

Two hundred.

His makeshift torch sputtered, the flame starting to die.

Harry stopped. Holding the board between his knees, he fished out his matchbox with his left hand. He shook out a match, then transferred it to the fingers that stuck out of the cast and struck the match.

He held it to the burning end of the stick and managed to get the flame to perk up some.

He dropped the box back into his vest pocket and resumed walking.

Three hundred.

Four hundred.

The tunnel, he was near certain, had leveled off. Six hundred.

Seven hundred.

Eight hundred.

Up ahead Harry saw a stone wall and a heavy oaken door. A large padlock, rusted with age, dangled from it.

"This had better be a way into the damn castle."

Harry thrust the end of his torch into the large upper hinge and it stayed there, giving him a dim, flickering light.

He squatted and tugged at the lock.

It broke apart in his hand. At that same moment the torch died.

Blackness took over the tunnel.

Tiny clawed feet started coming closer across the stones.

He felt for the doorknob. He caught it and turned. Then he pulled at the door. For about a half a minute it didn't budge. Slowly it began to come open. He tugged with his left hand and the available fingers of his right.

Beyond the door stretched a stone corridor. At its end it was joined by two other corridors sand in them oil lamps were burning.

Leaving the heavy door open behind him, Harry started toward the light.

* * * *

Returning to the clouded mirror over his bureau, the Great Lorenzo took another admiring look. "Marvelous," he pronounced. "The entire populace of far Cathay would be fooled."

The magician had tinted his visible skin a pale saffron hue, pasted on a drooping mandarin moustache and made his eyes look a bit more Oriental.

Pleased, he retreated from the mirror. "But unless Harry and the fair Belphoebe return shortly, I won't be able to do much beyond a slapdash makeup job on the lad." He glanced out a window at the declining day, consulted his pocket watch yet again.

Back at the mirror he gave his disguise another approving inspection.

"Might be worthwhile to use my Shanghai Coffin illusion during this engagement. I could step into the box as myself, reappear downstage an instant later as the Emperor of the Forbidden City of—"

A faint tapping, almost a scratching, sounded on his room door.

The Great Lorenzo trotted across the thin carpet. "Yes?"

There was no response.

Looking down, he noticed that a pale yellow sheet of folded notepaper had been slipped beneath the door.

Puffing, he stooped to pick up the note. "Can it be that the statuesque Senhora Picada has suffered a change of... Damn!"

The hand-lettered note read:

> Mr. Lorenzo:
> Please inform the authorities that we have Miss B. Stowe. Her life for the obelisk. Details will follow.
> O.
>
> P.S.: We are addressing you rather than Mr. Challenge, since we fear he's dead and gone.

The room's only armchair groaned when the magician dropped into it.

He read the letter twice again, shaking his head, and then let the crisp sheet of paper drop to the floor. "Is Harry no more?"

Shutting his eyes, the Great Lorenzo strained to summon up a vision.

The best he could conjure was a strong hunch.

"Harry's alive and at the castle." He stood, hurried to the door. "I've got to journey there right now."

Chapter 16

Harry let himself into another underground room. This one was large and had a vaulted ceiling. It was lit by a row of gas lamps that had been strung along one of the walls. There were weapons everywhere, some set up and ready to demonstrate, the rest in cases and crates.

Making his way slowly through the maze of arms, he spotted cases of repeating rifles, bayonets, sabres and even double-barreled eight-gauge elephant guns. Sitting on a cleared space on the dark stone floor were two wheeled Maxim automatic machine guns, loaded and ready to be fired for prospective customers.

"Zaytoon's pursuit of the obelisk hasn't gotten in the way of his business anyhow."

Harry sat down to rest for a while on a crate of Navy Colts. His ribs were commencing to bother him some. He scanned the room, taking a quick inventory of all the weapons stored there.

"Oh, I say, this is a deuced jolly surprise."

Turning, Harry saw Bertie Pennoyer standing in a doorway across the wide room. "Been hoping I'd run into you."

Pennoyer yanked a .45 revolver from the waistband of his tweed trousers. "One hopes you're not in a foolishly vengeful mood, old boy." He chuckled behind his free hand. "Hurt the old wrist, did we? Pity. Still, could've been worse, eh?"

"I came to get Jennie," he said. "And Professor Stowe."

"That old duffer I'd almost give you gladly, don't you know. Stubborn as a ruddy ox and won't do a blessed thing he's told." Pennoyer came down the three stone steps into the room. "Zaytoon, don't you know, got a bee in his blooming bonnet that he ought to have the sod working for us rather than for that great blubbery Orchard-son. Why, for pity's sake? I mean to say, who wants a bunch of silly mechanical bats flapping about. Not that the bloke's consented to finish a single one since we've had him nattering about the place."

"How come," asked Harry, not moving from his perch, "you're working for Zaytoon?"

Pennoyer gave another masked chuckle, then rubbed his thumb and forefinger together. "The lucre, old man," he answered. "Pennoyer fortune's been, thanks to my excesses and those of some of my like-minded kinsmen, just about used up. That bloody expedition nearly broke me and the Musée des Antiquités didn't pay anywhere near what they'd promised. Wasn't even able to smuggle much in from Egypt. Nearly on my uppers until recently."

"What's Zaytoon paying you for?"

"I got onto the secret of the obelisk, old man." He leaned casually against the wall, the gaslight making his monocle flash. "Actually, to be perfectly frank, I pilfered old Fodorsky's notes soon as I got wind of what he'd stumbled onto. Fodorsky himself sold the information to that pig Orchardson."

"There really is a secret?"

"Jolly well better be," said Pennoyer. "Turns out the blooming obelisk has a hollowed out section near the tip. Held in that in an ivory casket is a supply of some fabulous lost Egyptian drug that can extend life."

Harry grinned. "You believe that?"

"Inclined to, yes," he said. "Mostly, you know, because old Zaytoon does. Why does he? Because the bloke is actually nine hundred years old. Staggering, what? Nine hundred if he's a day. Means he was born back in…um…oh, around the year 1000 A.D. Well, when he was still living out his original three score and ten, don't you know, he came across some of this same stuff. Been taking it ever since and he is, as the chaps say, living proof that it works."

"His original supply is running out?"

"Ran out last week. I'd heard rumors he was scouring the blasted earth for more some months ago," said Pennoyer. "So when I was tipped to what old Fodorsky had found and got hold of the info, why, I approached Zaytoon. The rest is history."

"Why didn't Fodorsky just take the stuff out of the obelisk?"

"Ain't that easy, old man. After he got the heiroglyphs all translated and realized there was a code message hidden in them, he worked that out," explained Pennoyer. "That told him that the stuff was in there, but that it was sealed up tight as a drum. Only way to get at it is to saw into the blooming rock with special tools and all that."

"That's why Zaytoon was trying to scare off the workmen."

"Exactly. We could've done the job in one night and been off, safe as houses, by dawn."

Harry stood. "I'd like to see Jennie."

"Afraid not, old man. Since Jennie Barr knows just as much about the whereabouts of the real obelisk as you do, we don't need you at all," said Pennoyer. "You're going to expire right here in the bowels of the—"

"Jennie doesn't know anything about it. But I do."

Pennoyer hid a chuckle. "Nice try at a bluff, but afraid it won't work. You and she were intimate, don't you know. All you know, she knows." He swung the gun until it was pointing directly at Harry.

"This is hardly sporting."

"What?"

"Okay for Zaytoon to slaughter his opponents," Harry said. "Also acceptable for Orchardson. You, however, are a gentleman."

Pennoyer gasped. "Jove, I do believe you've got something there," he said thoughtfully. "Some things a gentleman simply can't do. Murder in cold blood's one of them."

"So how about a duel?"

"Duel, you say?" He considered. "Yet really, old chap, you're in no shape to—"

"Left hand." Harry held it up. "I say I can beat you with my left hand."

"You're suggesting what—pistols or sabres?"

"Sabres. There's a whole case of them right over there near you."

Pennoyer contemplated the open case. "I feel I must warn you, Challenge, that before I was sent down from Oxford, I excelled in fencing and—"

"Then there's no reason to be afraid."

"Afraid, is it?" He gestured at Harry with his .45. "First, old chap, take your gun out of its holster and drop it safely out of reach."

"Obviously you don't think me a gentleman or you'd trust me not—"

"Very few Americans are gentlemen."

Harry eased out his .38 and tossed it onto the excelsior in an opened case of bayonets. "Just pick out a couple of sabres and toss me one."

Pennoyer rested his own gun on a ledge. "Keep in mind, old chap, that I warned you about my skills in this sport."

"I will."

Pennoyer selected two of the British-style sabres. He gripped each in turn, hefted it, slashed at the air. "Yes, I prefer this one," he decided.

He flung the other three-foot-long blade to Harry.

Harry reached for it with his right hand.

The steel hit his cast, the sabre fell to the stone floor with a clang.

"Damn, forgot my cast." Harry bent to retrieve the sword, but only succeeded in kicking it under one of the standing machine guns.

"I say, if you're that bloody awkward, we can hardly expect a fair contest."

"Hardly." Harry made a sudden dive, got hold of the machine gun, activated it and fired a burst of shots over Pennoyer's surprised head.

"Here now, you—"

"Drop the sabre, Bertie. Raise your hands high."

"Jove, that wasn't at all sporting of you, Challenge."

"We've already established the fact," reminded Harry, "that I'm not a gentleman."

Chapter 17

The day was dying when the man Jennie Barr had never seen before came to fetch her. The shadows in her narrow stone room were deepening and she was lighting the chunky candle on her lame cot-side table.

The heavy door made its usual noises. Standing on the threshold was a thickset man wearing a dark suit and a pale blue turban. His face was pale, his whiskers a washed-out blond. "You will come with me, miss."

She dropped the matchbox to the table. "Odd hour for a firing squad."

"Hurry, please, miss." He held a lantern in his right hand, a .32 revolver of German make in his right. "Should you fail to cooperate en route, I will be obliged to shoot you. Not fatally, yet most painfully."

"Nicest invitation I've had since I checked into this dam hoosegow." She stood, hesitated, then picked up her notebook.

They walked along a twisting corridor, the turbaned man behind her with his gun barrel ready to prod. Up a long chill flight of stone stairs, along another serpentine stone hall, through a vast empty room paneled in dark wood, along a straight corridor, up a flight of hardwood steps, into a hallway that was paneled, carpeted and lit with gas lamps.

"Stop in front of the third door on your left, miss."

Jennie did.

Her guide knocked twice on the thick walnut door, paused, knocked three times again.

"You can go in, miss."

"After you."

"I'll be waiting out here, miss."

Shrugging, the reporter opened the door and entered the

room beyond.

The coffin was the first thing she saw. It sat on a low platform in front of the large canopied bed. An ebony coffin with fixings of gold. The lid was open.

The only light in the brown bedchamber came from an oil lamp resting on a claw-footed table beside the coffin. Jennie had the impression there was someone in the bed, muffled in the thick shadows.

"Come here, young woman."

Jennie inhaled sharply. "Beg pardon?" She wasn't certain if the thin, dry voice had come from the coffin or the fourposter.

"Here, beside the bed."

As she passed the open coffin, Jennie glanced in. The body of a young dark-haired woman reposed within on a bed of yellowed satin that was streaked with dirt.

There was an old man propped up in the bed. The remains of a man. There seemed to be almost no flesh on his face and Jennie had the impression the multitude of wrinkles were etched directly on the bones of the skull. His head was like some piece of cryptic scrimshaw. Atop the head sat a fezlike cap, crimson with a dark silky tassle. The cap had slipped down to almost the brow ridges of the -nearly fleshless skull. The man's neck was as thin as an axe handle and it rose out of the stained collar of the silk smoking jacket he wore. Under the jacket he had on a suit of faded long underwear and the topmost buttons showed. Both his hands were outside the tufted covers, folded over his sunken midsection. The wrists were sticks, the hands them- selves looked brittle and mummified.

"I am Anwar Zaytoon," he gasped in his dusty voice. "I discovered the secret of life eternal."

Jennie coughed into her hand. "I'm too polite to make the obvious rejoinder."

A strange, awful sound began rattling and wheezing around in his narrow chest. "You manage," he said, when he was finished laughing, "to be droll even when in danger, Miss Barr. Yes, I am full aware I look more like death than life."

"This secret you found, what does it have to do with the obelisk?"

Zaytoon didn't reply for a moment. "In Damascus in the year 986 A.D.," he began at last, "I discovered a supply of a rare drug developed many centuries earlier in my native Egypt. It was derived from the now extinct tana plant. This supply was sufficient to keep me alive, when administered in conjunction with certain mystical rituals, until this day."

"You're over nine hundred years old?" Her fingers tapped at the notebook she was clutching. "How does that feel? What are your reactions to the—"

"This is not the time for an interview, young woman," he cut in. "My supply of the tana drug has, at long last, run out."

"Haven't you been scouting before this?"

"Always, obviously," Zaytoon answered in his dim faraway voice. "In Tyre in the thirteenth century I found a small amount that had somehow been preserved, unbeknownst to its owners over the centuries, in a funerary urn. Another small quantity I was able to add to my store in the seventeenth century. It had been mistakenly stored with some Christian relics in a country church in Livonia."

"You killed people to get it?"

"When necessary."

"And the obelisk will tell you how to get more?"

"It contains more. There is nearly a pound concealed in a hollowed compartment inside the Osiris Obelisk."

"Did you find that out from Professor Fodorsky?"

"Only indirectly, since he chose to sell his knowledge to a rival of mine named Max Orchardson," said Zaytoon, his thin lips curling. "That man has committed more sins in one lifetime than I have in centuries."

Jennie asked, "A pound is good for how many more years?"

"At least five hundred," answered the old man. "In that time, given the impressive strides being made in the realm of science, I have no doubt that we shall be able to find a way to manufacture the tana drug synthetically."

"Then you could live for ever and ever."

"Such is my intention," he replied. "The tenor of death felt by an ordinary mortal is, I assure you, nothing when compared to those fears that plague me. The longer you live, the less inclined you are to—"

"You'd really want to live hundreds of years more in the shape you're in now?"

"Ah, but the tana drug also rejuvenates as well," he told her. "Once I begin taking it again, I'll soon assume the appearance of a relatively young man of fifty or sixty."

"Well, more power to you I guess," said Jennie. "Thing is, I can't help you at all. Since I have no idea where—"

"Don't tire yourself, Anwar. Let me question this stubborn young woman."

Jennie looked toward the coffin. The dark-haired young woman was sitting up now, smiling at her.

* * * *

It took Harry just under five minutes to pick the lock of Jennie's cell. If his right hand hadn't been in a cast he could've done it in two.

He straightened, pulled the door slowly open.

The stone room was empty.

"Damn, did Bertie give me a bum steer?"

He had the impression that Pennoyer, now trussed, gagged and stored among the weapons, told him the truth about where Jennie Barr was being held.

Glancing around the candlelit room, Harry noticed the stub of a pencil beside the flickering candle. "She was here."

After shutting the cell door, he stood in the grey corridor for a moment.

"Old Zaytoon ought to know where Jennie is."

And Pennoyer had also told him where to find the arms merchant.

Harry, somewhat awkwardly, reached inside his coat and managed to draw out his .38 revolver. He tucked it into his belt and started along the corridor.

Several hundred twisting yards later he came to the steep flight of stone steps Pennoyer had told him about. Harry climbed these and then hurried quietly along another snaking corridor.

He carefully opened the wooden door at the hall end. An enormous room lay beyond, its walls paneled in dark wood, its high ceiling crossed with thick beams. In the dust on the black and white floor he made out the recent footprints of a woman and a man.

The hall leading away from the room was hung with faded tapestries across which courtly knights and fair maidens rode in eternal pilgrimage. He went up another flight of stairs and found himself standing in an arched doorway.

Midway down the gaslit hall a broad man wearing a turban was leaning beside a door. His back was, thus far, turned to Harry.

Harry tiptoed along the carpeting. When he was about three feet behind the turbaned guard, he reached out and tapped him on the shoulder.

The stocky man flinched, started to spin around.

Harry hit him in the temple with the butt of his gun, holding the weapon in his left hand. Because of the guard's tuban and because Harry didn't have as much strength in his left as in his right hand, it took three whaps with the gun to knock the man out.

Harry caught him, dragged him along to a nearby alcove and dumped him in there. Using the turban, he gagged and tied him. He appropriated the guard's .45, stuffing it into his pocket.

"Spoils the look of my suit."

He returned to the door, opened it and walked in, grinning amiably.

"Harry," said Jennie happily. She was seated in a wing chair that had been pulled over beside the fourposter bed.

Naida Strand, wearing a floor-length velvet gown, was standing over her. The expression on her face mingled recognition, amusement and scorn.

The old man on the bed croaked, "Who is this audacious young man? What does he mean by—"

"This is my dear old friend Harry Challenge," said Naida, toying with the ruby brooch around her pale neck.

"Challenge? Pennoyer killed him, days ago."

"Apparently not," said Naida.

Harry took his revolver out and gestured at the dark-haired woman. "Jennie'll be leaving now."

Jennie stood, notebook pressed to her breasts. "Yes, I will," she seconded. "Thanks for having me."

Naida's smile was thin and cold. "You forget, dear Harry, that your gun can't harm me," she reminded. "Surely, after all your experience in matters occult, you know a vampire can't be killed with ordinary bullets."

He grinned again. "Yep, I know that, ma'am," he answered. "Which is why I have six silver bullets loaded in here. Had them cast while I was laid up in the hospital in Kaltzonburg. Took a fall off a train a few days back."

Jennie moved around the bed, walked by the coffin and came to Harry's side. "I'm glad you survived."

"I was sort of pleased myself."

"He's bluffing you, Naida," said Zaytoon. "Take the gun out of my bedside table and kill him."

She was studying Harry's face, still standing straight beside the chair. "I'm inclined to agree," Naida said. "Until you walked into this bedchamber, Harry, you didn't even know I was in partnership with Anwar Zaytoon. Therefore, you couldn't have prepared silver—"

"You put a lot more faith in Bertie Pennoyer than he deserves," said Harry. "He didn't kill me as instructed and he talked quite a lot about you folks before he escorted me off that damn train. Talked about Zaytoon, about the secret of the obelisk and about you, Nadia."

"You're bluffing, just as Anwar—"

"I let you live before." His voice was harsh now. "That was a mistake. This time I won't be sentimental."

She took a step back toward the table. "No, I don't believe you."

He raised the gun, aimed it directly at her. "Well, if this was a poker game, about now'd be the time to call," Harry said. "You go for that gun, Naida, and I shoot you. With real silver bullets. The kind no vampire can—"

"Damn you." She turned, ran suddenly for a window. Tugging it open, she dived out into the darkness.

"Bluff worked," he said.

Jennie said, "Harry, she committed—"

"Nope, there are balconies along this side of the castle. I spotted them when I was casing the place this afternoon," he said. "Naida's probably scrambling down the side of the tower now. Let's go, since I want to get you out of—"

"You'll go nowhere," cried Zaytoon. He was fighting with his covers, gnarled hands clawing at them. "I'll stop you myself."

The old man managed to throw the covers aside. With an enormous effort he rolled to the bed edge and thrust his stick-thin legs out and to the floor. He stepped free of the bed and stood up.

There was a brittle cracking sound, and another. Both legs snapped and the bones came poking through the yellow parchment skin.

Zaytoon gasped with pain but made an attempt to get to the table for the gun. Instead he fell to the carpet.

More cracking, splintering sounds. His ancient body was crumbling, breaking up.

"My god, Harry," whispered Jennie.

"C'mon." He took her arm. "We still have to get Professor Stowe out of here."

Zaytoon was a tumble of twisted clothes and splintered bones. The nightcap had fallen free and lay next to the chair leg, the tassle was powdered with the scaly dust that had been the old man's skin.

"He was nine hundred years old," said Jennie as Harry hurried her across the room.

"Should've picked up a little wisdom in all that time."

He opened the door.

Chapter 18

Professor G.P.R. Stowe said, "That is typical of my daughter, all too typical." He was a short, rumpled man with frizzled grey hair. "Arranges to have me rescued, do you see, and neglects to send sufficient hands to take care of all my luggage."

"We don't have time for baggage," explained Harry. "Zaytoon is dead, but there's still a castle filled with toadies and thugs who don't know that."

They were standing in the middle of the professor's combination bedroom and workshop. Stowe was swaying some, a cut-glass decanter of rum in his hand. Stretched out on the unmade bed was a nearly completed flying bat.

"Someone will come back for your stuff later," promised Jennie.

"I notice, more in sadness than in anger, that Belphoebe did not even see her way clear to—"

"She was carried off by one of your damn bats."

"Why ever did she let that happen to her?"

"It was more Orchardson's idea," said Harry. "I made sure, in a recent conversation with Bertie Pennoyer, that Zaytoon doesn't have any of your gadgets in operation yet."

"How can he, when the first is lying yonder upon—"

"We'll go now," said Harry.

"Young man, you do not seem to comprehend—and considering you are a gentleman friend of my daughter your denseness is accounted for—you do not understand my position. I am tired of being kidnapped by all and sundry and each time losing more and more of my personal and business—"

"There are two ways you can leave here," Harry cut in. "Willingly or unconscious."

The professor blinked, took a swig of rum, wiped his mouth

on his lab coat sleeve and frowned. "Are you threatening me, young man?"

Harry grinned. "You're damn right."

"See here, I...um...very well." He'd noticed Harry's left hand turning into a fist. "I, I assure you, Belphoebe is in for a severe dressing-down."

"We have to get her back from Orchardson before you can do that," said Harry.

* * * *

Harry, Jennie and the stumbling, muttering Professor Stowe were coming down a splendid carved wooden staircase and were only a few hundred feet from the main door out of the castle when three large, swarthy men in evening clothes entered the immense hall below.

They noted the strangers on the stairway and proceeded to draw revolvers and a dagger.

"Far be it from me to criticize, young man," said the frizzle-haired professor, "but attempting to exit by the most obvious—"

"Been lucky bluffing so far," said Harry. "I thought we could work it once more."

"Maybe we can," said Jennie.

Harry stepped ahead of the other two. "You men down there," he called. "Hurry, run to the kitchen and start boiling plenty of hot water."

"Gar?" The biggest of the three men was crouched at the foot of the stairs with his revolver in his fist.

"I'm Herr Doctor Hauser," Harry explained, "and I have just come from Herr Zaytoon's chambers. I fear he's had a serious relapse and must be—"

"Kill the infidels!" shouted another of the guards, the one with the knife.

"Death to intruders! By the Eye of Osiris!"

The three large men started up the stairs, howling, waving their assorted lethal weapons.

"You convinced me you were a medic," said Jennie.

"Duck behind me." He reached for his gun.

"Halt, you craven dogs!" boomed another voice down below, "lest the wrath of Isis vist you."

"Gar?" The guards halted, still fifty feet from Harry and Jennie.

A plump Oriental gentleman had appeared out of a dining room off the hallway. He held his silken-sleeved arms high. "I must request that you cease this unseemly display of mean-minded behavior at once," he informed the perplexed guards. "For not only am I a guest at tonight's buffet supper, I am a most powerful Eastern wizard."

"Kill him, too," suggested the guard with the knife.

The Great Lorenzo sighed, his Oriental moustache drooping even further. "You gents give me no choice," he said. "Lando Zambini Marvelo!"

From out of nowhere great sputtering clouds of thick green smoke began to billow. They came rolling up the stairs to engulf everyone. Blood-chilling shrieks were heard, strange ominous shapes danced in the dense green swirls.

"Get down here fast, my boy!"

Harry caught Jennie's arm and the professor's. "Let's go," he said. "Keep over to the far left."

"This latest nonsense," muttered the professor, "is almost more than I can stand."

Chapter 19

The main square in Kaltzonburg was filled with morning mist. The Great Lorenzo slackened his pace and then stopped in front of a frail old woman who was vending violets. "A moment, Harry," he said. "Be so kind as to give me a bunch of your very best blossoms, dear lady." He pulled a gold coin from behind his ear, handing it to her.

"Why, you must be the Great Lorenzo." She accepted the money and gave him the flowers.

"Ah, little mother, you've seen and enjoyed my magical extravaganza?"

"I fear I can't afford it, sir. But I saw your portrait, which hardly does you justice, in the newspaper only yesterday."

He upended the bunch of violets, shook them. Two tickets fell into his palm. "Here are a couple of free passes."

"God bless you, sir."

Taking hold of Harry's arm, the magician resumed their walk. "I never get over the gratification that fame brings."

"Did I notice greasepaint on that sweet old grandmother's face?"

"She is not a shill, my boy."

"Good, because I'm already impressed by your many abilities. No need to hire a—"

"Here I brighten the poor old wretch's otherwise drab existence by giving her a choice pair of seats in the second balcony and you suggest that—"

"There's Inspector Swann."

The French policeman was seated at a bench and facing one of the tables set out for chess and checker players. "Good morning, monsieurs," he said. "Thanks to your communication of last evening, Harry, I was able to alert the Kaltzonburg police and we raided Zaytoon's castle."

"What about Jean-Pierre Pastoral and the rest of your men who were on the train?" Harry seated himself on the opponent bench.

"All alive and being kept prisoner in the castle."

"We didn't have time, or the forces, to rescue them all last night."

"One quite understands." Reaching into his breast pocket, he brought out several sheets of folded paper. "First I... Ah, very impressive, M. Lorenzo."

"Hum? Oh, the stogie." The magician, leaning against the back of Harry's bench, had picked a lighted cigar out of his handful of violets. "Care for a smoke?"

"Not at the moment." Swann spread a page of pale grey paper

out on the inlaid checkerboard. "This Bertie Pennoyer we found exactly where you told us he would be. He is being held on a number of charges, including kidnapping and train hijacking. Of Mlle. Naida Strand there was no trace. Nor did we find the remains of Anwar Zaytoon."

Harry said, "What was left of him was right beside the bed. In the same room with the damn coffin."

Shaking his head, Inspector Swann said, "We found no coffin either."

"The dark lady returned after we took our leave," suggested the Great Lorenzo, "to do a bit of tidying up."

"Sooner or later I'm going to catch her," said Harry.

Swann unfolded another sheet. "Here is the latest communication from Orchardson," he said. "In your absence, M. Lorenzo, I took the liberty of intercepting this. It arrived last evening while you were otherwise occupied at the castle."

"What's he want?" asked Harry.

Swann handed him the sheet of pale green notepaper. "See for yourself."

The note read:

> The obelisk is to be delivered to the red hunting lodge on the north shore of Lake Langweilig at 4:00 P.M. this Friday. Miss Stowe will be turned over to you at that time. No tricks, if you please.
>
> O.

"This particular lake," said Harry, "is about thirty miles south of here. As I recall from my map studying of the other day."

"Twenty-seven miles, yes," said Swann.

"Okay, so we have three days to get everything ready."

"What do you have in mind?"

"First, we have to open up the obelisk," said Harry.

"The baron will never allow such a valuable—"

"When he hears what's inside, he will," Harry assured him.

"Almost everybody's interested in immortality."

"Eh? Do you mean such an awesome secret as—"

"That's what's inside the obelisk, yep."

"Even so, how are we to gain access to—"

"I've already arranged for that," said the Great Lorenzo, puffing on his cigar. "Thanks to kindhearted Prince Rudy, and a few of my own local connections, I have both a crackerjack safe blower and a gifted stonemason standing by. The latter fellow specialized in mournful angels for high-class tombs, but he can saw through stone like—"

"We also have to put Professor Stowe to work on a device he was explaining to me on our ride back from Lowen last night," said Harry."

Another flying machine, monsieur?"

"Nope, something that can control the ones that exist," answered Harry.

* * * *

"...then there was the redhead who was the understudy for the part of Little Eva in a traveling company of a German version of Uncle Tom's Cabin," Jennie was explaining. "He settled with her for $25,000. Next came an American girl named, so help me, Pansy Dorf. She was a sharpshooter with a rundown wild West show fronted by Colonel Buckskin Dan. Her attorneys claimed—"

"To sum up all your digging into the baron's background," interrupted Harry, "the guy is fond of women."

"Fond may not be a strong enough word." She glanced up from her notebook. "Do you want to hear about the tattooed Swedish girl known as the Portable Museum?"

"Nope," decided Harry.

They were on the wide terrace of Baron Felix Groll's chateau in the wooded hills above Kaltzonburg. The morning mist had gone but the midday sunlight was thin and pale.

Jennie closed her notebook. "In residence at the moment is a lady calling herself Lulu Cortez," she said. "She was stranded in

Urbania four months ago when the touring Graustark National Ballet Company went bankrupt."

"How old is she?"

"Twenty-two."

"And the baron is...what?...fifty-five?"

"Claims fifty-five. Actually, he's fifty-nine."

Harry nodded. "He's about to join us."

One of the French doors facing the terrace opened and a slender man in a blue blazer and grey trousers came walking toward them. His short-cropped hair and beard were grey. "Ah, it is Herr Challenge and Fraulein Barr," he said, bowing, smiling, clicking his heels. "Much have I heard of both of you." Taking hold of Jennie's hand, he bent and kissed it. "Your series on the tenements of New York City brought tears to my eyes. Ah, and your articles on the recent unpleasantness at Blackwood Castle caused my hackles to rise as I perused it, my dear."

"Why, thank you."

Harry said, "We didn't mean to get you out of your sickbed, baron. But since we're working against time, I—"

"Sick? Who is sick? I have been up for hours attending to my business affairs."

Harry grinned. "Excuse me. It's only that you seem... Well, I guess for a man of sixty you don't look all that bad."

"Sixty? I am but fifty-four." He frowned at Harry, then returned his attention to Jennie. "You are one of the most perceptive and objective reporters in the world, fraulein. I put it to you, do I appear to be sixty years of age?"

"No, I wouldn't peg you at anything beyond fifty-nine."

Baron Groll paused to breathe in and out. "I must inform you, Herr Challenge, that you are not putting me in a receptive mood to grant any favors," he told Harry. "I am informed you wish to make a—"

"You'll have to forgive us," said Harry. "It's just that I've got this rejuvenation drug on my mind. Naturally, I'm going to be doubly aware of the sad effects of aging on a once handsome and vital—"

"Rejuvenation?" said the baron. "I was told some lunatic wanted my lovely new obelisk in exchange for a young woman. By the way, she is beautiful?"

Jennie began. "Plain as a—"

"Belphoebe Stowe is quite a handsome woman," said Harry, nudging Jennie. "And she'd be eternally grateful to any man who—"

"Might we return to this talk of rejuvenation?"

Harry rested his backside against the marble railing that guarded the terrace. "I'm going to confide an enormously important secret in you, baron," he said. "Inside your obelisk, hidden for centuries, is a supply of tana."

"Of what?"

"It's a powerful drug," explained the reporter. "Anwar Zaytoon used the stuff and he lived to be nine hundred."

"Nine hundred? But that's imposs—"

"And up until the very end he didn't look a day over sixty."

"Fifty," suggested Harry.

"Fifty," amended Jennie. "That's right. Zaytoon was nine hundred, yet he appeared to be younger than you."

The baron stroked his beard, gazing thoughtfully out at the green woodlands surrounding his château. "You are certain this drug is concealed in my obelisk?"

"It is," Harry assured him. "As the owner of the obelisk, anything inside it is yours."

"I could look even younger," he inquired, "and never die?"

"That's the idea," said Jennie. "Harry knows exactly where the stuff is and how to get it out without damaging the obelisk much at all."

"Can have my crew here within the hour," Harry said.

Baron Groll asked, "What do you want in return?"

"The loan of the obelisk."

"Loan? As I understand it this decadent mystic wants it for good and all."

"We'll take the obelisk apart, extract the cache of tana, put it back together and borrow it for about a day."

"Merely borrow?"

"Harry has a way figured out to prevent Orchardson from keeping the thing."

"Then I will have this miraculous drug and my obelisk?"

"That's right."

"Very well, you have my permission to do what must be done," the baron said. "Ah, but you must not mention any of this to my friend, Lulu Cortez. I want to surprise her."

"Not a word," promised Harry.

Chapter 20

The Great Lorenzo rotated his hand in the twilight. His gold watch climbed free of his waistcoat pocket, floated up to his hand. "I must be off, children," he announced.

"Curtain time in two hours."

Harry and Jennie were again on the terrace of Baron Groll's chateau.

"The crew you provided ought to have the damn obelisk uncorked any time now," said Harry. "Why not stay and—"

"It is my motto, my boy, never to keep my eager public waiting." The magician manually returned his watch to his pocket. "Besides I have a feeling... Ah, but no need to play the wet blanket. Farewell until the morrow."

"Whoa now," said Harry.

"You're not going to leave," said Jennie, "without giving us the benefit of your latest magical insight."

"'Tis not a vision," he told them, "merely a hunch."

"And?" asked Harry.

"You—or rather the anxious baron is in for a bit of a disappointment perhaps." The Great Lorenzo adjusted his top hat, adjusted his cloak and went striding off across the terrace and down the marble staircase that led to the front drive where his carriage waited.

"What's he hinting at?" Jennie watched the magician disappear into the gathering dusk.

"That maybe there's nothing inside the obelisk."

"But there has to be. All these people couldn't be chasing after nothing."

"Wouldn't be the first time." He walked over and sat on the marble railing.

She perched beside him. "We ought to be back inside. Thing should be just about open."

"Inspector Swann'll holler," said Harry. "Unless you feel your readers could use a few more details on granite sawing and—"

"Darn it, Harry." She punched his arm. "Just lay off me, okay?"

"I didn't mean to—"

"We're both pretty enthusiastic about our jobs," she said. "You wouldn't drop a case you were investigating to come off with me. So don't razz me when I—"

"Sure I would. Where do you want me to come off to?"

She turned to study his profile. "Paris wasn't so bad. Let's go back there."

"When?"

Jennie sighed. "There's the same darn snag," she said. "You won't leave Urbania until Belphoebe Stowe's safe. I won't pack up until I file my story on the rescue."

"We'll both be finished by Friday," he said. "By Monday we can be back in Paris."

"The Daily Inquirer owes me a week of vacation," she said. "At least."

"Okay, then we'll spend a week in Paris. But without giant bats or—"

"Walking mummies or—"

"Aggressive Zouaves." Harry put his good arm around her waist, leaned and kissed her.

"Ahum," came the voice of Inspector Swann from an open French door. "They are ready to open it." He went away.

"And no obelisks," said Jennie.

* * * *

The stonemason was a small, dark man in smock and work trousers. Covered with granite dust, he was crouched at the tip of the lying-down obelisk. A makeshift scaffolding was supporting the apex.

"Easy now, chum," advised the dapper safecracker. A tall, lean man, he was standing close by with a stethoscope dangling from his left hand.

"We are ready," said the mason.

The safecracker dropped the stethoscope into his coat pocket, took hold of the tip of the obelisk. The mason did likewise.

Baron Groll was pacing along the canvas that had been spread out on the floor of his conservatory. "Get on with it," he urged.

"Lend a hand," Inspector Swann told the two uniformed Kaltzonburg policemen who'd been standing watch.

Grunting and puffing, the four men lifted the apex free of the obelisk and let it rest on the scaffolding.

"The mason mentioned earlier," said Swann to Harry, "there is evidence that's been taken off before and very artfully replaced."

"Sure, they did that back in ancient Egypt when the—"

"More recently than that, monsieur."

Jennie tapped Harry's arm. "Lorenzo's hunch," she said quietly.

The safecracker was on his knees, shining a bull's-eye lantern into the opening that was now visible. There was a hollowed out cube about the size of a shoebox. "Got to be mighty careful," he said. "On the lookout for poisoned needles and other such engines of destruction."

"There's a small ivory casket in there," said the baron. "Get it out, will you?"

"All in good time." The safecracker rubbed his fingertips on his palms.

"Ah, I have no more patience." Barol Groll pushed him aside and thrust in his hand. He pulled out a casket of gold-trimmed ivory. "Is this it, Herr Challenge?"

"Ought to be."

"Foolish," muttered the safecracker. "Don't know what sort of trap them old Gypsies set."

The baron, hands shaking some, put the casket on a marble-topped table. He took hold of the lid.

"Could also be," said the safecracker, "they rigged a spring device in the lid to shoot a—"

"There, I've open..." Baron Groll stared into the open casket. "There is nothing...only this folded piece of paper."

Harry had moved to the table. He lifted the page from the box and unfolded it. "Well, now."

"Harry," said Jennie, "what is it?"

"I'll read it to everybody," he said. "'To whom it may concern: Should anyone else ever solve the cipher, I offer my sympathies. I have already taken the tana drug but left the casket and this note. The work was done in the hold of the ship bringing this ugly artifact back from Egypt to Paris. My colleagues, a simple-minded lot, know nothing of this. Quite frankly, I don't believe anyone else will ever be clever enough to find out, as I have, the secret of the obelisk of Osiris. Yet my vanity prompts me to write this down and take claim for solving a riddle that eluded all others for thousands of years. The drug is mine and I am now assured of living forever. Most sincerely yours, Sir Munson Bellhouse.'"

Harry let the note drop to the tabletop.

"Orchardson killed Bellhouse," said Jennie.

"To keep him from learning the secret of the obelisk," said Harry.

"The current whereabouts of the tana drug," said Jennie. "Only Bellhouse knew that and he's dead now."

Baron Groll glanced from Harry to Jennie and back to Harry again. "I can't follow all this," he said, "yet I have the uneasy impression I'm not going to live forever or even be rejuvenated."

"That about," said Harry, "sums it up."

Chapter 21

Friday was grey and misty. When they reached Lake Langweilig, a light rain began to fall.

The Great Lorenzo had been expecting rain and was wearing a yellow slicker and matching hat. He and Harry were sharing the driver's seat of the lumbering circus wagon the obelisk was being hauled in. "Is that our destination I espy across the placid waters, my boy?" He flicked the reins of the four sturdy draft horses who were pulling the wagon.

Harry lowered his binoculars. "Only red hunting lodge in sight."

"Red's a handsome color."

"For circus wagons."

"I rather like this vehicle. Its crimson exterior and gilded bars add a nice touch of brightness to 'a drab day," said the magician. "And the words enscribed above the cage—The Wildman of Sulu—are rather fetching. All in all, I'm delighted I borrowed it from some of my old circus cronies."

Harry was studying the lodge, which was still two miles away, through the glasses again. "Looks like somebody's inside the place," he said. "And...yep...I'm near certain there's at least one of Stowe's flying machines roosting in those trees beyond the lodge."

"Then your scheme ought to work," the magician said. "If you can keep the professor sober back there."

A coach, with Inspector Swann at the reins and Jennie and Professor Stowe inside, was following behind them.

"Jennie'll see to that."

"An admirable young woman, my boy," he said. "Were I you, I'd settle down with her in a little bower by the side of the road in some quaint small town in the hinterland of America and there—"

"She's not the settling down kind."

"Ah, but love can work—"

"Nor am I." Harry lowered the binoculars.

"Do both of you intend to keep galavanting around the world until you're as long in the tooth as the late Zaytoon?"

"We'll keep on about like this for a while, bumping into each other now and then."

The Great Lorenzo sighed. "Let us turn, before my tender heart breaks, to more mundane topics," he suggested. "Is that gadget of Stowe's really going to do the trick?"

"He assures me it will."

"The professor, brilliant fellow though he is, fails to inspire my full and unqualified confidence," said the magician. "Possibly that impression was created when I found him flat on his back and snoring on the floor of the temporary laboratory you fixed up for him at the baron's."

"He's got a fondness for the bottle."

"So I concluded when the fumes from his sprawled carcass made me tipsy."

Harry said, "There's really no way to test that control panel he built for us. He claims he can use it to take over control of the flying machines from Orchardson. If he can, then that'll be the easiest way to nab Orchardson."

"And even if not, we'll still be able to exchange this dornick for the fair Belphoebe."

Harry nodded. "I want Orchardson, too," he said. "Any hunches?"

Shrugging, the Great Lorenzo replied, "Nary a one. We'll simply have to trust to chance."

* * * *

The crimson steps of the hunting lodge creaked as Max Drchardson came down them. He wore a tweed suit and hiking boots. "Look around you, Challenge," he advised.

"Already have." Harry had climbed down from the circus wagon and was standing near the edge of the misty lake.

The Great Lorenzo was at the rear of the wagon, unlocking the cage that held the obelisk.

"Three of my men, all armed, are out there in the woods,"

Orchardson came thumping toward Harry. "As well as two of my highly dependable aerodromes."

"I noticed."

"There are, in addition, three armed men inside the odge," added the immense, pale Orchardson. "One, armed with a shotgun, stands guard over Miss Stowe in the room Erectly above the entryway."

"We didn't come to make trouble or get into a brawl," Harry assured him. "You take the obelisk, we take Belphoebe Stowe."

"And you're welcome to her." Orchardson started waddling toward the rear of the circus wagon. "I thought her wretched father was the most quarrelsome person on the face of the planet, until I took this young lady under my roof."

"That's one of the drawbacks of kidnapping: you don't mow how your victims are going to behave."

"Not a bad remark, Challenge. I may be able to fashion it into an epigram." Stopping at the open cage, he squinted at the obelisk. "Appears to be authentic." From a coat)acket he took a magnifying glass. First he tapped the granite base with the handle, then he scrutinized it with the lens. "I hear tell, by the by, that Anwar Zaytoon has fallen on hard times."

"He's dead."

"Delightful." He continued to inspect the obelisk. "Were you responsible for his shuffling off?"

"Indirectly," said Harry. "The official cause of death was old age."

"Yes, one can see where it would be." Orchardson slipped the glass into a tweedy pocket, took two rocking steps back. "I am satisfied, Challenge. If you and your fat friend will now retreat to the vicinity of your coach, I'll give the signal for Miss Stowe to be released."

"Fine. Pleasure doing business with you."

He and the Great Lorenzo started walking toward the coach, which was parked several hundred yards down the shore of the lake.

All at once leaves rattled on their left.

From out of the woods a giant mechanical bat came flapping.

"Watch out." Harry shoved the magician down, dived to the pebbly ground himself.

The bat ignored them and sailed over. It hovered above Orchardson for an instant, then grabbed him up.

"Fools, what are you doing?" cried the fat man.

The bat rose up, carrying the thrashing, struggling Orchardson in its clawed arms.

It rose higher and higher and went flying out over the lake.

Crouched, Harry watched. "Damn, Stowe moved too soon."

"Demon rum has dulled his perceptions perhaps." When the flying machine was four hundred feet above the waters of the lake, it opened its claws.

Orchardson plummeted, screaming, down through the afternoon. He hit the water with an enormous slamming splash and sank at once.

Chapter 22

Harry tugged, left-handed, his revolver out of his belt. "Give me a diversion, Lorenzo."

Yanking off his yellow slicker hat, Lorenzo started hopping on the beach. "El Carim Zanzibar Zatara!"

Purple smoke commenced pouring from the hat, great thick clouds of it. The smoke engulfed the circus wagon, covered a long stretch of the lakeshore and surrounded the lodge. It hid Harry from the gunmen in the woods and from those still inside.

"Excuse my using the same trick twice," called the magician.

Harry went sprinting for the house, revolver in his left hand. He could barely make out the steps, but he went charging up them and shoved on into the lodge.

Just inside the front door he collided with a large coughing man. The man was heavyset, puzzled and carried a .45 revolver absently in his hand.

"The whole place is on fire," warned Harry. "Get all the

women and children out fast."

"To be sure, sir…what children?"

Smoke came spilling into the rustic living room, blurring everything.

Harry dodged the distracted guard, ran up the wooden staircase to the second floor.

Purplish smoke was forcing itself in through the open windows and the hall was clouded with it.

"Fire!" yelled Harry. "Fire and pestilence!"

"How's that again?" A bald-headed man, cradling a shotgun, stepped out of the room where Belphoebe Stowe was being held.

"This whole lodge is going to blow sky high," explained Harry. "Get out while you can."

"A moment, sir. I recognize you as Harry Challenge, a fellow who's opposed to our…oof!"

Harry hit him hard in the midsection with his cast. He punched him twice more in the temple and stepped clear as he slumped to the hardwood floor and was covered by billowing smoke.

"Belphoebe?"

"Mr. Challenge." The blonde young woman appeared in the doorway. "Whatever is going on?"

"Essentially, this is a rescue." He took hold of her arm. "Your nitwit father seems to have murdered Orchardson and that's meant a bit of improvising."

"What is the cause of all this dreadful smoke?"

"Lorenzo. He had some left over from a stunt he pulled the other night," he answered, heading her toward the back stairs. "C'mon. Run."

"I truly appreciate your efforts on my behalf."

They hit the stairs and went rushing down.

Harry was reaching for the back door handle when a third guard stepped out of the purple smoke and pointed a pistol at them. "Be so kind as to stop."

"Oh, nonsense." Belphoebe, who was three steps from the bottom, leaped through the cloudy air and executed a perfect tackle.

The nonplussed guard fell over backwards, fired a shot into an elk head mounted on the wall.

Harry jumped, stepped on his wrist. The gun went spinning from the man's grasp.

Stepping over him after grabbing up the gun, Belphoebe followed Harry out of the lodge and into even denser smoke.

The Great Lorenzo called to Harry, "How many guards did he mention were lurking amidst the flora?"

"Three." Harry aimed his reply at the spot he assumed the magician was standing.

"I thought as much," the Great Lorenzo said, walking closer and materializing out of the smoke. "In that case, I've succeeded in rendering the lot of them unconscious with a blackjack once presented to me by a fellow who claimed to be a former member of the Gashouse Gang."

As the smoke began to lift, Jennie came running along the beach to Harry. "You're alive," she said, smiling and hugging him.

"I am," he agreed, kissing her.

Inspector Swann, gun in hand, headed for the lodge. "I shall take care of any loose ends within," he said. "You two, let me add, displayed much inventiveness this day."

Belphoebe was watching Harry and the red-haired reporter. "This bears out all I have heard about the behavior of Americans."

"No one would consider you unladylike, Miss Stowe," said the Great Lorenzo, "should you demonstrate your gratitude to your rescuers in some physical way."

"Yes, I believe I shall." She marched over to the magician, kissed him, briefly, on his cheek. "My heartiest thanks."

He put his yellow rain hat back on, tugging it down. "I'm deeply touched," he informed her. "Harry, my boy, we'd best hog-tie the Orchardson forces scattered in the woods and then collect them into our barred wagon."

"Soon as I ask the professor why in the hell he—"

"Revenge," said Jennie. "That's what he told me while I was

trying to struggle with him and get him to put Orchardson down gently on dry land."

"Our original plan was to pluck him up with one of his flying bats after Belphoebe was free and before he could start off with the damn obelisk."

"He claims the sight of Orchardson brought back all he's suffered at his hands," said Jennie, nose wrinkling.

"It sounds as though my deplorable parent has caused yet another—"

"Belphoebe, my beloved child!" The door of the coach came flapping open. Stowe tumbled out, hit the beach with a sloppy thud.

"There are times when I truly wish my loyalty to that awful man was not so strong."

"Help me up, will you? I seem to have developed a cramp from sitting so long in this drafty conveyance." Stowe got to his knees, rubbing at his thigh.

Belphoebe took a few unenthusiastic steps in his direction. "Mr. Challenge informs me that you came very close, father, you wicked old man, to undermining the entire plan."

"Can you blame a father for revenging himself upon the very man who defiled his firstborn jewel and—"

"Orchardson was not at all interested in women, as you well know. Even if he had been, I could easily have eluded the advances of one so grossly over—"

"Yes, yes, go ahead. Scorn and malign me for risking life and limb to save you from a fate worse than—"

"Father, I suggest you climb back inside that coach at once and cease your unseemly behavior."

The professor was upright, more or less, at last. He brushed dirt from his wrinkled suit. "The ingratitude you're displaying, dearest, is more unseemly than—"

"Did you mention, Mr. Lorenzo, that you are in need of assistance in tying up some of those dreadful, debased brutes who have been my captors?"

"All help is most gratefully accepted," he told her. "Come

along into yon forest glade with me."

Professor Stowe jerked a wad of handkerchief out and commenced sobbing into it.

"Would you mind, Harry," asked Jennie, "if I rode back on the wagon with you?"

Chapter 23

The Great Lorenzo tipped his top hat and six milk-white doves came fluttering out.

The enthusiastic audience in the packed Spielzeug Theater applauded.

"Tonight, ladies and gentlemen, I am pleased to introduce yet another brand-new and never before seen illusion," he announced, winking in the direction of the box occupied by Harry and Jennie. "Or is it an illusion? Can a man, a mere mortal, actually walk through solid stone? Attend well, for you are about to witness what I call the Curse of the Obelisk illusion."

The houselights dimmed, the gilded curtains behind him slowly parted.

"Not a bad replica," said Jennie, nodding at the pinkish obelisk that stood in the spotlight, flanked by two handsome young women in diaphanous and vaguely Egyptian gowns.

"Obelisks aren't my idea of entertainment," said Harry.

"Well, you can't blame Lorenzo for wanting to cash in on all the notoriety," she said. "The obelisk is news."

"Thanks to you."

"And most of the newspapers around the world who picked up my stories."

"...imprisoned within this solid granite, dear friends, and then bound with sturdy chains of..."

"We're going to have to leave before this final encore," reminded Harry, "to catch the last express to Paris."

"He'll be hurt."

"Not Lorenzo. Romance is more important to him than magic or—"

A polite tapping sounded on the door of their private box.

Harry stood and opened the door.

A red-coated young usher stood there with two pale envelopes in his gloved hand.

"Herr Challenge?"

"Yep."

"Fräulein Barr?"

"As well."

"Cablegrams. Urgent. I am to remain in case of any replies."

"Thanks." Harry took the cables and gave the young man a half-gulden piece.

"Let's not open them just yet, Harry."

He shook his head, passed her message to her and opened his.

It was from his father and said:

Dear Son:

You didn't do badly with the obelisk. Pack up at once and hightail it to London. Rich half-wit claims dead coming back to life and secret cult after him. Ought to be worth plenty.

Your loving father, the Challenge International Detective Agency.

Jennie finally pried her own envelope open and scanned the message. "Grand Duke Rupert has been assassinated in Bosnia," she said ruefully. "My darn paper wants me to get there right away and cover unfolding events."

Harry tapped his cable against his chin a few times and then returned it to its envelope.

"Young man," he said to the usher, "you weren't able to find either Herr Challenge or Fräulein Barr."

"I wasn't? But you professed to be the—"

"All a mistake. Fact is, I'm near certain they've both left the country for parts unknown." He gave the cables back, along with three more coins. "You never will find them. Understand?"

The usher smiled. "Ah, but to be sure. An affair of the heart." He took his leave.

"Parts unknown?" inquired Jennie.

"Paris, actually," said Harry.

"I advise you, ladies and gentlemen," the Great Lorenzo was saying down on the stage, "to watch the next part most carefully. You will be absolutely amazed."

AFTERWORD—THE FURTHER ADVENTURES OF HARRY CHALLENGE

Harry, Jennie, and the Great Lorenzo have kept plenty busy over the years. *After The Prisoner of Blackwood Castle* and *The Curse of the Obelisk*, our intrepid trio became involved in many other lively—and deadly—investigations.

Here is a catalog of their further exploits to date:

- "The Secret of the Black Chateau," which appeared in the May 1985 edition of *Espionage Magazine.*

- "The Monster of the Maze," in the February 1986 issue of *Espionage Magazine.*

- "The Phantom Highwayman," in Marvin Kaye's anthology *The Ultimate Halloween* (iBooks, 2001)

- "The Woman in the Mist," in the December 2002 edition of *The Magazine of Fantasy & Science Fiction.*

- "The Incredible Steam Man," in *The Magazine of Fantasy & Science Fiction*, May 2003.

- "The Secret of the Scarab," in *The Magazine of Fantasy & Science Fiction*, April 2005.

- "The Problem of the Missing Werewolf, which appeared in the 4th issue (Spring-Summer 2007) of *H.*

P. Lovecraft's Magazine of Horror.

- "The Mystery of the Missing Automaton," which was in the 1st issue (Winter 2008) of *Sherlock Holmes Mystery Magazine.*

- "The Mystery of the Flying Man," which was published in the 2nd issue (Spring 2009) of *Sherlock Holmes Mystery Magazine.*

Two new Harry Challenge tales, "The Secret of the City of Gold" and "The Somerset Wonder" (involving a Superhero!) will be published, respectively, in upcoming issues of *The Magazine of Fantasy & Science Fiction* and *Sherlock Holmes Mystery Magazine.* (Another tale, "The Bride of the Vampire," has gone missing; hopefully, the author will find the manuscript somehow/somewhere.)

"In addition to the above titles," Ron Goulart states, "I have about seven or eight unfinished Harry stories sitting around, one that I set aside for various reasons—'The Elusive Cracksman,' 'The Phantom of the Ravenwood Tunnel,' 'The Problem of the Dead Man's Plans,' etc."

Marvin Kaye's Nth Dimension Books plans to publish these subsequent Harry Challenge adventures in a companion to the current volume.

52861369R00158

Made in the USA
San Bernardino, CA
30 August 2017